A ROLLICKING REGENCY

All the Tea
in China

JANE ORCUTT

Revell

Grand Rapids, Michigan

© 2007 by Jane Orcutt

Published by Fleming H. Revell
a division of Baker Publishing Group
P.O. Box 6287, Grand Rapids, MI 49516-6287

Printed in the United States of America

Library of Congress Cataloging-in-Publication Data
Orcutt, Jane.
    All the tea in China : a rollicking Regency / Jane Orcutt.
      p.   cm.
    ISBN 10: 0-8007-3179-4 (pbk.)
    ISBN 978-0-8007-3179-3 (pbk.)
    1. Title.
PS3565.R37A79 2007
813'.54—dc22   2006103331

1

I can abide neither a liar nor a cheat, but you may be wont to think me such while I here relate my little tale. Were I not your humble narrator, even now I would scarce believe it anything but mere fiction. I take pen in resolute hand to assure you that what I am about to recount is truth, not the least of which involves heartbreak, joy, a Chinese translation of the Gospel According to St. Luke, and, oh yes, a rather large sword.

Perhaps it is best that I start where my journey of a thousand miles began, not with a single step but with the dearest pair of pink silk slippers.

Soft as rose petals they were and embroidered with a bit of curious white design on the toes. They looked quite lovely peeping from beneath my new white muslin dress with a pink ribbon encircling just below . . . oh dear, let me simply say high above my waist. My modiste assured me the dress was the finest in the county and that during the party no one would be my peer.

I was, after all, preparing for social battle.

"This dress will accomplish the task," I said, twirling on the stool set in front of the mirror. "You do me proud, Flora."

My modiste tugged on the hem to allay my motion. She looked up from where she knelt before my stool, mouth full of pins. "I do not know why you asked me to stitch this in such a hurry. If you do not cease your movements, Miss Isabella," she mumbled, "'twill not be finished in time for the Ransoms' party tonight. Be still, child."

"Child?" I laughed. "I have five and twenty years, as well you know, and you have been with me for all of them."

Flora removed the pins from her mouth to permit an angelic smile. "And now the only child in attendance is when little Lewis visits with Frederica."

I resisted the urge to roll my eyes. Would I never cease hearing about my older sister's child? My nephew was a creation of God, indeed, but he was also quite possibly the most disagreeable baby upon which I had ever set eyes. Not only did he wail piteously whenever I attempted to hold him, but he also possessed some rather curious physical traits. It had been my limited experience that most babies lose the red, wrinkled skin and expression so common to them (and their mothers!) soon after birth. But this child—pronounced hale and hearty by the doctor—persisted in retaining the most distressingly mottled skin and ungainly form.

Shall I describe the child's face? In deference to his mother, I think not.

"You are far behind your sister. She already has a babe, yet you do not even have a husband."

Touché. The battle had already begun, and with Flora, no less! She had long been concerned with my future, since my mother and father passed away soon after my birth. A distant relative hired to care for Frederica and me, Louisa Florey had served as our nursemaid, governess, modiste, and confidante. "Miss Florey" had been shortened to Flora long ago.

Now that Freddie was happily wed, Flora had turned her attention fully to me. She often suggested particular young men in Oxford as potential husbands, never even attempting to cloak her matchmaking as idle speculation. Fortunately, I had learned to overlook her plainspokenness, for its source was always love.

"No one is more aware of my solitude, thank you," I said. "But I am not yet past hope of being wed." *I would be happy with even a disagreeable baby . . .*

Readjusting her position, Flora bumped against the stool, scattering the pins. "Only see what I have done!" She got down on her hands and knees, sighing. "That is probably my punishment for my insensitive words," she mumbled to herself as she hunted near the mirror and around the stool. "It is quite one thing for me to be a spinster, but you . . ." She looked up and smiled, determined to soften her words. "It is as you say, dear Miss Isabella. You are not yet past hope."

7

I smiled. "Then this should please you. Catherine Ransom told me there would be an extra guest tonight." I paused for best effect. "A male guest."

"So *that* was the reason for a new gown. And now, I suppose, that you with your spontaneous notions have already begun to contemplate the wedding."

In truth I had pictured myself standing beside an elegant groom at Christ Church's chapel, but I feigned shock. "Why, Flora! I only wanted a chance to show off your beautiful handiwork."

"Pah. It is my French blood. Only the French know how to sew a proper fashion."

"You are but one-quarter French, I believe."

She let out a dolorous sigh. "To think what fame could be mine if my ancestors had taken more care with my lineage."

I smiled and slipped an arm around her shoulder. "Were Napoleon himself your father, you could not be a better seamstress."

"Were Napoleon my father, I would refer to myself as fully British," she said. "Let us pray then that my work shows off to your advantage tonight. Do you like the new slippers?"

I wiggled my toes happily. I had small, delicate feet, about which I confess to an equally small, delicate vanity. "They are beautiful, Flora, and the fit most comfortable. Not like that last pair that pinched to no end."

"That is peculiar, for the shoemaker used the very same pattern for this pair." Flora brightened. "Perhaps it is a difference in the silk. When I inquired after his best fabric, he made sure that no one was watching, then he drew out a small bolt of this pink silk. 'Newly arrived from the Orient,' he said. 'It put me right in mind of your Isabella Goodrich, and no one else should have it,' he said. Then, when the slippers were finished, I saw that his wife had added the embroidery. I could not bear to refuse to pay, because the poor woman is near blindness. The white stitching does look lovely . . . though a trifle peculiar."

I bent to stroke one of the slippers and felt an odd little thrill. The design on the toes must be some sort of Chinese symbol, then, if the fabric was Oriental silk. I could envision Solomon's wife painstakingly copying the patterns, and I was touched by her efforts. "Did he say why he thought of me, in particular?"

Flora shrugged. "I never know why old Solomon says what he does. One cannot trust everything he says. After all, *he* is not French, for all that he tries to fashion shoes."

I covered a smile.

"Did Catherine Ransom say anything about this mysterious stranger that is to visit tonight?" Flora said.

I shook my head, and she sniffed. "Thankfully *she* is already married, though I would not put it past her to steal this man's attention too."

"Flora! She is a lady, after all. As well as my friend."

She sighed. "I am sorry to speak of it, Miss Isabella, but she is no friend to you. I cannot find it in my heart to forgive her. Or Mr. David." She waggled her finger in my direction. "And I do not doubt for one moment that Catherine

Ransom has some other mischievous plan tonight. It is far too suspicious that she would advise you about a male visitor to tonight's party—she who has never had your interests at heart!"

Studying the mirror, I adjusted a dark ringlet at my cheek. "She wants only to pair me for the evening with someone suitable. Is that implausible?"

Flora's reflection scowled at mine.

"Very well," I said, turning to face her. "I will be *en guard* tonight against Catherine Ransom and her wiles."

Flora cocked her head. "Truly? Do you pledge it?"

"I do," I said firmly, with the certainty that one day soon—surely!—I would be repeating that expression in the matrimonial setting for which it was properly intended.

By the time I prepared for the party, my hands were trembling. Flora helped me into the finished dress, then adorned my hair with strings of pearls. She argued in favor of flowers, but when I studied the pearls, they accidentally slipped from my hands to the floor. I looked at Flora triumphantly.

She sighed. "I suppose you will insist that is the right choice, then."

"Of course." I was not superstitious, but I did believe that sometimes decisions were ordained for us. To my estimation, young ladies should be careful (though Flora called it impulsive) to pay heed.

Her eyes shone as I departed, and she whispered in my ear that I should remember every fashion detail. She also squeezed my arm and warned me not to spend too much time with Uncle Toby, who would no doubt encourage me to more intellectual conversations than a young lady of my age should pursue.

Tobias Fitzwater, my uncle, had raised my sister Frederica and me but was better known as the dean of Christ Church at Oxford. Though he had never claimed to understand the dreams and whims of girls or young women, he had taught Freddie and me—just as he did his students—to reverence God first and education second. My sister scorned her knowledge once she reached her first Season, but I embraced it heart and soul.

If Uncle Toby knew nothing of proper behavior for girls, I could claim equal ignorance. When, as a child, I observed some of his students fencing, I demanded to take up the sport. My dear uncle readily indulged my desire, and I had no maternal figure to advise against its impropriety. Flora was as devoted to my uncle as she was to me, so she guarded our secret even when my practice grew more scandalous as I gained in age.

Uncle Toby and I rode in silence to the Ransoms' until he squinted in the dim light of our carriage. He angled his spectacles further down his nose. "Do I see a new pair of slippers on your feet?"

"You do," I said proudly, sticking out a foot for his inspection.

He studied it, then checked the other slipper, his expression sober. "Where did you get these?"

"Flora had them made for me. Solomon said it was a

11

special pink silk that made him think especially of me. Why do you ask?"

"This is Chinese writing on the toes, were you aware?"

"I assumed as much. Solomon said the silk came newly from the Orient." I twisted my neck to study the symbols from Uncle Toby's perspective. "Do you know what they mean?"

"I am afraid not. Far be it from me to judge society, but I cannot help but think it will frown upon such foreignness in fashion."

That was odd. Uncle Toby had never commented negatively on anything I wore. Still, he was so involved in his studies, he scarcely took notice of his own appearance, let alone anyone else's. "I am sure that Catherine Ransom and all the other ladies will have more to worry about than the slippers on my feet," I said with a light air.

Uncle Toby raised an eyebrow. "You are not hoping to impress anyone tonight, are you?"

"Why do you ask?"

He shifted uncomfortably in his seat. "I have been meaning to speak to you of this for a while now, Izzy, but have worked up neither the courage nor the proper words. Perhaps I should best be plain."

"By all means." I nodded. Uncle looked quite serious, a rarity for a personal exchange between us. Our conversations, though oftentimes lengthy, were usually limited to scholarly discussions.

"Not all are intended by God for matrimony," he said.

"Indeed," I said, wondering why he spoke of himself.

Uncle Toby had never wed, preferring to pour all of his affection into his studies—and in raising Freddie and me, of course.

Uncle Toby nodded.

I waited for him to proceed. He looked away, obviously flustered. I continued to wait.

He shifted uncomfortably. I shifted as well, studying the tips of my slippers as though some answer could be found there. At last it dawned on me that Uncle Toby did not intend to say more.

I smiled broadly, then felt an involuntary chuckle tickle my throat. Uncle stared as though he were riding with a lunatic. "I did not envision humor as your response," he said.

"I did not envision matrimony as a subject you would broach tonight." *Or rather, broach then retreat!*

He looked troubled again. Apparently the situation was uneasy for him, but I could not imagine what sort of participation he sought from me.

"Sometimes," he said, then seemed to draw courage. "Sometimes men are so enamored with finding a diamond that they fail to see the pearl among them."

I shook my head, bewildered. Now he was speaking of jewels. I patted his hand. "You are quite a riddle, Uncle Toby."

His shoulders slumped in a sigh of evident defeat, then he smiled at me fondly. "I fear that I am, my dear. I fear that I am."

Sir Henry Ransom waited at the doorway to greet us as we alighted from our carriage. He ushered us inside his spacious home, and anticipation fairly took my breath. Or maybe it was the smoky aroma of the multitudinous candles. The crystal chandelier glowed above the generous main room, while wall sconces reflected their own kindred flames. Striped and solid velvet chairs were artfully arranged for conversation. Later, I knew, dinner would be served in the massive dining room. The Ransom home was as comfortable as it was large, like a portly woman with her finest jewels.

All of this might have been mine, for David Ransom and I had been friends since childhood. He and his family rusticated in Oxfordshire every year, and we played explorers and pirates together while young, then later began to eye each other with keener interest.

Then Catherine Allbright became the object of his affection. No words of explanation passed between David and me, but none were needed. We had exchanged no promises save those of a pirate king to his fair lady. Though I would never dream of voicing my doubts, I was at a loss as to David's selection in Catherine Allbright. Unless it was her well-lined purse. She was the daughter of a prosperous landowner, after all, and I but an orphan. I wished them well on their wedding day.

"Will you be all right alone for a moment, Izzy?" Uncle Tobias asked. "Sir Henry wishes to show me his latest art acquisition."

"Enjoy yourself, Uncle," I said, smiling, as he took his leave. "I shall be all contentment."

"Isabella!"

Then again, perhaps not.

"What a perfectly lovely dress!"

"Catherine!" I returned, kissing the cheek of the blonde beauty who had claimed my childhood friend for her husband. I took note for Flora that Catherine had donned a beastly green silk that made her complexion look like the underside of a trout. "You look lovely too."

"Not for long." She leaned closer for a confidential whisper. "I am with child."

My heart sank. Could crueler words be spoken tonight? "Really! That is . . . wonderful. Truly wonderful. You and David are quite blessed."

"To be sure. David is the most devoted of husbands," she said, demurely touching the front of her dress in a maddening way, as though the babe were already making its presence known. She snapped to herself and smiled. "And you? Any prospects?"

"If the Lord is willing, I shall breathe and rise again tomorrow," I said with a smile. Prospects, indeed! As though I were in search of a situation!

Catherine smiled blandly. "How many years has it been since your final Season? No, wait. Let me guess." She counted on her left-hand fingers and unfortunately soon moved to those on her right. "I remember now. It was the year David proposed to me. My, but that *has* been a while."

"I—"

15

"Excuse me, dear." Catherine patted my arm as though she were my elder, and since she had wed, I suppose she was. "Lady Ransom has asked me to stay particularly close to her tonight. For protection, I suppose, since I am in charge of the family heir." She giggled in what I knew she hoped was a light manner, but which sounded more like a donkey's bray. When we were younger, she had confessed that she pursued all manner of different laughter, but there was no getting around the horrible sound.

"Yes, of course," I said with a curtsy, but she was already sailing across the room like a stately maternal ship. I had neglected to ask about the unattached gentleman who was supposed to be in attendance tonight, but if Catherine Ransom entertained the notion that I would beg for a man . . . !

Sighing, I surveyed the room to see who was available for conversation, but at the moment everyone seemed to be paired off. I retreated to the Ransoms' inner hallway, where I studied Flora's beautiful handiwork in the gilt-edged mirror.

Oh dear! Was that a smudge along the neckline? I leaned closer for further inspection, studying the offending spot. What a pity that—

"Unless your vision is poor, you will not find your image improved by pressing against the mirror. Though I'll not gainsay that many ladies oft believe it otherwise."

"Oh!" I whirled about with a start, finding myself face-to-face, nay, nearly nose to nose with the most unusual-looking man. He appeared to be but five years my senior, yet he wore thick spectacles, which magnified his eyes most alarmingly. His dark hair was pulled back in a queue, though such style had been out of favor for many years. He also wore an ill-fitting, odd sort of faded silk jacket, along with near threadbare inexpressibles.

In short, I felt sorry for someone so out of tune with simple fashion. Surely it was my Christian duty to be kind to such a person, no matter his manners. How he had snuck up on me so silently, without my knowledge, was beyond all reason. Why he had spoken to me without introduction was beyond all propriety.

"Sir, I confess not to vanity but to a wish not to offend others with any displeasing physical display," I said, attempting a light tone. Surely he would understand a lady's dismay at seeing her new dress soiled, no matter how slightly.

"Perhaps what you desire, if you so truly wish not to offend, is the raiment of a monastic, complete with cowl. Then every displeasing aspect of yourself would be truly hidden."

With great effort, I kept my mouth from dropping open. Christian duty forgotten, I willed myself to stand straighter and attempted to brush past him. "Excuse me, sir. You forget yourself." The man thought I was preening! Moreover, he inferred I was unattractive! I did not like to give anyone the cut, but his behavior was inexcusable.

He moved in front of me, impeding my progress. "Did I offend?"

"To ask the question is to answer."

He smiled knowingly. "Ah, but if *you* answer the question, it will admit the need for a deeper reflection than any mirror can provide. But perhaps you disagree? Or are you merely . . . disagreeable?"

I opened my mouth but was checked by a hand on my elbow. "There you are, Isabella." My hostess had impeccable timing.

"Lady Ransom," I said with a curtsy. "I had the pleasure of seeing Sir Henry at the doorway, but you were detained elsewhere."

"Yes, and for that I beg your forgiveness." She pointed her fan at the strange man and smiled. "I see you have met our distinguished guest."

He bowed slightly in our direction. "I confess that we have not, Lady Ransom. We were merely commenting on your mirror here."

She tutted. "What a ghastly piece of work it is. But if you two admire it, then I shall consider it fine enough. Mr. Snowe, Miss Isabella Goodrich. Isabella, Mr. Phineas Snowe."

I curtsied, and somewhat to my surprise, he followed decorum by bowing.

"Mr. Snowe is visiting us from China, Isabella. He is with the uh, the uh . . . what was the name of your organization, Mr. Snowe?"

"No doubt you have heard of the London Missionary Society," he said somberly.

I could feel the blood rush from my face. I had no idea he was one of God's workers. Uncle Toby held such men in high regard and had taught me the same. "Why, yes."

He smiled, bowing low. "I am traveling with a husband and wife who seek to become missionaries themselves."

"Unfortunately, the Tippetts were called away to London and could not join us tonight. And now I shall leave you two alone," Lady Ransom said, tapping me lightly with her fan. "I am never one to meddle in discussions of the heart or religion, and something tells me that one or the other is about to transpire. If you will excuse me."

Left alone with Mr. Snowe, I felt the obligation, if not quite the desire, to apologize. And yet he was, I reminded myself, practically a foreigner, which explained his lack of fashion sense. I should at least be forgiving in that regard.

Meanwhile, he said nothing but stared at me until I felt irritation rise anew. "I suppose your travels have kept you away from England for a good many years?" I ventured.

"A *great* many," he corrected, as though I had made another grievous error.

"In China alone?"

"Among other places."

This was certainly awkward. One had to wonder how he could minister to the masses when he could barely speak to a fellow countrywoman except in innuendo or insult. "And these other places are . . . ?" I asked, resisting the urge to tap my foot.

"Miss . . . Goodrich, was it?" he said. "You need not feel you must entertain me. Sir Henry invited me tonight not for social, but financial reasons. I am here to raise money for my work. Is there a Mr. Goodrich with whom I should speak—your father? Or perhaps your betrothed?"

At least we had lack of forbearance in common! "I fear not, Mr. Snowe. You might, however, find favor with my uncle, Mr. Fitzwater, that white-haired gentleman conversing with Sir Henry."

"Not Tobias Fitzwater?" His eyes gleamed. "The Oxford dean?"

"He is a dean, yes. You have heard of Uncle Toby?"

"Indeed I had hoped to speak with him, as he was a major reason for my visit to Oxford. I understand that he has an interest in Oriental studies."

Perhaps that explained why Uncle Toby had recognized the language on my slippers, if not its meaning. "I did not know that about my uncle," I said, vexed that Mr. Snowe knew anything about Uncle Toby. "Have you perhaps mistaken him for someone else?"

He pursed his lips. "Tobias Fitzwater is the dean of Christ Church, is he not?"

I nodded. How did he know this?

"And he has been at Oxford for, oh, thirty years now, yes?"

I nodded again.

Mr. Snowe shifted. "What I fail to understand, however, is how you fit into the picture."

"And which picture is that?" I replied, blinking in what I hoped was the manner of all innocence.

For a moment it seemed that his face darkened, then

inexplicably brightened. "Forgive me for nattering on so, Miss Goodrich. Would you be so kind as to introduce me to your uncle?"

"I should be quite at a loss without your company," I said. "But follow me."

I did not wait for a reply but sallied forth across the room. I could not be rid of Phineas Snowe any too soon. I was only sorry that I would be handing him over to Uncle Toby, who was far too kind.

Be kind yourself, Isabella. He is a missionary. Be charitable.

I drew a deep breath as we approached Uncle Toby, who was just finishing a conversation with Sir Henry. Our host bowed, excused himself, and left us alone.

"And who is this?" Uncle Toby smiled in the stranger's direction.

"Phineas Snowe, sir." He bowed. "But *you* need no introduction, Mr. Fitzwater. I feel I am acquainted with you already."

Uncle Toby bowed, looking at me curiously, as though I could explain this peculiar man's ways. "He is visiting from China," I said and watched in revulsion as Snowe sidled closer to my beloved uncle. Odious man! "Obsequious" must surely have been his original Christian name.

To my distaste, Uncle Toby's face brightened. "Ah, yes, the missionary. Sir Henry told me about you. You are here to—"

"To endeavor to raise funds that we might spread the Good News among the heathens in China," Snowe said, reaching into his coat pocket. "In fact, I brought along this

21

newly translated account of the Gospel According to St. Luke. I believe you have heard of Robert Morrison?"

"Yes, yes. Quite," Uncle Toby said, putting on his spectacles and accepting the volume. He flipped through it carefully. "Unfortunately, I do not read Chinese, but I am sure that it is a faithful translation."

"You may be certain," Snowe said, smiling from one side of his mouth.

"Izzy, did you look at this?" Uncle Toby asked, handing the volume to me.

Snowe smirked as I accepted it. I felt my cheeks flush. "I do not read Chinese either," I said, pretending humility that I did not feel.

"I would not expect you to."

"Isabella is quite accomplished in other languages, however," Uncle Toby said, "and I have no doubt that given time, she could learn Chinese as well."

Snowe laughed until the spectacles slid down his nose. He pushed them up again, still chuckling. "Forgive me, but it is a very difficult language. I doubt that it could be acquired by even a woman who wore it on her best slippers."

Uncle Toby had been right that someone would notice. I had had no notion that it would be a man. How embarrassing!

Uncle Toby looked interested. "Would you please be so kind as to translate for us, Snowe? Isabella and I were discussing those very symbols today."

"Not at all." He turned to me. "If you will hold out one of your feet."

22

Face flushing, I extended one. I felt that I should die of mortification, knowing that he had ample glance at my ankle in the perusal.

"Well?" Uncle Toby asked.

"They mean," Snowe said thoughtfully, as though trying to decide. "They mean *love*."

Oh my. That was rather forward.

Love?

Uncle Toby looked amused. "I am not surprised, Izzy. It seems the sort of notion that would pass as fashion for you young ladies."

"I must disagree, sir," I said, "for I never felt that young ladies were much concerned with love but with making a good match. The two are seldom the same, in my personal estimation." David's marriage to Catherine had taught me that.

"How wise you are, Miss Goodrich," Snowe said. "A lady who settles for love generally settles beneath herself. You, I am certain, are too clever to claim less than a marriage that is . . . what did you call it? A good match?"

I could not tell if he was jesting at my expense, but I suspected as much.

"Isabella can have a wonderful life without love or marriage."

"Uncle Toby," I murmured. He seemed determined to defend my honor.

"Really?" Snowe gave me his full attention. "And why are you above both love and marriage?"

"But I do not think myself so," I said. How on earth

was I to repair this conversation? My dear, it was beyond repair. It was in dire need of termination. I had heard that a lady's swoon could bring an entire room to a standstill. Dare I attempt it? Yes, I must. One, two . . .

"Perhaps our Lord has called Isabella to a different life," Uncle Toby said. "I am certain that a man of God such as yourself, Snowe, can well understand how the Almighty sometimes sets the feet of his children on different paths from others."

"Indeed I can. No doubt God will reveal that path to you in his good time, Miss Goodrich."

Bewildered by the conversation's turn, I was nonetheless pleased. Phineas Snowe had uttered what I believed were his first sensible words all evening. "I await his command," I said.

Snowe pressed his hands together in a soundless clap. "Spoken like a true disciple! Miss Goodrich, I am delighted to have met you. Mr. Fitzwater, might I have a word with you about my mission work? Miss Goodrich, you will not mind if we excuse ourselves? I fear that our conversation will be entirely too boring for your tastes."

"On the contrary, Mr. Snowe. I find discussions of foreign lands most intriguing." China! The Orient! Oh, to see all the foreign sites and peoples of such places as my imagination could only invent from my reading. Surely I could forbear Phineas Snowe long enough to hear his firsthand tales.

Uncle Toby pressed my hand. "The Ransoms are in want of your company to keep the party amiable." He smiled. "You must not waste what should be a convivial time."

"Of course, Uncle," I said, knowing that I was being dismissed. Perhaps it was for the best. I had yet to make note of any gown save Catherine's, and Flora would want a full accounting when I returned home. And there was still the eligible man who was supposed to be in attendance. "You will want this back, Mr. Snowe," I said, handing him the Chinese translation of Luke.

He bowed, his thick spectacles sliding down his nose. He pushed them back as quickly as he rose, his smile peculiarly unctuous. "It would honor me were you to keep it."

"Thank you," I said, curtsying as he and Uncle Toby headed for a quiet corner. I could hear Snowe's voice, cheerful and animated now, and wondered again at the strange man.

As for other strange men, it was far past time to search for the eligible one who was due to be in attendance tonight. I oddly sensed that my future depended upon him.

Finding myself unengaged, I tried to watch the doorway to see the mystery man arrive. He should be handsome, certainly, but even if he were not, a pleasing disposition and intelligent demeanor would suffice. Despite her faults, Catherine knew men, and she would match me with no one less than I deserved.

Unfortunately, my watch was curtailed when I was drawn into a conversation with which obligation demanded I pay strict attention. Mrs. Marston complained bitterly about her verrucas, and though I would have liked to politely disengage myself from discussions of oozing and the merits of potatoes planted in the garden at midnight, she was the oldest woman in attendance and therefore due the courtesy of my attention. Lady Ransom soon joined us and proceeded to expound upon the vagaries of the Methodists. Here, at last, was a discussion with merit, though of course I could not share the extent of my true opinion. Freddie had repeatedly warned me that I should never reveal the depth of my mind or then I would have nothing left to show.

Several other women joined us, and I gradually realized that no one in the circle was within twenty years of my age. The other young women, all engaged to be married or already wed, huddled in conversations of their own. In between discussions of Mrs. Marston expounding on colonics and elderly Mrs. Gentry bellowing (she being rather hard of hearing) herbal remedy suggestions, I could hear the prittle-prattle of my peers.

". . . scandalous education . . ."

". . . uncle even permits her to use a sword!"

Of course I knew their talk to be directed at me, but one gaze in return, and they smiled charmingly at me as though I were a child or a pet dog begging for treats.

Dinnertime arrived at last, and I consoled myself with the thought that surely Mr. Mysterious had managed to sneak into the party without my notice. At last I would see him, for he could not possibly bypass the meal.

"Isabella, you simply must sit next to me," Catherine said, drawing me to her side at the lengthy table loaded with platters of food. "I have the most delightful person selected for your dinner companion." She leaned toward me confidentially. "The man of whom I spoke, Izzy."

"Really?" I tried to hide my excitement, craning my neck to watch the others as they sat at prearranged places. Deep in conversation with Mrs. Marston (but hopefully not about her verrucas), Uncle Toby took a seat directly across from me.

"Here he is," Catherine said, holding out her hands past me. "How good of you to grace our humble table with your presence, Mr. Snowe."

My heart sank nearly to my knees as I watched Phineas Snowe take her hands. "The pleasure is all mine, Mrs. Ransom."

Catherine brayed with laughter, then placed her hands on my shoulders. "I have taken the liberty of seating you next to—"

"Isabella Goodrich, was it not?" His eyes seemed to twinkle maliciously behind those horrid spectacles.

"You two are well suited as dinner companions," Catherine said, her face a warm mask of smiles.

"But he is not, that is . . ." I searched the doorway, hoping desperately to see my dashing, ideal gentleman at last. "We met earlier," I finished lamely.

"I am delighted," Catherine said. "For I can imagine no two people more predisposed to like-minded conversation. After all, Isabella, you have always been the intelligent one among our little crowd." She took the arm of her doting husband, David, who seated her with great solicitation. "Isn't that right, my love? You always said that Isabella Goodrich was quite the bluestocking."

27

David glanced at me for a moment, then away, his cheeks flushing.

My mind was all sixes and sevens as Phineas politely held out my chair. *He* was the man Catherine had in mind for me all along? As I settled into my seat, I glanced around the table and saw that save for Uncle Toby, Phineas, and myself, everyone was paired off like animals preparing for Noah's ark.

Suddenly it seemed that every set of female eyes was trained on Phineas Snowe and me. Their gazes were quick but not enough so for me to miss their shift to Catherine. Out of the corner of my eye, I noticed that she smiled triumphantly, and when the other women turned to their husbands or betrotheds, I knew that somehow they, too, had been a part of my public humiliation. For as surely as I knew my name, they were setting me in my place.

This was what Uncle Toby had tried to relay in the carriage but had not the spirit to make plain. Or perhaps I simply had not the ears to hear. But the truth was that I *was* past hope of finding a husband. My place in life had suddenly been reduced to gossiping with the matrons and entertaining this foreign man, a social stray.

In society's eyes, I was officially on the shelf. The battle was over.

Or was it?

Through the years, I had learned that one of the greatest mistakes in fencing occurs when one does not allow proper distance between himself and an opponent. You simply cannot be hit if you maintain a more than adequate separation. Maestro Antonio had repeatedly emphasized that I should always set the distance between myself and him as one small step beyond where I believed the tip of my weapon could strike him. Time and again, his advice had proved advantageous, and I trained to perfect my lunge across the gap.

Catherine Ransom had failed to leave herself just such adequate space to avoid my riposte to her parry. I would let her think that she had done me a favor by pairing me with Phineas Snowe, though the thought turned my stomach. She and every woman in the room would see that Isabella Goodrich was not done for, that they need not consign me to spinsterhood just yet. Though he had been rude beyond measure, Snowe was only a man, after all. I abhorred flirting, but that did not mean I was ignorant to its methods and results.

I turned my most beguiling smile to my dinner companion, taking care to lower my eyes a trifle and peer through the fringe of my hair. "You have already spoken to Uncle Toby, but I should love to hear about your travels if you do not mind the repetition. I am certain that you can moderate your speech so that even I can understand."

Snowe glanced at my uncle, who was still in conversation with Mrs. Marston, then presented me with a thin, oily smile. "I would not mind at all, Miss Goodrich."

2

Ever the romantic, Flora once said that every young woman should have at least one secret vice. I would hate to disappoint with something so seemingly useless, but mine was fencing. Uncle Toby had taken me, as a child, to view a student fencing exhibition, and I was enthralled by the flash of blade against blade. I insisted upon being shown the basics, and Uncle laughingly obliged what he thought mere whimsy by hiring a fencing master. We worked first on footwork, then added wooden swords. Both the master and Uncle assumed I would weary of the endeavor, but they indulged my increasing interest as the years went by. Eventually I graduated to real swords and a more skilled fencing master, for time sown in persistence reaped undeniable skill.

I thrilled to the sport for its cat-and-mouse qualities, each thrust and parry designed to work an opponent to my will. When I fenced, I felt as though I were a human chess piece, as well as the player, calculating and executing moves in sequences designed to ensure victory. Had I been born male, I have no doubt I would have been drawn to the military or, more imaginatively, to life as a benevolent highwayman, like Robin Hood. I understood implicitly that fencing should only be employed with the purest of motives, though I, like many other fencers, romantically desired to execute a *botte secrète*—a perfect thrust that would ensure victory.

To guard my reputation, my practice remained secret for many years. The rattling tongues at the Ransoms' party only reinforced society's opinion: young women simply did not fence. How long my rule breaking had been common knowledge, I could not say. But I would not let a few clucking guineas stop me from my favorite pastime. I met my instructor in his *salle d'armes* the very next day.

Signor Antonio and I sparred diligently, as was our custom. Our fleurets met, parted, and met again, our blades clanging with metal against metal. However, I could scarce keep my concentration as I daydreamed about the Ransoms' party of the previous night. Flora's superb work on the new dress still enthralled me, as did the memory of the slippers. They had been works of not only beauty but comfort too. After dinner, we had adjourned to the ballroom, where a four-piece orchestra played for the remainder of the evening.

"Ah! You are slowing. Too much dancing last night, eh?" Signor Antonio beamed. I could see sweat forming behind his mask as we broke. "If you must participate in useless exercise, you must know your limits. Reserve your strength for fencing."

I nodded as we continued. If only Signor Antonio knew that I had not set even one of my beautifully slippered feet to dance. Phineas Snowe had kept me cornered all night with his fustian chatter, waving off all who approached. Not that any man would willingly dance with me!

Signor Antonio broke free, gesturing with dismay. "Signorina Goodrich, it is not like you to lose your concentration. If you are not willing—"

"I am sorry, Maestro," I said, bowing. "Please forgive my lack of attention." I assumed the stance.

Uncle Toby paid poor Signor Antonio handsomely every week not only to keep my unladylike secret but to train me well. Why, I do not know, but I had accepted my practice all these years without question. Before my first failed social season, however, I fretted that the skill would be all for naught. When I thought I would marry, I knew I would eventually have to put away my sword as a childish plaything; it would serve no purpose in my womanly future.

Now, however, I could foresee a future of freedom to pursue my beloved sport. Oddly, the idea of being a spinster did not sadden nor frighten me, but it did leave me yearning for some divine call. An evening with Snowe had showed me one thing: a high purpose would no doubt help me fill the many days of solitude ahead of me. Most of the men with whom I was acquainted were men of leisure or academicians. The former seemed to have no desire for busyness, and the latter found employment enough in mental athletics.

Snowe, however, was a man with purpose. He could

scarce sit still for ten minutes last night without resorting to a nervous pace. I could see the hunger in his eyes as he talked about the poor heathen Chinese. He had obviously spent much time among them and desired to improve their lot in life, particularly regarding the spread of the gospel.

If only I had not been forced to play the simpleton young woman. I would have dearly loved to ask Snowe an intelligent question about his work. Most of the evening he spoke down to me, but on an occasional moment, his eyes seemed fixed on a distant spot, and he seemed to speak a trifle more freely. Almost as if he had quite forgotten I was even present.

I felt the faintest tip of a fleuret at my heart. A touch. Signor Antonio had not landed one so lethal for years. "Be careful, Signorina Goodrich!"

I could almost see him smile as I bowed. "I am sorry, Maestro."

"Bah! That is all for today. You are wasting my time." He waved his hands in the air, pretending anger, but I knew he was secretly pleased. Signor Antonio was not usually a teacher to berate me for carelessness, thank goodness. In truth I believe we both knew that I had surpassed his abilities as my teacher several years ago. Old age and dissipation had overtaken his better days. Signor Antonio had trained under Domenico Angelo, both of them Italians who excelled in the French school of fencing. Though Uncle Toby and I never spoke of it, we knew that Signor spent most of his payment on the wine he loved dearly. After every lesson I somehow managed to send him 'round to Cook for some hearty victuals before his next lesson. Despite his once-proud reputation, he had lately been shunned by many of the students in favor of other fencing masters, ones who taught fencing as a competitive sport and not as a true martial art. I worried about the leanness of Signor's purse and feared he did not sup well during the week.

We finished, bowing low to each other. "I believe Cook said something about making two extra meat pastries today by mistake, Maestro. She would be pleased if you would help by eating one now and taking the extra one for later," I said.

"*Grazie*, Signorina Goodrich," he said as he did after every lesson. "I would not mind just a taste from your kind uncle's kitchen. Just a taste, *per favore*."

After I changed from my fencing clothes back into my morning dress and adjusted my hair into a less disheveled style, I walked home, accompanied by Flora. We spoke little, for I felt as sober as a vicar. Was fencing to be the highlight of my future? Was there no higher goal to which I should aspire? Surely there was some lifelong service on which I could fix my sights!

Our home, the deanery, was a residence in Christ Church's main quadrangle, affectionately known as Tom Quad. Normally I marveled at the fountain in the center as I passed, but instead I hurried Flora and myself home. As we entered, I thought to spend time alone in my room, in contemplation of my future, when I passed Uncle Toby in his study. I doubled back. Because he spent much of his time here, it was our accustomed sitting room. Full bookshelves lined the walls, and cozy chairs were arranged in front of the fireplace. Silhouettes of my mother and father—created, I am told, a few years before my birth—stood on the mantel as though watching us. Down through the years, Uncle Toby, Frederica, and I had passed many a pleasant moment together before the fire in either solitary reading, chess matches, or long discussions of political or religious nature.

Now he sat in his favorite leather wing chair, pondering a dusty tome between his hands. Unaware of my presence, he smiled faintly to himself, and I knew him to be lost in a world of literature that excluded all reality.

I cleared my throat at the doorway to gain his attention. Uncle Toby had been known to read straight through dinner if not alerted.

"Oh! There you are, Izzy." Uncle Tobias looked up, peering at me through the spectacles perched on the end of his nose. He gestured to the high-backed chair beside his own and waved the book in his other hand. "I was just reading the most amazing story. Have you time to share your opinion?"

I admired that he thought me an academic equal, but at the moment my conscience was preoccupied as I sat. "I am afraid not, Uncle Toby, but perhaps you can answer a question for me. How do I learn my life's calling?"

He shut the book and removed his spectacles. "I had feared that last night would reveal the truth to you. I hoped to soften the blow beforehand, but I—"

"You were nothing but kindness, Uncle." I patted his hand fondly. "I was a silly goose to be enamored with my new slippers when you tried to speak to me about my future." I straightened in the chair, feigning maturity as I folded my hands in my lap. "So now I am all attention. How do I learn my life's calling?"

Uncle Toby smiled anew. "Society would tell you that it is to become some fortunate man's wife."

I lifted my nose a trifle. "Society has not helped much in that regard, then. Perhaps I like being unwed."

His eyes twinkled, and he chucked my chin. "I am not sure that I quite believe you on that, dear Izzy, and I wish I could help where you feel society has not. I have no doubt that my poor dead sister would despair to hear you say such words."

I swallowed, glancing up at the silhouette. From what Uncle had told me of my mother, I knew his words to be truth. Mother would have reveled in Frederica's chosen life and no doubt been appalled to have a younger daughter turn out to be a . . . dear, I hate to use this word, but it is becoming more true each day. I am a spinster.

I squared my shoulders. "Nevertheless, Uncle, I know God chooses a path for each of his children. If it is not marriage, I would like to know mine. A life of solitude, perhaps?"

Uncle Toby smiled. "I do hope it is not in a cloister, Izzy. You are far too intelligent to seal yourself away in a life of contemplation."

"All that seems left to me is to be a governess then."

I sighed. "Some days I fear that is my only ordained path."

He raised his brows. "'Fear,' Izzy? Do not embark on a journey of unhappiness, for I do not believe that we are called to tasks that make us miserable, but rather those that bring joy not only to others but to ourselves, as well."

"Then I should be a modiste, for I love fashion."

He frowned. "You are also too intelligent to spend your days hunched over fabric and thread."

"But I am on the shelf, Uncle. No man has seen fit nor apparently ever will see fit to claim me for his wife." I sighed. "I know that God orders our every path, but I must confess that I am puzzled. What would he have me do?"

Uncle Toby touched my cheek. "Ah, Isabella, I fear it is my fault."

"Yours?"

He nodded. "I have raised you with too much inquisitiveness and too much of a thirst for knowledge. It is true that you have learned the ways of fabrics and fans, but you have not, apparently, acquired the secret art that women pass so heartlessly from one generation to another—flirting."

"Is that the sum of all skills to acquire a husband?" I asked, arching a brow.

"You see?" He laughed. "You are too straightforward by half. Ah, well, I shall look forward to my niece attending me in my dotage then, if no one will speak for you."

"But Uncle, did you not hear me? Perhaps God has another plan for me. If it includes you, that is good and well, but sadly, I worry that it may not."

37

"Then I shall look forward to your telling me of its nature," he said, reopening his book, then winking. "Once you find it. Good day, Isabella."

"Good day," I replied, rising, knowing when I was dismissed.

"Isabella?"

I turned. "Yes?"

"I do not mean to belittle your worry for your future. You are my dearest niece and a great comfort to me. I hope you know that."

I smiled fondly. "Indeed I do, Uncle."

He returned to his book, his mind already wandering from me. "If your presence will not intrude on Signor Antonio's meal in our kitchen, please inform Cook that we will expect one more for dinner tonight," he said.

"Oh?"

Uncle licked his finger and turned a page. "I invited Phineas Snowe to dine with us. I should like to hear more about his charitable work. You two seemed to enjoy each other's company last night. I also thought it would be a good chance for you to further your conversation."

I opened my mouth, but no sound came out. "I'll make sure Cook knows," I finally said, turning to leave.

My head began to ache as I headed for the kitchen. Must I endure another night of Phineas Snowe and his condescension? Because I had already acted a role at the Ransoms', I would be forced to repeat it tonight as well. The thought of smiling endlessly and nodding gamely at his every pronouncement . . . It would take a great deal of not only physical strength but mental agility to continue the missish role.

I came to a full stop in the hallway. "But why should I? I owe nothing to Snowe."

Last night had only been a chance to hold my own with Catherine Ransom and the others. Uncle Toby would not expect me to be anyone other than who I truly was, and in the safety of our own home, that is exactly who I would be!

Phineas Snowe arrived at our doorstep at the precise hour for which Uncle Toby had issued the invitation. Flora ushered him into Uncle Toby's study, raising her eyebrows at me behind his back. She knew from my description of Snowe last night that he wore the same threadbare attire tonight. Either he was more destitute than I believed or he truly had no sense of fashion. I was quite sure that if I had mentioned the name of the dandy Beau Brummel, he would have stared at me like a sapscull.

"Ah, Mr. Snowe," Uncle Toby said, rising from his wing chair. "It is so good of you to join us."

He gestured Uncle back down. "Pray do not stand on my account, Mr. Fitzwater," he said, then bowed in my direction. "Miss Goodrich, you look well this evening. Is your health compatible with your appearance?"

"I am afraid I cannot answer that, Mr. Snowe."

"Indeed?"

I nodded. "If I answer yes, I might stand accused of conceit."

He frowned. "How so?"

"To answer yes might be construed that I took your comment to mean that my appearance, while 'well,' was equivalent with 'pleasing.' However, if I answer no, then you would, of course, inquire as to the nature of my negative response. Then I should be forced into prevarication by inventing some imaginary ailment to appease any further questions."

Snowe glanced at Uncle Toby. "Is it always this difficult to exchange pleasantries with your niece?"

Uncle smiled blithely. "Sometimes it is more so." He rose. "If you two will excuse me, I will see about procuring a bit of wine before dinner."

Snowe bowed, and I curtsied at Uncle's departure. I thought Snowe would continue the subject, but he affected a solemn sort of smile. "Miss Goodrich, I owe you an apology."

I blinked. This was most unexpected. "Whatever for?"

"I fear that I nattered on at far too great a length last night about my work. You must think me the most dreadful of bores."

"On the contrary, Mr. Snowe, it is I who should apologize to you. I am sure that any number of guests could have held up their end of the conversation better than my feeble attempts." I paused. "I was not quite myself last night."

He smiled. "You were kind to allow me to discuss my life's mission. It must seem a simple life, compared to what you are accustomed here with your uncle in a thriving town like Oxford."

"You must be mistaking our location with London, sir,

for one could hardly accuse our humble town of much notoriety or excitement."

"Notoriety can well lay claim here if only for the university and its history. To think of Cranmer, Ridley, and Latimer losing their lives here as martyrs for the church . . ." He shook his head in contemplation. Uncle Toby entered with a tray of wine, and Snowe gestured in his direction. "Perhaps your uncle would do me the honor of showing me the locations of their martyrdom at Oxford. It would be a privilege to stand on such ground where three holy men were burned at the stake for their beliefs."

Uncle presented us each with a glass of wine. "If you speak of Cranmer, Ridley, and Latimer, I am certain that Isabella would be honored to show you the locations. She is most familiar with that history."

"Are you indeed, Miss Goodrich?" Snowe turned his bespectacled eyes on me.

I cast a glance at Uncle Toby. I was beginning to believe that he was *trying* to bring Snowe and me together. Inviting him to dinner was one thing, but sending us on a historical tour was quite another. "History is of great interest to me, Mr. Snowe. Particularly church history."

Snowe sipped his wine. "What was it Latimer said as encouragement when the flames consumed him? 'Be of good comfort, Master Ridley and . . . and . . .' Oh, the words escape me."

"'Be of good comfort, Master Ridley and play the man! We shall this day light such a candle, by God's grace, in England, as I trust shall never be put out,'" I finished.

"Yes. That's it, Miss Goodrich. Well done. You *are* rather conversant in church history."

Was he jesting? Any churchgoing child could recite the words!

"She is an historian indeed." Uncle Toby beamed. "Izzy, tell Mr. Snowe about the paper you wrote on the Reformation."

"I am sure Mr. Snowe would not care to hear of it, Uncle," I said.

Snowe took a long sip of his wine. "Thank you, I would not. While I admire theory and history, I find that quiet lives of useful service are more in keeping with Christ's commandment to go ye therefore and teach all nations."

"Why, that is Izzy herself." Uncle Toby beamed. "Lately Isabella has been much taken with the Methodists."

"Have you done much charitable work, Miss Goodrich?" Snowe asked, his accusing gaze turned on me.

"Flora and I made some simple frocks and knitted mufflers for the poor," I said. "Perhaps you would care to discuss your work in China?"

Snowe smiled smugly. "Your own work is a trifling effort, but an effort nonetheless. I wonder that you have not been challenged with more personal work."

"And what, exactly, is *your* personal work in China?" I persisted.

He put a finger to his lips, thought a moment, then smiled. "Mr. Fitzwater, I have a unique suggestion."

Uncle Toby leaned forward in his chair. "Yes?"

"Would you and your niece be interested in joining me

tomorrow with another from my group as we endeavor to bring some comfort to the poor? Along with my friends, another young lady desires to serve in China."

"Oh, will your friends join us?" I must admit I was curious to meet the Tippetts. I had never heard of a married couple desiring to serve the Lord together.

"Sadly, no. But we all desire to repay the town of Oxford for its generous hospitality. Tomorrow we will deliver baskets of food and blankets to some of the less fortunate, and I would like you and your uncle to join me."

My heart stirred. I too often forgot about those beyond our university setting. Oxford had its share of thriving trade and prominent town members, as well as the academicians and servants of the university. Yet Christ Church itself hovered above a collection of unseemly and no doubt disease-ridden hovels, which were too easily ignored in the constant quest for learning and commerce.

Uncle Toby peered at me. "Is this something you wish to do, Izzy?" he asked softly, evidently reading the expression on my face. To Snowe he said, "My niece is tenderhearted to a fault."

Snowe rocked on his heels, digesting this bit of information, one finger still at his lips as though preventing himself from saying more.

"I would see your group's work in action, Mr. Snowe," I said. "Provided Uncle Toby and I will not be a burden to you."

Uncle chuckled. "Not me, dear child. I have work to attend to tomorrow. Flora may accompany you. Mr. Snowe,

I trust my niece's curiosity will be satisfied. And perhaps her heart uplifted."

Snowe positively beamed. "Miss Goodrich?"

I glanced at Snowe then Uncle Toby then back to Snowe. "I . . . would be delighted," I said, hoping that once again I had not spoken or acted in haste.

What dress does a young lady wear to serve the poor?

I brooded over it at great length until Flora solved the issue by thrusting a white cotton batiste with vertical blue stripes into my hands. "This will look lovely on you, Miss Isabella. Especially with that new blue-ribboned poke bonnet."

Thank goodness for Flora. I had an eye for fashion and normally knew just what to wear, but I was quite at a loss that day. I certainly was not dressing for Phineas Snowe, but I suppose I wanted to make an impression on the young lady who would be joining us. It is quite true that ladies do not dress for gentlemen but for other ladies.

Mr. Snowe arrived promptly as scheduled, escorting Flora and me to the waiting carriage. There we were introduced to a Miss Julia Whipple, and I knew instantly that all fashion worries had been for naught. She was clothed in the most unimaginative brown cotton dress and matching bonnet I thought I had ever seen. Oddly, she did not seem to notice my clothes, glancing away shyly as we were introduced. No wonder she sought to become a missionary. She obviously lacked the fortitude for society and its graces.

We spoke little during the ride, which was blessedly

short. As the familiar streets around the university gave way to a meaner, dirtier area, Flora drew close to me. Ragged children with dirty faces ran after our carriage, shouting to us for money. Old men in tattered clothes staggered aimlessly down the dirty, unpaved road. A woman wearing an entirely too revealing dress and garish shawl called out to Phineas as we alit from the carriage carrying baskets of food and blankets. He approached her, and she smiled, angling the shawl off her shoulders. However, he spoke a few quiet words, then handed her a loaf of bread. She shrugged but accepted it, then called out to a young girl, who took the bread and ran up the street while the woman moved in the opposite direction.

"Flora," I whispered, "is that a Cyprian?" I had heard of women who accepted money from men in exchange for favors.

"Yes," she said, her lips tight. "I am sorry that you should see it."

I knew such existed, of course, but instead of revulsion, my heart melted. The poor girl was younger than me, I was certain. Miss Whipple seemed equally disturbed, glancing away to shield her eyes, obviously shocked by the brazen display, or perhaps she was afraid.

I felt a moment of fear myself, then inwardly chided myself. Snowe would not bring us to a desperate situation. He had chosen to do God's work, but he was also a gentleman. He would not put three ladies in danger.

Behind the spectacles, Snowe's eyes seemed sad, or perhaps it was merely a reflection of the sun, which oddly enough did not seem to shine so bright in these sooty streets. He took Miss Whipple's arm. "Are you all right?" he said.

She nodded, squaring her shoulders. "Where should we begin to serve?"

I had no designs on Phineas Snowe, of course, but something in the way he beamed at Julia Whipple's eagerness made me want to be noticed as well.

"Perhaps we should split up," he said. "Miss Goodrich and Miss Florey can take one side of the street, and Miss Whipple and I the other."

"If I may differ, perhaps we should all remain together," I said.

"I agree," Flora said, pulling her pelisse closer as several children raced past, their grimy hands outstretched.

"Very well," Snowe said. "Let us begin."

He walked boldly to the nearest door and knocked. A girl of perhaps four and ten answered, her face expressionless as Snowe stated we were there to provide food and clothing.

She stepped back without a word, hanging her head. We entered the cramped home, or should I say hovel, for though it was obviously carefully tended, there was no ignoring the decrepit nature of the rotting beams and walls, the decayed wood floor, and the bugs that scuttled into the walls. A poorly ventilated chimney allowed smoke to seep into the room, while something vile smelling bubbled in an iron pot over the fire. We ladies coughed. Loud snores emanated from behind a curtain in the corner of the room.

An elderly woman rocked in a chair by the fire, staring at us blankly.

To my surprise, Snowe knelt beside her and spoke softly. "Is that your husband behind the curtain?"

She nodded, yet she never ceased rocking. "I wouldn't try to speak to 'im, though. 'E's a bit cup-shot, sir."

Snowe touched her hand. "I am sorry to hear that, madam. Please accept some of the food we have brought for your family. Do you need blankets?"

The gentleness of his voice—still a great surprise to me!—must have swayed her vacant expression, for she turned to him then to the rest of us. "Bless ye. Thank ye. We could use a bit of warmth for the cold nights."

Snowe nodded at me, and I reached into the large basket I held and placed two coarse woolen blankets on the table. He turned back to the woman. "I wish we could do more," he said.

She nodded as if to say she understood. Snowe rose to his feet, and he and Miss Whipple left bread and cheese on the table beside the blanket. He motioned us to leave, and the expressionless girl showed us out.

Back on the street, I somehow found my voice. "Why was her husband abed in the middle of the day? I have never heard of an ill person snoring like that."

Snowe sighed. "He is given to much drink. It is sad enough for him but sadder still for his family."

"He should provide for them as a gentleman should," Flora said.

"He is no gentleman, Miss Florey," Snowe said. "He has

not the benefit of birth as many in England and therefore finds it difficult to make a better life for himself. I am in agreement that he should provide for his family, however, and I pray that someone will show him the error of his ways. Unfortunately, it cannot be me, for I must return to China."

"They are so poor here," I murmured, glancing back at the house, my heart stirring with pity.

"They are indeed," Snowe said. "Yet even they would be richer than many in China."

I had no response, for I could not fathom such poverty. I had read of such situations, of course, but literature often made the condition seem noble or the poor at least responsible for their dire situation. The woman and her daughter could not be faulted for the man's decision to drink. What could I do to help?

Mr. Snowe took Miss Whipple's arm again and led the way to the next house. Flora and I fell silently in step behind them, clutching our baskets as though for dear life. I felt like a kitten who had just opened its eyes for the first time and, upon opening them, was quite shocked to learn of its surroundings.

"My soul and stars," Flora said, laying a hand over her heart as we entered our home later that day. "I am thankful to be here."

I watched through the crack in the closing door as Phineas Snowe drove away in his rented carriage. I reluctantly closed the door. "What is that you said, Flora?"

She removed her shawl and straightened the mob cap she insisted on wearing in public because she thought it made her look French. "Run upstairs and divest yourself of your clothing, dear. All of it. I plan to boil everything thoroughly before wearing it again. Phew! What a misbegotten part of town."

"Those poor people cannot help where they live, Flora," I said gently. "It is the best they can afford. It is true that some of the men are not good providers for their families, but there were so many widows and children . . . women grateful for the least crumb of bread we brought them. They have no one to turn to, the poor lambs."

Flora removed my shawl, grumbling. "That missionary group would do well to stay in Oxford and help them who need it. Instead, they fancy themselves missionaries out to save the Chinese." She snorted. "At least the Methodisticals stay mostly at home."

"The London Missionary Society has a different calling than the Methodists. Both lives of service are worthy."

Flora put her hands on her hips. "Listen to you, Miss Isabella. You sound just like that Phineas Snowe. 'We intend to go into all nations and serve,'" she said, mimicking his somber voice, "'and in China there is a great need for not only food and blankets but the gospel.' Such talk! Now upstairs with you, and I'll draw a bath. Tobias Fitzwater would have my hide if you get a horrible disease from our experiences today."

I obediently trotted upstairs and soon found myself unceremoniously tossed into the tub we used for bathing.

Flora not only drew my water—as hot as I could stand, I might add—but stayed to scrub me with one of her fancy soaps. "Nothing but French milled will work against this grime," she muttered under her breath as she attacked even my nails with a scrubbing brush.

"Ow! Flora, I am quite certain that no vermin could escape your ministrations. Though the soap smells divine."

"I got it from Gemma, who visited Bath this summer with the Pembertons."

"She is a governess?"

"Yes." Flora attacked my hair with the same vigor as my skin. "She's given up on finding a husband and resigned herself to life with a merchant's family."

"I have abandoned all hope as well," I said thoughtfully.

Flora stopped scrubbing and sat back on her heels. "Now, Miss, you have your uncle and me to look after you. And while we're not the same as a husband and family of your own, we care about you."

"I know you do, Flora. No one could love me more, I am certain. But I must find something to do with my life. I must be of some useful service, or I will go mad with pining. I live within one of the world's largest and most prestigious universities, and yet I am not allowed to use the knowledge I have gained from the many tutors Uncle has chosen for me. I cannot believe that God would have me content to read books with no one to discuss them with nor to write papers for no one to read."

"Miss Isabella . . ."

"And what is unused learning, anyway, but puffed-up

vanity and pride? It is not as though I can teach anyone else, as Uncle Tobias does." I shook my soapy head. "No, Flora, there must be something higher to which I might aspire. If I pray about it, I am certain that God will reveal his answer."

She sighed. "You pray then, and I will retrieve your rinse water."

And while she did that, I did exactly as she suggested. After I had dressed, I chanced upon the Chinese version of the Gospel According to St. Luke that Mr. Snowe had given me. I thumbed its pages, marveling at the mysterious foreign characters. They held the very wisdom of God-breathed writing, surely no less in substance than my own authorized King James version. I concluded my prayers and contemplated instead on deciphering the curious Chinese characters.

I picked at my dinner that night, thinking about all the poor Flora and I had seen that day. What were they dining on this evening, if at all? Flora was right that their existence was squalid and, I must confess, somewhat repulsive. But I could not attach their circumstance to any lack of moral character on their part, as some did. The women kept their homes as tidy as possible and often tended to far more people than their strength allowed . . . not only children but parents, grandparents, and the occasional drunken husband.

The weight of these women's fates seemed heavy on my

shoulders, and I wanted to pitch forward into my sumptuous food and weep.

"Is everything all right, Izzy?"

"Oh, Uncle . . ."

He patted my hand. "If it will make you feel any better, I sent word to Mr. Snowe that I would return him to China with a contribution for his missionary efforts. Your recommendation was all I needed."

"That is wonderful, but what have I to contribute?"

"Why, whatever is in my name is in yours as well, dear Isabella."

I shook my head. "If you could have but seen the women and children in need of the common things . . ."

Uncle Toby's expression softened. "I have tried to shield you from such ugliness in life. The poor we will always have with us, true, but you were born to a better station. It is our responsibility, of course, to help those less fortunate, but you must not let it discourage you from leading your own life."

"But I have no life," I mumbled. I was close to wallowing in self-pity, a most undesirable state, but the emotions of the day had coupled with my own.

Flora bustled to the table, teapot in hand. "Miss Isabella, would you like some tea? It is a special blend straight off His Majesty's most recently arrived East India ship. Cook got it at the market just today."

"Where is the tea from?" I inquired listlessly. "India, I suppose."

Flora shook her head, smiling as though to burst her apron strings. "China! Wouldn't Mr. Snowe be impressed?"

I glanced at Flora, and the beginnings of a smile tipped my mouth. She stared at me. "Miss Isabella, are you all right?"

I turned my attention to Uncle Toby, a full smile in bloom now.

"Izzy?"

I clasped my hands in my lap, trying vainly to contain my joy. "I prayed that God would show me my purpose today, Uncle."

"And?"

"The tea! It is from China. Just like the Gospel According to St. Luke that Mr. Snowe gave me. My pink slippers also were presented to me with Chinese letters."

Uncle Toby and Flora stared at me.

Did they not understand? It was obviousness itself. "All three are answers to my prayer. I know what my purpose is! God intends for me to travel to China with Phineas Snowe's missionary group."

Teapot in hand, Flora stood frozen. Uncle Toby as well, until a smile lit his face. "I cannot discount any message from the Lord, but you *are* prone to spontaneity, Isabella. I must wonder if your deduction has been reached in haste."

"I cannot believe it has been. I feel such a . . ." I drew in a deep breath. "A *rightness* about this."

Flora set the teapot on the table and fled the room, apron at her mouth.

"Why, what is wrong with Flora?" I said.

Uncle reached across the table to take my hand. "It is not

every day that a gently bred young woman announces her intentions to give up civil life for that of a missionary. In a country halfway around the world, no less." His expression softened. "I have my own doubts, Isabella."

My resolve crumbled. I thought they would be pleased. "But . . . it is a worthy calling."

"Indeed it is. For someone like Phineas Snowe. He is a single man with no encumbrances of family."

"As am I! . . . Except that I am not a man, of course."

"Of course. But my dear, have you forgotten Flora and me? Your sister Frederica and her family—Lewis, your nephew?"

I doubted that, of all people in Britain, little Lewis would mind my absence. "I would miss you all, Uncle, but my religious duty must come first."

"God and king, Isabella?" Uncle smiled.

I nodded. "Please, would you speak to Mr. Snowe on my behalf to ask if I might sail with his missionary group? He told Flora and me that they are to leave in two days. Surely it is not too late for me to join them."

"Well . . ."

"Please, Uncle." I tried to signal my earnestness with my expression. I would never resort to the lowly feminine trick of tears, but to my surprise, moisture welled in my eyes.

Uncle Toby, who could spare me little and knew that I seldom asked for much, sighed. "I will ask him, Isabella. Your agreement must be that you will abide by his decision if he says no. I will warn you in advance that I believe that will indeed be his answer."

Joy lightened my heart. Of course he would say yes! Had he not complimented me today on my patience as I held squirming, squalling children and fed feeble elderly mouths? His answer would be yes just as surely as it was already God's!

3

You may think me insane to have wanted a future with Phineas Snowe, since he was most peculiar. I marveled at my decision as well, but I can recount with all honesty that Snowe was a different man when he was about the Lord's work. He spoke gently with the poor, offering comfort and aid.

His assistant, Julia Whipple, also did the missionary society proud. I did not care for the dark brown clothing she wore, but I supposed it was necessary for the required physical labor of a missionary and as good a detriment to a lady's vanity as anything. Miss Whipple spoke little but dispensed food and medicines and bandages with a shy, cheerful demeanor that greatly lifted the spirits of the destitute, I am certain. I longed to serve beside her in China.

Besides, surely Snowe and I would not have to work in close proximity.

Uncle sent word to him that very night, at my insistence, of course. I am happy to report that I did not resort to tears; indeed I was ashamed that they had manifested themselves earlier. I choose to believe that Uncle Toby thought them merely strong evidence of my sincere desire to serve the Lord in China.

I knew that no answer would be forthcoming from Snowe that evening, yet I waited with keen impatience. One of Uncle's friends, a dean from another college at Oxford, called on us after dinner. With no family of his own, Erasmus Howe often warmed himself before our fire and exchanged intellectual conversation.

I tried in vain to work at an embroidery Flora had insisted I begin, but the threads refused to lie flat. My fingers, representatives of my inner being I am certain, trembled with eagerness for Snowe's answer. Normally I enjoyed Mr. Howe's visits, for he was too old to disapprove of my joining the discussion with Uncle Toby. Tonight, however, I found no pleasure in even their spirited argument about the philosophy of Jean-Jacques Rousseau.

"The development of the sciences and arts have contributed to society's moral corruption," Howe said, wagging his finger.

Uncle Toby shook his head. "Old friend, I am afraid you overlook the inherent evil of man himself. His academic and aesthetic reaches are only reflections of corruption, not the root cause."

"Bah!" Howe crossed his arms. He turned to me. "What say you, Isabella? Will you not side with me?"

I set my embroidery in my lap, sighing. "I am afraid I have no worthwhile opinion tonight at all, Mr. Howe. If I were to choose sides, however, I would say that each of you possesses a modicum of truth in that your belief is so fervent."

"So then belief is all that is wanted for truth?" Howe twisted further toward me, settling in for further discussion.

"Isabella, would you please ask Flora for some more tea?" Uncle Toby asked softly, gesturing toward the doorway with his eyes.

I gratefully laid the embroidery aside altogether and rose. I would have hurried off to find Flora right away, but something told me to tarry. I was not given to eavesdropping, but Uncle Toby's dismissal had been extraordinarily abrupt.

"What is wrong with Isabella tonight?" Howe said. "She does not seem quite herself."

Uncle Toby sighed. "She wants to go to China."

"China! Whatever for?"

"She has a notion that God intends for her to become a missionary. Because of Phineas Snowe and his fellow servants of the Lord, she is convinced that is her calling, as well."

"But perhaps it is!" Howe said. "Admit it, Fitzwater. You would welcome the chance to travel again."

A long pause ensued. "I would," Uncle finally said. "Even at my advanced age, I wish I could travel to the Continent. With the war on, it would not be safe to take Isabella. But, oh, to visit France again. Germany. Italy." He sighed. "So many places of historical interest. So much literature to be read in their original languages."

"Can you not let Isabella decide about the risk for herself?"

I shamelessly moved closer to the door.

"Even so, she would be a burden," Uncle Toby said. "I would be obliged to look after her welfare to the point that my research would be impeded. No, Howe, I am afraid it is a dream that will remain unrealized."

I shivered as though someone had pushed me outside into the cold. Poor Uncle Toby. I was apparently an impediment to his resumption of the life he had lost so many years ago when Frederica and I were thrust upon him. Oh, how the reality of my spinsterhood these recent days must have rankled.

"Isabella!"

I started. "Flora. You gave me a fright."

"Whatever are you doing away from the fire?" She wrapped her shawl closer about her shoulders. "It is a chill night."

To be certain.

"I . . . I was looking for you, Flora. Uncle Toby has requested more tea."

"I was on my way into the study to see if more was needed. I am sorry you were indisposed."

Hearing Uncle and Howe's chatter in the room beyond, I drew Flora away, whispering, "It is well that I was, for I have learned an unsettling truth."

Flora clapped a hand over her mouth. "Phineas Snowe will not take you."

"No!" I glanced over my shoulder to make certain we had not been overheard. I lowered my voice. "At least, I do not yet know his answer."

"Then what?" Flora took my hands in hers and rubbed them. "Lord love you, child, you are chilled. Tell me about this dreadful truth you have learned."

I repeated Uncle Toby's exact words. Flora ceased rubbing my hands yet still held them. "You know that he did not mean for you to hear that, Isabella."

"Of course he did not. Uncle Toby would not hurt my feelings for the world. But I cannot ignore his own desires and dreams."

"His desires and dreams are your well-being. They have been such since the day you and your sister arrived in this home."

"I heard his words, Flora," I insisted. "If he would not hurt my feelings, I would not hurt his."

Flora gave my hands a final pat and released them. "It will all be well, dear one."

I repeated her words to myself as I lay in bed that night. Just before sleep overtook me, I reminded myself that God had called me to be a missionary in the Far East. Phineas Snowe would send an affirmative answer that I could join his group, and both Uncle Toby and I would have our lives laid out for us. Why did I worry when both our problems would soon be solved?

The letter arrived the next morning. Flora showed it to me, and we examined it together. Addressed to Uncle Toby in florid handwriting and sealed with the wax impression of a cross, it could only be from Phineas Snowe.

I clutched the letter between my hands. "Oh, Flora, this is my future life. Where is Uncle Toby?"

"I believe he's in the study with one of the students—"

I hurried down the hallway.

"Though I do not think he would care to be disturbed!" Flora called after me.

Outside the closed study door, I drew up short. I raised my hand to knock, then took a moment to straighten my skirt, pat my hair, and compose myself. Then I knocked. When Uncle Toby gave me entrance, despite my best efforts, I fairly flew through the door. I am not sure who looked more startled—Uncle Toby or his student, James Beatty. Beatty was an overly anxious young student who often turned red in the face, particularly in my presence. My impression of him was as a large puppy with feet still too big for its bearing.

Uncle Toby adjusted his spectacles and closed the book he and Mr. Beatty studied. "Here," I said without preamble. "It must be my answer."

Uncle Toby accepted the paper. "Mr. Beatty, we have studied enough for the day."

"Yes, sir," Beatty said. "Thank you, sir."

Uncle Toby waited until the young man had presented us with a fumbling bow, then stumbled his way from the room. I took the chair he had vacated and leaned toward Uncle while he used an opener to unseal the wax. His expression never betrayed his emotion as he read. How long could the missive be?

"Well?" I finally asked.

Uncle Toby removed his spectacles, rubbed his eyes with one hand, then put the spectacles back in place. "He says no."

Hope dashed, stomach churning, I reached for the letter. "He said *no*?"

Uncle handed the paper to me, and I scanned the lines, reading aloud. "*. . . flattered that she envisions herself . . . however . . . gently bred . . . certain she will make a fortunate gentleman a caring wife . . . sail tomorrow . . . wish you both God's blessings . . . your generous contribution will not go unrewarded . . .*"

Dazed, I let the paper fall to my lap. This rejection was far worse than David Ransom's. Or Catherine's, for that matter.

"I am sorry, Isabella. Surely it is for the best."

I glanced up. Uncle Toby's eyes were filled with sadness. Did he mourn my loss or his own?

"This belongs to you," I said, handing him the letter. Half of the broken seal pulled away from the paper and dropped to the rug. When I bent to retrieve it, I saw it was the half with the top of the cross. I clutched it in my palm to dispose of later.

Uncle Toby peered at me. "It is for the best, Isabella," he said again. "Do you understand that?"

I nodded woodenly, unable to speak. Perhaps later I would comprehend what he said, but at that moment only shock and disbelief were my companions. I had been so certain of Snowe's answer, so certain of God's call . . .

Uncle accepted my farewell, seeming to understand that

I needed time alone. I contemplated seeking Signor Antonio. It would feel good to have a sword in my hand and an obstacle that I could face. Then I remembered that I would have any number of days to practice my fencing and decided instead on a long walk to think matters through.

"Where are you going?" Flora met me at the door.

"I need a walk. Phineas Snowe has refused my request."

"Has he?" I could tell Flora was trying her best to keep the joy from her expression, but she was not wholly successful.

I headed for the rack and grabbed my pelisse. "I'll go with you, Isabella," Flora said, retrieving hers, as well.

"I need to be alone, please."

Flora set her mouth. "Wounded heart or not, you cannot leave this house unattended. I pledge to walk beside you as quiet as a mouse."

I could not help smiling in spite of myself. "A mouse who will try her best to give me counsel."

Flora placed my bonnet on my head and tied the ribbon under my chin, as she had done when I was a girl. "You have always sought my advice," she said calmly. "Would you cease now, even when you are in such haste to leave me forever?"

I thought about her words as we headed outside. We passed through the quad and Tom Tower, the college's main entrance at St. Aldate's Street. A light wind blew, and I wrapped my pelisse closer. Flora and I locked arms, and we headed down the street—toward what, I did not know. They had paved the streets at Oxford when I was a baby, and some said they were as fine as any of the best in London. Not that I traveled even so short a distance with great frequency!

Oxford is a university—and town—with unique architecture. Many of the buildings have spires that reach skyward, nay, toward the heaven of God himself. I longed to raise my arms in mutual supplication. *Why was I not chosen to do your work?*

As we walked together, silent, I thought long and hard. Flora had often called me impulsive, but my destiny, I was certain, lay in the Far East. Surely this was only a test of my resolve to answer God's calling. Did he not challenge his children in the Bible? If I were to accomplish my task, however, I would have to evade Flora. She was loyal to a fault, but she would not, I feared, hesitate to alert Uncle Toby if she felt my plans endangered my life. I would have to strike a balance between telling the truth and withholding pertinent points of my plan. It was not exactly lying, I reasoned. Merely omitting some of what Flora might perceive to be an unpleasant truth.

"I do not want to leave you or Uncle Toby," I said at last. I gestured at the buildings of the university as we passed. "But look around us, Flora. What are behind these walls but men striving to learn?"

"Is that not a noble cause?"

"For men, yes. For me, nothing. I believe God wants me to commit myself to a life of service."

"Then why not here in Oxford? There are plenty in want of Christian charity. We saw them yesterday."

"That is true, but I feel called to China. After looking at

the Gospel According to St. Luke that Mr. Snowe gave me, I felt a peculiar kinship with the strange marks. I have already learned Greek and Hebrew and several other languages. I feel that I could conquer Chinese as well. Surely they need a woman's touch in that heathen land."

"Like Miss Whipple, the lady in Mr. Snowe's group yesterday," Flora allowed.

I nodded. "Yes! And when I inquired, she admitted that she does not speak Chinese. Miss Whipple stared at me as though such thought were folly." I stopped short in the street. "God has given me a brain, Flora. I am certain that he wants me to use it. Did he not give me three instances of China—the slippers, the Gospel, and the tea?"

"The tea, I believe, was mere coincidence."

"I do not believe it was. Nonetheless, I am determined. I must speak to Mr. Snowe myself."

"If he still refuses your entreaty—"

"He won't," I said firmly. "I intend to meet him at dockside tomorrow."

"Miss Isabella, no! That is no place for a young lady."

"That is why you are going with me," I said. "I knew that if you would not allow me on a walk by myself that you would certainly not allow me to speak to Mr. Snowe alone. Though heaven knows I should be perfectly safe from him," I added, mostly to myself.

"You want *me* to go with you?"

"You said yourself that I could not go alone."

Flora raised one eyebrow. "You are only going to talk to him?"

"I would go today, but I do not know where he is lodging. I am sure to find him at the docks tomorrow."

Now it was Flora's turn to stop dead in the street. "You know that there are no docks in Oxford. He is leaving from London. No doubt he is already there."

"Then we must take a coach."

"A coach?" Flora recoiled in horror. "Two women alone?"

"It has been done before," I said mildly. "Really, Flora. What do you fear? I hardly think we need worry about highwaymen."

"But . . . but . . ."

I raised my eyebrows. "Yes?"

"But Mr. Fitzwater . . . what will he say?"

"He will know nothing about this," I said firmly. "We will go to London, speak to Mr. Snowe . . ." I fell silent.

"And then what?"

"And then perhaps he will see that I am in earnest," I said, trying to sound as positive as possible. I prayed that Flora would not be quick enough to speculate what might happen next, because I did not want to imagine hearing a negative answer from Snowe. Surely my perseverance would please not only him but God, who had called me to a life of mission work.

"How will we get to London?"

"Mail coach, I should think." I breathed an inward sigh of relief. Flora would follow me anywhere. Indeed, I could not live without her companionship. She was old enough to have been a very young mother to me, but she had always been much more.

"It would be the fastest," Flora said, thinking aloud. "No stopping to pay tolls along the road."

"Then it is settled. We must go home and pack some clothes."

"And tell your uncle."

"No!" I lowered my voice, aware that we had gathered onlookers. "He would not let us go, Flora. Once we are in London, we will send word that we are well."

"Or more likely, we shall simply return, errant, and be chastised."

"Perhaps," I said, but I knew that Flora was wrong. She had to be.

I packed a few things but was not overly concerned about weighting myself with possessions, including too much money. I took what few coins I had in my possession, but I wanted to rely on God to meet all of my needs. After all, I would start a new life in China. I did take the Gospel According to St. Luke, knowing that it would be useful in that foreign land.

I glanced around the room where I had grown up—my neatly made four-poster bed, the gently worn Aubusson carpet, my writing desk, the cases of my neatly arranged, beloved books . . . My heart seemed to expand then constrict. I could not imagine living anywhere else but here, but I would meet this challenge with determination, just as I had successfully studied fencing so diligently all these years.

The one possession I almost could not bear to leave was my sword. Signor Antonio had purchased it for me years ago, a sword forged by the finest craftsmen in Toledo. A fencer's skill is determined not only by talent but also by the capability of his weapon. I daresay mine was one of the finest in England. Yet by leaving it, I acknowledged that I intended to abandon selfish desire and anything short of my calling. So be it.

I penned a note to Uncle Toby, explaining my situation. I asked his forgiveness for leaving so abruptly and begged him to pursue the academic studies and travel he had once hoped to undertake. He should consider me as a newly married woman now, for though I had no husband or family, I was determined to wed myself to helping others.

I left the note on my bed, knowing that I would not be missed until after dinner. Uncle Toby would be teaching students all day, and he knew Flora would take care of me when needed. Yet I did not like to think of the look on his face when he learned I had left . . .

Flora and I carried our bundles to the Angel, an inn from which coaches left during the day. Oxford was quite the traveling town, a stop between many routes—London, naturally, a primary destination or origination.

"Maybe we should look for Mr. Snowe," Flora said. "If we are lucky enough to spot him, it will save us a trip to London."

She spoke a certain amount of logic, so we proceeded inside the inn. When I was finally able to secure someone's attention, I inquired whether they had seen Snowe. His was an easy description to relay, but unfortunately, no one had seen him. I was not surprised. There were so many coaches going in and out of Oxford that there were several stops. Perhaps he had even left the day before . . .

We secured our seats in the mail coach. Only four people were allowed to sit inside, even though the seats were abominably small. It was unladylike of me, but I had to elbow a rather ghastly man of corpulent stature to gain seats for Flora and me. I could not imagine that someone would refuse to give up a seat for ladies, but there is no accounting for manners—or lack thereof. Unfortunately, Mr. Corpulent was forced to sit atop the coach, and as we drove off at breakneck speed, I prayed that we would not topple over.

I had no illusions that the drivers or the guard would accommodate passengers. We were secondary to the mail and only allowed to ride with it, Uncle Toby had told me long ago, to help allay the expense of its travel. Passengers on their maiden ride might believe that the nattily scarlet-clothed guard was there for their protection, but I knew better. His presence was strictly to oversee the mail safely stowed in the boot underneath his post at the rear of the coach. He carried a yard-long tin horn to signal innkeepers of the mail's arrival, as well as to call passengers back to the coach and blow at the toll keepers, who rushed to open the gates.

By the time we reached London some six hours later, I was quite pleased to be rid of the whole traveling arrangement. I thought I might never rid myself of the seemingly constant blare of that tin horn, nor the guard's continual hastening and corralling of us passengers from each stop back to our seats. The ride itself was no bargain either. Flora and I both felt as jostled as potatoes in a poor man's sack. I believe Mr. Corpulent fared poorly during his ride atop the stage. His fingers seemed curled into a permanent state from clinging to his seat.

When we had collected our baggage, we found ourselves at loose ends. Flora, of course, had been to London as often as I, yet she could not stop gawking at the ladies who passed us by.

"Look at that darling shawl," she said. "And the stitching on the hem of that skirt. Why, I could accomplish that with a little work, as well."

"Flora, we are not here to study the latest fashion," I reminded her. "We must find our way to the docks. It would be dreadful if we missed Mr. Snowe."

After much inquiry, we found another coach, this one public, to take us to the East India Docks. It seemed no time at all before we were on the main street outside the entrance to the docks. We watched in awe as carts conveyed loads and loads of spices and tea up the Commercial Road.

"Where are they headed?" Flora said.

"The East India Company has warehouses in the City," I said. "I believe they sell their wares at auction there."

Flora gripped my arm and pressed so close to the coach window that I half feared she would hang her head outside like a hunting dog spying its prey. "Look," she said, her eyes wide.

The street was thronged with vendors, sailors, and people of both dubious and reputable natures. I could not imagine that such sights should provoke her curiosity. "What is it?"

"There," she whispered, pointing beyond the dock walls.

"Where? I don't—"

Then I saw where she gestured, above the dock walls, for I, too, could see the masts of many ships. The thought that they conveyed people and cargo beyond our native soil made my flesh tingle. Oh, adventure! Surely it was meant to be mine at last.

When the carriage arrived, we scrambled to disembark, find our luggage, and avoid the crowds that pressed against us, milling to and fro with much more purpose than we seemed to possess. We spent much time gawking until we had the presence of mind to begin inquiries as to the location of Phineas Snowe's ship.

A kind sailor tipped an imaginary cap. "Sorry, miss, but this here are the West India docks. Ships headed to India. You must be wanting the East India docks, where the East Indiamen sail to China."

"Yes, of course," I answered stupidly, grateful that the pleasant worker pointed out the direction where we should be. Normally, the distance—a good half mile, I estimated—might have necessitated that we find another means of conveyance. Our prospects did not look good, so—grateful that we had brought only one bag each— Flora and I hefted our baggage and walked. By the time we had passed between the proper dock walls, Flora was panting with exertion. Sailors and dockhands and even the occasional well-dressed man of commerce jostled us without thought.

I pulled Flora to the side of a vendor hawking food to the workers. She clutched her chest, and I worried that her heart was amiss. I searched her face. "Are you all right?"

"I just . . . need to . . . catch my breath."

"Poor Flora." I smiled. "I forget that you are unaccustomed to such exertion."

She leaned against the wall, closing her eyes momentarily. "I will be to rights in a moment," she said.

I stood on tiptoes and craned my neck, anxious, I must admit, to proceed with our mission. Suppose we missed Mr. Snowe? I was certain that I could convince him of my earnestness—as well as my suitability—for mission work in the Far East.

Flora must have sensed my anxiety, for she patted my arm, smiling wanly. "If you want to go look for the proper ship, I will wait right here. You can come back for me. Perhaps you will even get a chance to talk to Mr. Snowe, and this foolishness will soon be over."

"Thank you, Flora," I said, relieved that she had given me permission to leave her. It was uncharacteristic of her, to say the least. Yet no one seemed to frequent this area, so I felt certain that she would be safe long enough for me to investigate the various ships and find Snowe. I would be safe as well, for I did not intend to waste time or risk my welfare by asking questions of anyone other than a ship's officer. "May I leave my bag in your care so that it will not impede my progress?"

"Of course," she said. "I will keep them both safe right here and not twitch a whisker until you have returned."

"Will you be all right?"

Flora straightened. "I had three older brothers, Miss Isabella Goodrich, who taught me to care for myself. Now off with you!"

I gave her a final grateful smile, then headed toward the ships. Oh, what glorious works of man! Each one taller and larger than the rest. My head grew dizzy trying to look up at the top mast. Men scurried to and fro like ants on a hill, loading cargo. I knew that the East Indiamen often took on passengers such as Snowe and his group, so I was not surprised to see women, as well as men who were obviously not sailors.

More ships than I could count weighed anchor at the docks. I would never find Snowe this way. Scanning the crowds for someone who seemed trustworthy, I finally spied someone in uniform. A captain, perhaps? I knew nothing about naval dress or insignia.

"Excuse me, sir," I said, feeling uneasy about speaking to a man without formal introduction. "I'm looking for a ship sailing to China."

He smiled. "You have come to the right location, but as you can see there are many ships."

I tried to keep the shock from my expression. Were all these ships embarking at the same time? "I am looking for an East Indiaman that is leaving today and—"

"Most likely you want *Dignity*, ma'am."

Dignity? I knew it was not propitious to approach a

stranger, but he was an officer. I hoped. "I . . . I beg your pardon?"

He pointed down the lane of ships. "The HMS *Dignity*. See the East Indiaman with the three masts in between the smaller vessels? She is the only ship sailing for China today that I am aware of."

Good heavens. "Thank you," I said. "You are most kind."

"Not at all, miss." He touched his cap then turned away.

I looked back at where I had left Flora, wavering. Should I return for her or press on? Perhaps it would be best to make certain that this *Dignity* was, indeed, Snowe's ship.

I pressed on.

The crowds grew thicker as I made my way down the dock. I heard language that made my ears pinken, but I held my head high and lifted my skirts just enough to keep them from being splashed by the standing water. Thankfully my adorable pink slippers were stowed safely in the bag with Flora.

Wouldn't it be wonderful if I ran into Phineas Snowe without having to locate the ship and go aboard? I scanned the crowd for him, or at least another fellow missionary, but saw no one who looked likely.

Never did I imagine that ships could convey such grandeur and importance. Why, they were veritable countries unto themselves, it seemed, with sailors climbing the ropes to the dizzying height of the tallest masts, polishing and mopping the decks and their features, touching up the prows of the ships with a bit of fresh paint.

Why on earth were they dragging lowing cattle aboard? Poor Bossy. I should not like to be towed in such manner either, and I would put up just as much of a fuss were I an unwilling passenger!

I reached the gangplank and encountered someone who I felt certain was an officer, though perhaps a trifle young. He was decidedly not a captain! He gave commands in a voice that was still breaking with the change of youth, and I could see his resolve to act as a man in this role. "Excuse me, sir," I ventured, hoping that the mature title would flatter him into helping me.

"Yes, what is it?" he barked, then, when he saw me, had the good grace to flush. "I beg your pardon, miss, but I am in a bit of a hurry. We are about to cast off."

"Indeed?" I tried to quell the rising panic. Where was Phineas Snowe? "I am sorry to detain you, then, but I am looking for a . . . friend. I was supposed to meet him at the ship. Can you help me . . . Captain?" I blinked my eyes a little in what I hoped was a small bit of flirtation and flattery.

He reddened again, particularly when a nearby sailor stifled a hearty guffaw into a cough. "Miss, I regret for your sake that I am most certainly not the captain. Midshipman Bates at your service. Regarding your dilemma, however, I can tell you that most passengers do not board until Gravesend," he said. "It saves them some time aboard ship, though with our long voyage, I can't see that twenty miles makes much difference." He tipped his hat again. "Begging your pardon again. Most likely your friend will be boarding there, or even at Deal, where we'll await a good wind."

"I see," I said. "Thank you so much. I am quite sorry about the mistaken identity."

He tipped his hat again, then, obviously suffering from civility's restraint on my account, he snapped out another order to a sailor hefting a huge burlap bag.

Gravesend! How would Flora and I get there? We were rapidly running short of coinage. Why hadn't I foreseen the need for a great deal of money? Flora and I would have to pool our intelligence and come up with a way to—

"That's the last of the stock, sir," a sailor said, saluting the midshipman.

"Very well, then, thank you, Mr. Green. I shall inform the captain that we are ready to shove off."

Shove off? I had best remove myself from the ship before—

Oh, Providence, you are the answer to my bumble-bath! I did not stop to think of Flora's reaction, for my only thought was in getting to Gravesend as easily as possible. The best way to find Phineas Snowe would be to meet him aboard ship, of course! When I did think of Flora a few fleeting moments later, I realized that her worry would only be for a short period. If necessary, I could retrace my steps from Gravesend to London (by carriage this time, naturally) and rejoin her *and* Uncle Toby.

There was, however, the small matter of the success of my journey from these docks to Gravesend. I had no ticket, and I did not think it likely that they would allow me to work my keep for the twenty-mile journey. I was confident that I could pull and coil rope as quickly and neatly as the sailors doing so at the moment, because fencing had made my arms and legs much stronger than was reputable for a young lady. But it would behoove me to find a hiding place until Gravesend. Surely there I could reveal my presence and be forgiven for my unlawful means of passage. I was, after all, on a mission.

Where to hide? Why, the last place anyone would expect to find a lady.

I headed in the direction I had seen the sailor take the last cow.

Thinking that I would have to skulk to be undetected, I crept behind all manner of woodwork and iron mongery, but the seamen were so busy at casting off that no one seemed to pay me any mind as I made my way to the lower deck.

Until someone clapped a meaty hand about my wrist. My alarm grew as I stared up into the visage of a most unsavory sailor, surely worthy of any pirate novel. "What are you doing, missy?" he said, jagged yellow teeth prominent behind his bared lips.

I forced myself to avert a swoon. "I spoke with Midshipman Bates just a moment ago." There. That was not a lie.

He narrowed his eyes. "So you know where you're to go?"

I nodded, fearing that any further words would betray my purpose.

He unhanded me. "Off with you, then. I've work to do."

Alone again, I relieved myself of a sigh and continued my path. Where *were* those stairs?

At last I reached the lower deck, and aided by the sound

of more than one poor bovine bellow, I found the stable area, if that is what it can be called. Cows were separated from hogs like some religious gathering, no, that was sheep separated from goats. No matter. The hogs grunted at me dubiously, but as I had no fear of cattle, I entered their stall and made myself at home.

No doubt it would be a while before anyone bothered to check on the poor creatures, so I settled in. I had no fear of the great beasts, as I had often insisted on helping the dairy man with his chores when I was a girl—much to his delight. Of course I had been forced to cease the practice once I attained the age of young lady, but I could not forget the warmth of a bovine flank nor the gratefulness of expression when the milking had concluded.

"Here now," I said soothingly, rubbing the shoulder of one overly frightened Guernsey. "You will be cooped up for quite a while before you see true land again, I am sure, but you will be fed regularly and milked. Would you not like to be a Chinese cow? For that is where you are headed."

Bossy stared at me with large brown eyes as if she understood. The other cows quieted too, but the pigs squealed uproariously.

"Traitors," I mumbled. "Cowards." I had never liked pigs. Loathsome, dirty brutes.

After I had tired of admiring the cows, which took all of twenty minutes, I found a tidy corner to sit in and began to consider my present predicament. Poor Flora must be watching and waiting for me. How could I leave her stranded at the dock that way?

Remorse set in with a vengeance. I braced my hand against the wooden rail to rise and was suddenly thrown back to the straw. The ship moved!

"In for a penny, in for a pound," I muttered. "My decision is made. Again, Providence, I am sure."

Though my heart felt resolved, I mourned Flora. In the unlikely event that my plan failed, our reunion would be all the sweeter and our laughter all the heartier. She would scold me for being impetuous, then we would be on good footing once again.

But surely my mission would not be deterred.

As the hours wore on, boredom sank in. I had the Chinese Gospel According to St. Luke tucked in my pocket to keep me company, and from my memory of some of the verses, I studied the characters as though deciphering a code. I was pleased to find several symbols repeated in several places. I could learn this language!

When I tired of this, I realized my stomach was rumbling. I had no notion of the time of day nor how I would ease my hunger pains. I weighed the prospect of venturing above deck in search of food, then realized that if I were found, I would no doubt be smartly put ashore at Gravesend, perhaps without ever seeing Snowe. I could not bear the thought of all my efforts ending in vain, so I ignored the rumblings and sang softly to myself.

At some point I realized that I faced danger of discovery on another front. Someone was bound to feed and water the cattle sometime, and then my presence would certainly become known.

"Perhaps if I feed you on occasion," I murmured to the nearest cow, "anyone coming below deck to check on you will find you already fed and assume that someone else has seen to the task." I paused. "Perhaps."

It did seem to be a totty-headed scheme, but it was all I could concoct at the moment.

Surely I would be safe for today, so I would not worry about feeding the cattle until tomorrow. If only I knew for certain when that might be . . .

4

I dozed off and on, disoriented by the lack of sunlight or a timepiece. I had no notion what day it was or whether we were yet in England or Timbuktu. One thing of which I was certain: I knew with a certain smugness that I was not prone to seasickness as so many had recounted in literary works. I must be made of sterner stuff. That was altogether a good thing, since I would no doubt encounter a dreadfully long voyage to China.

Only one person had entered my hiding area, and I am not sure but that he took the wrong turn. I cowered behind a trough, but when he heard the cows moo, he uttered a curse and stamped loudly back up the stairs. To ensure that no one took me unawares while I slept, I remained behind the trough, cramped in an unnatural position with my limbs pulled to my chest and my arms tight around my knees.

At some point I awoke with a start and, after recollecting my surroundings, realized that we were no longer moving. I had grown quite accustomed to the gentle lull of the water, the trampling of feet overhead, the various calls from one seaman to another. My stomach rumbled pite-ously, like a kitten, no, make that a roar like a tiger, for I had evidently missed many a meal. If we were stationary, I thought, perhaps I should risk going aboveboard to gauge my situation.

I stretched my arms and legs only to be greeted by im-measurable pain. How long I had been tucked into my womblike position, I knew not, but it was obvious that I must regain the use of my limbs before I could even fathom climbing the stairs. With the trough as support, I rose slowly, like Flora on a cold morning, and tried to work the cramp and stiffness from my body. When I felt a bit more to rights, I took stock of my other immediate needs, chief among them, water.

"I don't suppose you have any to spare, do you?" I mut-tered to Bossy, who only stared back. She looked as though she could use something to drink herself. Did no one tend these poor—

Wait! She was a milk cow. The dairy man from my child-hood had actually taught me the milking process. If I could find . . . yes, there was a bucket hanging on a hook near the stairs. "I would be most obliged if you would allow me to milk you," I said soothingly to Bossy as I reached for the bucket. "I imagine it will do us both good, yes?"

I continued to croon to her softly as I arranged myself on a stool. Fortunately, she was as sweet as I imagined and stood placidly, barely twitching her tail as I milked her. When I had enough to last, I all but plunged my face into the pail and drank heartily.

82

The milk slaked my thirst and fortified my stomach. I scarcely noticed any aches or pains and indeed felt revived enough to see what was happening on the rest of the ship. Once I took stock of my rumpled dress and realized that my living quarters were much more fragrant than at first because of the cattle's natural eliminations, I questioned my ability to mingle with any passengers who might have boarded. No doubt I was a bit more fragrant as well. I would have to be careful about returning to the main deck.

Signor Antonio had taught me to be a superior fencer, but his lessons had not included any espionage skills. I longed for them as I crept as quietly as possible up the stairs, poking my head through the hatch to the deck. The sun hit me square in the face, and its brilliance forced me to duck back a bit into the lower darkness. I had not realized that it was so easy to become unaccustomed to full light. I gave my eyes time to adjust, then, still shading them with my hand, I carefully ventured topside again.

Sailors scurried to and fro, and to my delight, I saw regular passengers now aboard. I should be able to blend in better.

I stared down at my dress, which was sadly rumpled and somewhat smudged from my time spent in the straw. If only I had foreseen the necessity of bringing my bag! Still, what I had left behind for Flora to guard, God would no doubt provide. I smoothed my dress as best I could and brushed at the dirt.

When I spied a group of passengers coming my way, I waited until they had just passed, then I scurried up the steps and onto the deck, blending in with their group. No one seemed to be the wiser, and hopefully Midshipman Bates, if he saw me, would think me merely reboarding.

My plan called on me to find Snowe, however, and soon. If he would vouch for me (and surely he would when he learned of my earnest desire), he could no doubt see to my accommodations and perhaps some new clothes. I hated to dispel any noble missionary thoughts, but the idea of a new frock and a comfortable bed for that night gave me the strength to proceed. Bossy's milk had satisfied my growling stomach for the moment, but it would not last for long. Heaven help me, I desired meat.

I walked the length of the ship without detection, keeping a keen eye out for Snowe and his group. I did not know how long the ship would lay in harbor, but I did not want to miss him. I observed another group of passengers boarding, but they did not look familiar either.

I caught several glimpses of Midshipman Bates and stayed clear. No need to run into him unless necessary. I did see another, even younger midshipman—whose rank I recognized by an identical uniform to Bates's—and stopped him. "I am sorry to detain you," I said. "But I am looking for Phineas Snowe. Has he boarded yet?"

The young lad recoiled for a moment, his nose wrinkling. Then, as though remembering an elder's admonition, he relaxed. "I believe he has, miss. I saw him near the cabins."

I could have kissed the lad! "Thank you so much. You are doing a marvelous job, truly. I am certain you will be promoted as soon as possible."

He flushed, touched his cap, then turned to more pressing matters. I turned heel and rushed toward what I hoped was the direction of the cabins. I took a set of stairs at the opposite end of the boat from the cattle and, just as I headed down them, whom should I run into but Phineas Snowe himself.

His eyes went wide. "Miss Goodrich!"

How odd. He was not wearing those horrid spectacles. "Mr. Snowe." I curtsied.

He bowed stiffly. "What are you doing here?"

Under his cold eye and manner, the speech I had prepared fell apart on my lips. I clasped my hands to steady my nerves. "I . . . I have come to join your group. I want to go to China to serve in whatever capacity the Lord has prepared."

He stared for a moment, then smiled as though speaking to a child. "Come, Miss Goodrich. The Orient is no place for a lady such as yourself. What could your uncle have been thinking to bring you as far as Gravesend? I trust he will see you safely back to Oxford."

"But I came alone, Mr. Snowe. I knew that Uncle Toby would protest, but this is God's plan for my future."

Snowe's face darkened, and I involuntarily stepped back. Without his spectacles, his eyes appeared opaque, his countenance more serious than I could have imagined. I had always thought him out of place somehow, but rather than being a step behind most people, he suddenly seemed to want to be two steps ahead. He almost seemed a different person.

"Foolish girl," he mumbled, then reached into his pocket. "Here." He pressed several coins into my hand. "This should see you back to Oxford. I am sorry if you misunderstood my attentions toward you. My purpose was to discuss my work with the mission, not to court you. You have no need to follow after me like a poodle."

He compared me to a dog! I sputtered. "If I am a poodle, then you, sir, must be compared to a lady at court. For that is the human companion for such a breed." I managed a laugh. "Upon my word, I believe that is quite insult enough . . . to the ladies at court."

He drew a sharp breath. "Miss Goodrich, I have wasted enough time bandying with you. Have the goodness to take my money and leave this ship."

"*Your* money, Mr. Snowe? Did you not manage to secure more than coach fare from my uncle?"

"He gave it to me for the mission." He smiled. "Yet I believe I secured something from you as well. You cannot say that you did not enjoy my attentions while in Oxford. I am certain that it was quite a privilege for a bluestocking such as yourself to be treated so affably. Your . . . friend, I believe, Catherine Ransom all but begged me to entertain you at her party. She said that you were near starved for attention, and now I see that truer words were never spoken. As well, your uncle was so delighted to see you occupied with a man's company that he was willing to contribute a great deal of money toward my work."

I stood aghast. Cathy had not only schemed to throw Snowe and I together, she had asked him in advance to attend me. Uncle Toby, too, had not been interested in my opinion of Snowe's mission, rather only that Snowe had shown me attention.

I was both the laughingstock and the pity of Oxford.

I clutched the coins in my palm until my nails cut into flesh. "I am sorry for the misunderstanding," I said in a low voice. "I will leave at once."

He bowed slightly, formal in his victory. "Have a safe journey. Rest assured that your uncle's money will be of good use in China."

Somehow I curtsied, dazed, and headed for the boarding area. I was conscious of activity around me, much scurrying and loading of passenger possessions, but I could only realize that my future was gone. I had believed it my calling to go to China, and now to find that not only that dream was shattered but my place in Oxford as well . . . No one would ever be able to pass me in the street without whispering, "There goes Isabella Goodrich, poor girl, the bluestocking. She claims she was destined to work at a mission in China, but it is said she was only interested in the missionary himself."

I started down the gangplank, trying to force myself to think about how I would return home. First, I must find a coach to London. Once there, Flora—dear Flora!—would cosset me, let me weep, then together we would make our way to Oxford. Uncle Toby would love me, of course, and perhaps between the two of them and lessons with Signor Antonio, I could continue life within the walls of the university. Everything I needed could be found in books and—

No! I could not foresee such a life. Had I believed that God called me to a life of service or not? Would I give up on my dream only to return to a life of shame?

I turned and marched resolutely back up the gangplank. The young midshipman recognized me and smiled, my flattery apparently remembered. "May I help you, miss? The ship is leaving in just a moment. You are not a passenger, are you?"

I smiled, opening my clenched fist. "These coins belong to Mr. Snowe. I am such a goose that I forgot to give them to him. I will return them then disembark."

He looked flustered, as though he had many duties that needed attention. Yet chivalry prevailed. "Perhaps I should go with you—"

"I know just where he is. I shan't be a moment. No need to trouble yourself about me." I waved a dismissive hand. "You have much more important things to think about, I am certain. You are a credit to East Indiamen everywhere, Mr. . . . ."

"Mr. Calow, miss." He blushed under my praise. "Thank you, miss. Please hurry."

I curtsied. "Thank you."

I headed back toward the cabins, then when the midshipman's back was turned, I reversed course and proceeded directly toward the cattle. I knew exactly where to hide.

Later I scolded myself for not having secured some food while I was above deck. Thankfully, Bossy seemed pleased to see me again, or rather, she did not object when I returned to my home in the straw. It appeared that someone had mucked out the area, for which I was grateful. I knew that someone would find me eventually, for it was foolish to think that I could make the voyage all the way to China without discovery. Following the biblical admonition to let tomorrow take care of itself, I determined merely to live through one day at a time. And perhaps to find some manner of securing food.

Once again I was plunged into darkness, with no notion of the passage of time. I could have been there a week or several hours. I tried to stay hidden as much as possible, cramped into the corner, but naturally I was forced to stand up and stretch on occasion, and even to move around. Bossy was obliging with her milk, even seeming to appreciate my relieving her of its burden.

"When we get to China, I shall see that you have only the finest of pastureland," I solemnly promised her. "You have been a faithful companion when everyone else has forsaken me."

Even as I spoke the words, I knew them to be untrue. As hunger and (evidently) time wore at me, I had visions of Uncle Toby and Flora grieving for me, and regret gnawed at my empty innards. Had my impulsive nature been not only my undoing but theirs as well? I was not selfish enough to believe that I was the center of their worlds, but I knew that I shared a goodly portion of them. No doubt my unexplained absence had rent a tear in the fabric of their lives.

Light-headedness came and went in a manner that soon not even the consumption of milk could ease. I found myself little able to move and huddled in my corner. To make matters worse, I realized that I had quite misjudged my immunity to the effects of a ship upon water. Evidently the journey from London to Gravesend on the Thames was no match for an ocean voyage, for I soon realized the ship swayed and rocked in a manner that could only indicate we had encountered a good wind and were out to sea. At first it was only a mild annoyance, but soon full *mal de mer* overcame me, and I retched more than once into the straw.

Surely it was days that I lay nearly immobile, hardly caring if—and indeed close to praying that—the ship might be struck calamitous and all aboard drown. God must be sorely testing me, I could only reason, or perhaps, like Jonah, my foolishness was bringing ill fortune to all aboard. I could not be the only one to suffer from the ship's lurching back and forth, up and down, back and forth . . .

At some point I knew instinctively that I was near death. Having been raised in the Church of England, I did not, of course, believe in Last Rites, but I tried to confess my sins, not the least of which was an apparent misunderstanding of God's purpose for my life. As I lay in the straw, something hovered over me, and I determined that it was either Bossy or the angels come to take me to heaven. I felt myself lifted from the straw, and I was helpless to resist.

"I am . . . sorry . . . for my foolishness," I mumbled, in case they were, indeed, celestial beings. I did not want to enter the presence of the Almighty without having offered one final, blanket apology.

"We all are," the being muttered in response.

To my surprise, I came slowly to a conscious realization that I still walked among the living. *Walked* being a fanciful word, however, as I could no more walk than sit up at the moment. My limbs felt weighted, but the ship no longer seemed to lurch underneath me like a wild stallion. I felt a gentle sway, however, and realized I was in a hammock.

I endeavored to force my eyes open and received a blurry impression of a rather cramped cabin and Phineas Snowe lying in a hammock on the other side. Obviously I had been mistaken, for I was not in heaven but instead in Hades.

"Wha . . . wha . . ." I mumbled, trying to speak but sounding like a babe.

He was at my side. "Miss Goodrich, can you hear me?"

I nodded. If Snowe was the devil, I did not want to speak. Even if I could.

"I am glad that you are all right. Do you think you could tolerate some broth?"

I listened to my stomach. Yes, it seemed to say. Broth would be better than milk. Indeed, the sooner the better.

I nodded.

"Good. I'll have some brought to you." He headed toward what must be the door, then turned. "I know you will recover at your own rate, but it is imperative that you understand this now. For purposes of this voyage, you are my sister. Is that clear?"

I would not speak even if I were able. *His sister?*

He approached me, his eyes burning. "Is that clear, Miss Goodrich?" The tone of his voice indicated he would brook no deviation from an affirmative answer.

91

In my weakened state, I had no choice but to agree. At that moment, I could only think about the impending bowl of broth, and somehow I sensed it might be withheld were I to cross Phineas Snowe.

"Yes," I whispered.

Before he could leave the room, I closed my eyes in resignation and slept like one dead.

The next thing I knew, I was fully awake. Not dragged from sleep against my will, but a willing, nay, eager participant. My return from death's lair was no doubt a miracle, and I said a hasty prayer of thanks.

Once finished, I took stock of my current situation. I had not dreamed the crowded cabin nor my hammock bed, as I had supposed, but found them to be reality. If such was the case, then I could only assume that Snowe's insistence that I call him brother must be reality as well. Or at least his version of it.

Besides the two hammocks lining opposite walls was a large trunk I assumed to be Phineas's on his side and a wooden crate on mine. I was also fortunate, I suppose, to have a porthole, which was partially open. A gentle sun streamed through, and I caught a glimpse of blue sky. I could smell brine and hear water lapping against the ship.

Physically, I seemed to be mostly to rights, though I felt as weak as a newborn calf. I could not remember if Snowe ever procured the promised broth, but my stomach allowed that it was doubtful, for such a rumbling could only signify its emptiness. I could not remember the last meal I had eaten, somewhere back in Oxford, I believed. Heaven only knew how long ago that was.

Though I lay covered with a thick blanket, I had been divested of my muslin dress in favor of some sort of night dress. I blushed to think that Snowe had anything to do with that, though common sense told me otherwise. After all, where would he have procured such? He was an odd man, but surely not one given to the possession of ladies' night clothes.

The door opened, and though I expected Snowe, a buxom brunette in the most adorable green satin dress smiled at me. It seemed to me somehow to be daytime, and the dress seemed a trifle too fancy to wear before dusk. The way it rode about her person also did not speak to the fashion of society but of something else.

"So you live, after all," she said. "Phineas said so, though I thought it simply one of his fanciful notions." She laughed, and despite her attire, she seemed to be void of malice, at least toward me. Something familiar rested in the way she moved, the flutter of her hands, the sharpness of her features, but I could not recall.

I thought it wise to be agreeable, so I smiled. Her eyes connected with mine as though we shared a secret, and my memory was restored. Though previously she had worn a nondescript brown dress with a faded gray pelisse, there was no disguising her plainness of face nor sharpness of eyes. She was the missionary in Phineas Snowe's group who had accompanied us to feed the poor.

"You are Julia Whipple," I said.

She nodded. "I look a bit different now, I suppose."

"Why, yes." It would be impolite to inquire, but I wondered if there were some missionary rule about saving one's finest clothes for travel.

She gestured at the clothing she wore. "Fortunately for you, I brought those horrid things with me on the trip. Along with that nightgown you're wearing."

It was not the height of fashion to be sure, but it seemed a perfectly decent nightgown. "What happened to my dress?"

She shrugged. "I tried to wash it as best as I could, but I don't know as you'll want to wear it again." She paused. "You've a lot of gumption in you, I'll say that. I pegged you as a lady, but I wouldn't have dreamed you'd be able to hide for so long in a cow stall."

"How long was I there?"

"Three days since we left England before you were discovered."

"I thought it was angels who attended me."

Julia laughed. "It was a sailor sent to muck the stalls. Fortunately for you, one of those young officers was with him, and he connected you with Phineas right away. Snowe accepted the blame for your presence and had you brought to his cabin."

Despite my previous anger at him, I felt a flush of gratitude. "I hope he was not chastised unduly for my behavior."

"Another time the captain might have been angered, but your weakened state made your welfare everyone's primary

94

concern. But the ship's doctor pronounced that a decent rest and some food should revive you. Are you hungry?"

"Famished," I said.

"Then I'll bring you some broth and let Phineas and the captain know that you're awake."

While I awaited her return, I pondered over the fact that she constantly called Snowe by his first name, a behavior that was most unseemly in polite society. Even if they worked the same mission field in the Far East, she should certainly follow conventional address.

I greedily ate the broth that Miss Whipple brought and felt quite revived. I felt even more so after she brought a bowl of water and a cloth so that I could clean myself. When I grew faint, she whisked the bowl from my hands and set about wiping my face and arms herself. At last she smiled at me, giving the tip of my nose a little swipe as though I were a child. "That's enough for today, Miss Goodrich. We've a long voyage ahead of us and plenty of time for cleaning away the grime."

She set the bowl on a small table, her movements steady and sure as she wrung water from the cloth. She was obviously accustomed to service work, for none of my Oxford friends—except Flora, of course—would have managed with such efficiency. Cathy would have giggled and avowed that she knew nothing of cleaning or bathing an invalid.

"Your service must be needed greatly in China," I said.

Miss Whipple set the cloth in the bowl and turned toward me. "I hope so."

"Have you ever been there before?"

She shook her head.

"But you have done charitable work in England? London, perhaps? I do not believe I have seen you in Oxford before that day I joined you and Mr. Snowe."

"Yes, I have been in London. If I lived in your hometown, I daresay you would not have ever made my acquaintance, though."

My conscience pricked. I had not always been a doer of charitable deeds, but surely she did not believe I would ever turn up my nose at more faithful servants. "I should have been glad to meet you," I said. "I have a notion that we would have gotten along splendidly."

She looked at me curiously for a moment, then burst into a smile. "You truly don't know, do you?"

I cocked my head, puzzled.

A knock sounded at the door, then who should enter but Phineas Snowe. "There you are," Miss Whipple said. "You can see that our patient is much improved. Her complexion seems to have more of a pinkish hue."

Snowe looked at me solemnly, then approached. Wood creaking, the ship listed a trifle, and the bowl of water nearly slid to the floor but for Snowe's quick catch. His movement reminded me of a cat, but he replaced the bowl on the table without a moment's hesitation. When he turned back to me, his eyes were unfathomable. "As you can see, Miss Goodrich, life onboard a ship is not for the faint of heart."

Miss Whipple laughed. "I think she did fine by herself these past days, Phineas. No need to give the girl a lecture."

He frowned at her. "She could have spoilt everything

and caused our delay. We will be fortunate not to incur the captain's wrath as it is."

"I'm sure you can explain it satisfactorily . . . if you haven't already."

"I've done my best. The rest is dependent on fortune. And Miss Goodrich's cooperation, of course."

"I am sorry for the trouble I have caused," I said, eager to put their minds at rest. "If I had not been so convinced of the rightness of my actions, I would not have undertaken to come aboard."

"You are a stowaway, Miss Goodrich. There can be no rightness in that."

I lowered my eyes. "I understand, Mr. Snowe. It is not a good way for a missionary to begin her life's calling."

He stared at me a moment as though seeing me for the first time. "Then you truly believe that you are to be a missionary? That is why you followed me to the *Dignity*?"

I nodded. He was abominably full of himself—believing that I followed him because he had courted me, indeed!—but he was still a man of the cloth. "Serving alongside you and Miss Whipple among the poor in Oxford convinced me of my calling. I do not seek a husband, as you supposed, but a life of service."

Snowe looked to Miss Whipple as though for help. She crossed her arms and smiled. "She wants to join us in China," she said.

"You know very well that is not possible," he said to her.

"But why?" I asked, bewildered that I was summarily

97

dismissed from the conversation. "Surely you have seen that I am resourceful. Despite my upbringing, I am not afraid of hard work. I am also most learned. I can read the Bible in Greek and Hebrew, I speak several languages, and I even brought the Gospel According to St. Luke in Chinese that you gave me, Mr. Snowe. I am certain that if Miss Whipple is willing to serve, that I can accomplish the same."

"I believe she means it, Phineas," she said.

He glared at her. "Julia, why don't you remove the bowl of water from this cabin. I will speak to Miss Goodrich alone."

Still grinning, she retrieved the bowl and held it against her hip, water splashing her green satin dress. "What are you going to tell her?"

He glared at her again, and she retreated for the door, laughing. When she was gone, he turned to me. "Miss Goodrich, your decision to follow me was most ill-advised. I am certain that your uncle must be heartsick."

At the mention of Uncle Toby, my own heart felt ill. "I left him a note explaining my intentions. He will know that I am in your good care since he approved of your work. You have already shown me great kindness by bringing me to restored health."

"Nevertheless—"

"Though why you wanted me to agree to your ruse that we are brother and sister is yet unclear. As I seem to have more of my wits about me than the last time we spoke of the matter, please explain."

"You are aware that this is an East Indiaman—a ship belonging to the East India Company?"

I nodded.

"Then you are also aware that it is populated primarily by sailors."

I clasped my hands. "You have only managed to state the obvious, Mr. Snowe. I assure you that I can handle much more information and certainly in a more timely fashion. I fear that we may be in China soon at the rate you are explaining yourself."

He raised a brow over one dark brown eye. Where had the spectacles gone to? "You prize directness, do you?"

"Yes, and I—"

He took a step closer. "Then let me be perfectly frank. I will have you put off this ship at the first available opportunity. Until that time, the sailors will be eyeing any unattached female, some with courtesy but some with less than Christian thoughts. Perhaps backed by less than Christian deeds, as well."

I thought of the sailor I had met when I boarded and nodded.

"I have explained your presence as my sister so that I may see to your safety. They will respect you if they believe us related."

"And what of Miss Whipple? Will they respect her too?"

His eyes leveled with mine. "Julia Whipple does not seek their respect. Only their coins. At least once we reach China."

"I do not understand."

99

"Julia is going to China for one reason only." He clasped his hands behind his back. "She hopes to set up trade with the Englishmen working in Macao."

"Then she is quite enterprising. A tradeswoman! Such a thing is practically unheard of in England. Is it easier in China for a woman to do so?"

"No easier than in England. She is involved in the trade at which women naturally excel."

Understanding dawned in a rush. "Oh!" I felt my face warm. "I . . . I understand now. But you . . . surely you do not approve? Why do you sponsor her?"

He paced a few steps, hands still behind his back. "She cannot have a good life in London as she was not born into society. I hoped that a change of continents might precipitate good fortune for her. Women, decent or otherwise, are in short supply in China, and who knows but that one of East India's finest might seek her hand. In the meantime, she helped me in my endeavor, and I with hers. It was a suitable arrangement."

I eyed him suspiciously. "But nothing more?"

He ceased pacing, standing directly in my line of sight. "It is you, Miss Goodrich, who is ensconced in my cabin. Not Julia Whipple."

5

I did not quite know what to make of such a statement. Before I could respond, however, he turned away. "I will see that you receive some fresh clothing. Perhaps one of the other women on board can loan you a frock."

"If there are other women on board, perhaps I should lodge with them rather than continue to be your cross to bear," I said.

"They are all married women, traveling with their husbands. I do not think they would find your presence acceptable in their cabins."

"No, of course not. And yet you find it acceptable for me to be in yours?"

He sighed. "Miss Goodrich, I feel responsible for your safety and well-being until such time as you can be restored to your uncle. Is it so difficult to believe that I can act as a gentleman?"

"Would a gentleman keep an unmarried woman in his room?" I countered.

"Perhaps you would rather return to your accommodations with the cattle," he suggested, "and whoever might choose to join you in the straw. I made a quick decision to claim you as my sister . . . for your protection only. Fortunately, the prevarication was believed, and no one will be the wiser if you act the part. As for me, I assure you that my intentions toward you are nothing but honorable."

Without waiting for my response, he left the cabin, and I was left to wonder at all that had transpired. He had said that he would have me put off the ship as soon as possible. That could not happen, as I still held to my original belief that I was meant to be in China. Besides, Miss Whipple needed me. Despite the fact that she was a Cyprian, I sensed a goodness in her soul that wanted validation. I had seen her work with the poor; it was no mere pretense. She had been as genuinely concerned for their welfare as Mr. Snowe had been. It had been the generosity of those two that helped me see my future. Perhaps if I stayed close to Miss Whipple during the voyage, we could become friends. After all, I seemed to have left certain social norms behind in Oxford.

I saw the logic in Mr. Snowe's claiming me as his sister, but I did not think much about it that first day I regained consciousness. I tried mostly to regain my strength, dutifully eating the broth that either Mr. Snowe or Miss Whipple brought me. Indeed, though we spoke of mere triflings during her ministrations, she and I shared each other's company rather well. I did not know if Mr. Snowe told her that I was aware of her situation, but after an initial wariness, she seemed to realize that I had no intention of chastising her. She smiled at me as before, and like Mr. Snowe, promised to find me some suitable clothes.

"You seem healthy to a fault. You'll be out of that hammock and strolling about the deck in no time," she said, handing me a bowl of broth. I had regained enough strength to spoon-feed myself. I tried not to gobble greedily, but I was famished. She pulled the wooden crate close to my hammock so that she might sit while I gorged myself like royalty . . . that is to say, ate.

"What is it like on deck?" I asked between swallows. "I have never been aboard a ship before."

"There is a variety of activity with the sailors. They are perpetually tasked with myriad activities for the betterment of the ship. They move cargo about, scurry above and below deck, raise the sails . . ." She put her hands around her knees, smiling. "I enjoy watching them climb the rigging, for it's a feat of daring I can only imagine. I get dizzy watching them so high aloft. They climb as high as the tallest sail sometimes. The captain said we caught a very good wind, so we are on our course, I suppose. I understand that with fair weather, the voyage should last only five months."

"I should like to know the stops we are intended to make," I said, thinking of Snowe's vow to put me ashore.

"I can't say that I know of them, except for Cape Town, of course."

I stopped with the spoon halfway to my mouth. "Cape Town," I whispered. "It sounds so exotic."

"I have heard of it but do not know where it is."

"Why, everyone knows that it is at the southernmost tip of Africa on the Cape of Good Hope," I said, then blushed with shame. Miss Whipple probably had not been given the education I had received. "I am sorry for speaking so knowingly. Mr. Snowe has called me a bluestocking, and I suppose he is right."

She leaned back, smiling. "I have heard of Cape Town for many years, but no one bothered to tell me its location. It *has* always sounded a bit exotic. What do you know of it?"

"Only what I have read. It has been in existence for some two hundred years. It is a business town where ships stock up on provisions. There is also lodging, I believe, and families who live there year round. It is located between two oceans, the Atlantic and the Indian. Oh, and some call it the Tavern of Two Seas because there is apparently no lack of strong liquor."

"Really?" Miss Whipple seemed amused by my last statement, her eyes taking on a calculated expression that worried me.

"I hope that you will tour the town with me," I said hastily. "As we seem to be the only two unmarried women aboard ship, I would enjoy your company."

She stared at me, and I felt that my impulsiveness had gotten the better of my speech. I should not have forced her to give me a cut. "Forgive me, Miss Whipple," I said. "I did not mean to presume an acquaintance that you may not desire."

"That *I* may not desire?" She continued to stare at me, and I felt quite unnerved.

I slurped the last of the broth in my anxiety then handed her the empty bowl. "Thank you so much. It was delicious. I appreciate your bringing my food."

"It is Phineas who secured it for you."

I made a face. "Then I thank you doubly for your service when he has thought himself either too busy or too important to bring it to me himself."

Miss Whipple broke into a smile. "You don't care much for him, do you, Miss Goodrich?"

"I care for his charitable work, but I cannot say that our personalities are well suited for each other. We seem to rub each other like flint and steel."

"I have noticed the sparks," she said, her eyes twinkling.

I flushed. "I should learn to curb my tongue. He has been kind to me of late, but I must convince him of the necessity of my staying aboard ship. He did promise to put me off at the first possible convenience."

"Most likely Cape Town, then." Miss Whipple rose. "I would like to hear more about your plans, Miss Goodrich. Especially what you hope to accomplish once we arrive in China." She turned when she reached the door. "I feel certain that if we chat a bit, we can arrive at a plan to convince Phineas to keep you aboard ship. For I am quite certain that you could be a valuable asset to him in the future."

"Since you have known him longer than I, I would appreciate any insight," I said. "You have been kindness itself, Miss Whipple. I am certain that God led us both to this ship for a reason."

"Let us hope that we both still agree to that thought by the time we have reached the end of our respective voyages—no matter where that might be," she said, then left the cabin and me to my own reflection.

Well fed and refreshed, I fell into a dreamless sleep that night. The ship no longer seemed to rock beneath me but rather soothed me like a babe in a cradle. It is a wonder that someone does not invent a device whereby people may fall asleep in the safety of their own homes, yet lulled to dreamland on gentle water's wave. I slept so deeply that I heard nothing save perhaps the ocean's rhythm.

I must confess that I gave but the barest moment of a thought to Mr. Snowe's presence in the cabin that night. Yet I saw him only once after Miss Whipple brought my dinner, then not again. When I awoke in the morning, feeling completely like my normal self, he was not present either. However, laid fast on the wooden crate upon which Miss Whipple had perched was a brown dress and various undergarments.

I rose to examine them. The porthole to my right was still open, and I could see that the cabin was located at the rear end of the ship. A bit of wet salt sprayed my face from the hypnotic wake trailing our mighty ship. I drew a deep breath. This was preferable, indeed, to solitude in the dark with the cattle.

I paced the cabin's length and width, if such it could be said to have, to regain my footing. I paused briefly at the large trunk on Phineas's side of the cabin. What could that large leather box possibly store? It looked quite big enough to hold several dead bodies, which, I realized, I would not put past Phineas Snowe.

At last I felt that I had use of what I supposed would be vulgarly referred to as my sea legs, and I determined to relieve myself of the nightgown, dress in the provided clothes, and survey my new home outside the cabin. The undergarments were acceptable, though far from fancy, but I wrinkled my nose at the dress. It was of coarse cotton—cotton!—and had not a shred of beauty to adorn it. Flora would have said that she'd see me naked rather than in such attire. I knew such talk to be mere jest, but I did believe that she would find the cotton dress highly unsuitable. I would acquire no more notice than a common wren.

Thankfully, my own black shoes had been salvaged from my feet after my discovery, but I did pause a moment as I slipped them on to remember the beautiful silk pair that were now, apparently, forever left behind in Flora's care. I would have taken some comfort in knowing that she, at least, could wear them herself, but as my feet were twice as small as hers, I knew the thought to be mere fancy.

The door opened. "Miss Goodrich!"

Thankfully, it was only Julia Whipple. I did not feel capable of seeing Phineas Snowe just yet. She approached me, concern furrowing her brow. "Are you quite well?"

"I believe that I am. And how fortunate that you have arrived at only such a moment, as I was about to venture forth from this cabin." I leaned forward in a conspiratorial whisper. "I fear I might need a steady arm yet, though I have managed tolerably well taking several turns around the cabin."

"I shall be only too happy to lend you my own," she said, crooking her elbow. "It's a beautiful day, and I know that the captain will want to make your acquaintance."

"Oh dear. I rather hoped that there would be no need for me to meet him before the voyage was concluded. I am sure he is quite displeased with my behavior."

"And *I* am certain that he is a Christian man full of forbearance and willingness to see only to your current welfare."

With that hope tucked away, I allowed Miss Whipple to lead me from the cabin. We passed through a dining area with a long table bolted to the floor. "This is the cuddy, the dining salon," she said. "The captain eats here every night along with some of the officers and invited passengers."

"Are there many passengers aboard?"

"Two married couples and you and Phineas." She paused. "And me."

"Yes, of course," I murmured. I wondered whether she preferred being the only unattached female, but then I remembered that I was unattached as well, so I held my tongue on that subject. "I thought I heard footsteps overhead, but perhaps it was just people here in the dining area."

"I'm sure it was people overhead, for your cabin is below the poop deck. I understand there is quite a lot of noise."

"Where is your cabin?" I asked. "Are you not near mine?"

She shook her head, smiling. "I sleep in the great cabin,

which is just below this dining area. I do not hear much noise at night, however, I have no window." She opened a door, and we stepped out. "And this is the deck."

The great ship lay before us. Men in sailor outfits bustled to and fro, moving barrels and crates, climbing the rope ladders that led up higher than I could see to the topmost masts. The sides of the ship creaked, and water seemed to lap on all sides. A sailor swabbed a portion of the deck with a mop and bucket amidships, and a higher deck stood at the bow. Behind us stood a similar raised deck, though not as large as the one at the front. "That is the poop deck?" I asked, recalling Miss Whipple's words.

She nodded. "Would you like to see it first?"

"Of course! I want to see everything on board the ship."

We climbed a small ladder and stood on the poop deck. I shivered. The sun shone bright, but the wind chilled. Overhead flew an East India Company flag, its Union Jack in the corner and red and white stripes snapping in the breeze. I felt somewhat disappointed, for other than the boards of the deck itself, there were only crates of squawking chickens and ducks. So I had not imagined their noise!

"Good morning, ladies," a sailor said, tipping his cap.

We nodded, watching as he fed grain to the chickens through their wooden cages. "Is it your job to tend to them regularly?" I asked.

"Yes, miss," he said, tipping his cap. "I am the poulterer, John Swinney."

Miss Whipple and I watched as he gave them their grain and made certain they had water, making soothing noises that sounded oddly akin to their own. I felt somewhat amused by the thought of fowl riding on water. "Do they have a great need for chickens in China?" I asked cheerfully.

"No, miss. These birds will depart from us long before we reach the Orient. They'll be food for the captain's table."

"I see." I wondered that I had not been intelligent enough to deduce this for myself.

Several large lanterns hung at the end of the ship. "Excuse me, Mr. Swinney, but what are these for? They are not intended as a side dish with the chickens, are they?"

Mr. Swinney grinned, rubbing his hands together to disperse the leftover grain. "No, miss. They are for signaling other ships. Excuse me, miss, but I wouldn't want the captain to find me dawdling about." He departed with a slight bow.

During our exchange, Miss Whipple had ventured to the edge of the ship. She stood transfixed, scanning the horizon behind us and the divided path of the water our ship made. "If you don't mind the fowl, it's quite beautiful here."

"It is interesting to see the wake of the *Dignity*," I said. "To think of where the ship has gone, and no one to know we were here . . . unless we are spotted, of course."

"And we pray that does not happen," she said. "I have heard tales of French privateers boarding East Indiamen. I have no desire to see crewmen or passengers killed in such an exchange."

"Of course not," I murmured.

"But come," she said, linking arms with me again. "Let's

110

put such horrible thoughts behind us and examine the rest of the *Dignity*. Who knows but that we might run into Phineas Snowe?"

The thought made my nerves jump. Naturally, I should thank him properly for rescuing me, but seeing him now somehow seemed too soon. "I believe I could travel the entire voyage and not miss his presence," I murmured.

Miss Whipple squeezed my arm playfully. "And yet you long to serve alongside him as a missionary?"

I could not respond. Uncle Toby and Flora had each told me—on separate occasions—that spontaneity was my dear friend but a more potential worst enemy. I sometimes rushed headlong like an adventurous calf but took no notice of the gate securing my safety.

I found walking a trifle precarious, but Miss Whipple assured me that I would quickly gain my sea legs. Amidships, she paused beside the lifeboats lashed to long, thick poles. "What are those?" I said.

"Spare spars. They can be used to replace a mast or boom or gaff."

"The poles that hold the sails?" I struggled to remember any nautical terms I might have learned.

"Yes," she said, then drew a deep breath of air. I did the same, thankful to be outdoors instead of cramped below deck or even in a cabin. The sun shone warm and the air held a tang of salt that tickled my nose in a not unpleasant manner. "It feels good, doesn't it?" she said. "I can understand why men long to go to sea."

"Have you been aboard a ship before?" I asked.

111

A peculiar expression crossed her face. "No, but I was raised in Portsmouth. I am familiar with ships and those who sail them."

Remembering her own reason for being aboard the *Dignity*, I endeavored to change the subject. "Perhaps, then, you can tell me the names of some of the sights, for beyond the three masts that I see, I am at quite a loss."

"I thought you had learned much from books?"

"I confess that I know a smattering of names and a general idea of their location aboard ship, but I cannot place the two together."

As we slowly made our way forward, I found myself clinging to Miss Whipple as my legs found their bearing on the unsteady deck. I also needed her emotional support as well in these unfamiliar surroundings. She, however, walked gracefully with her head high, nodding at the sailors, some of whom politely responded and others who only grinned and went about their business.

"Where are the other passengers?" I whispered. At Oxford, I was accustomed to being the only woman in sight, but there I was around gentlemen. Here I felt like a scholarly lamb among wolves, though Mr. Swinney, the poulterer, had been naught but polite.

Miss Whipple smirked. "The last I saw of the husbands, they were tending their wives below deck. Seasickness, still. You are fortunate to be past that. The sailors told me that sometimes passengers go ten days before they are well. At least the captain's table will be empty for a few days yet. Besides the officers, Phineas and I have been his sole companions since we set sail."

Canvas flapped above my head, and I stopped short. Miss Whipple released my arm, and I leaned back, trying to catch a glimpse of the highest sail. "I feel like a child beneath a laundry line," I murmured, feeling small and insignificant. "I am sure each sail has a name, does it not? And however do those sailors manage to climb the ropes?"

"It is called the rigging," she said. "And as for the sails, I am not quite certain. We shall have to ask the captain. Hello, sir."

Startled, I jerked my gaze downward to its normal level. A man of some three score with a white wig and resplendant uniform stood beside Miss Whipple. Fortunately, his ruddy complexion and poorly suppressed smile told me I had nothing to fear. "So this is our stowaway, eh?" he said, affecting gruffness.

I trembled nonetheless. "Y-yes, sir. I am sorry, sir."

"Miss Goodrich, this is Captain Stephan Malfort. Captain, this is Isabella Goodrich."

I curtsied.

"At your service, miss," he said with a bow. "Pray tell me what was so urgent that you risked life and limb to be with your brother?"

This I could answer without fear. I explained about my calling from God and how I must get to China. "It is a burning in my heart," I said, then pressed my case. "I am certain that it is not unlike your passion for the sea."

He smiled. "My passion is somewhat more pecuniary

113

than yours, but aye, there is something wanting in my soul that being at sea fulfills. Still, I can't imagine following a sibling to the detriment of my own health, not to mention avoiding fare passage, as you have done."

"I am sorry about that, Captain," I said. "I hope I can repay the money to the East India Company."

A shadow fell across the deck. "No need to worry about that, dear sister," Phineas said, looping an arm through mine. "I have already paid the captain for your rather unexpected passage. At least for the portion of the trip during which you will be aboard ship. But I must say that I am delighted to find you in better health."

I tried not to cringe at his touch. Miss Whipple looked on in amusement.

"Ah, Mr. Snowe," Captain Malfort said. "It is indeed a delight to meet your sister at last. But one thing troubles me."

The muscles in his arm seemed to tense. "Yes?"

"Why is it that you and your sister have different last names?"

He relaxed. "In truth, Captain, we are only half brother and sister, raised by different parents, of course." The lie sprang a little too easily from his lips. Not an admirable quality for a man of the cloth! "Miss Goodrich was raised by an uncle at Oxford, Mr. Tobias Fitzwater." That, at least, was not prevarication.

"Ah," the captain said, as though it explained everything. To my taste, it certainly did not.

Miss Whipple smiled. "Captain, just as you joined us, I

114

told Miss Goodrich that we should ask you for the names of the many sails above us. Would you do us the honor now?"

Snowe released my arm. "As I am familiar with such terminology, you will excuse me if I take my leave then, Captain. Miss Whipple." He bowed, and upon rising, looked directly at my eyes. "Isabella."

The sound of my name in his voice bred confusion in my soul. He headed aft, and I wanted to follow him, for I had many questions yet for Phineas Snowe. Captain Malfort, however, was already pointing up high. "The upper sail is called the main topgallant, below that the main topsail, and the one nearest us is the mainsail. That one is the main topgallant staysail, and the one aft is the mizzen topgallant."

Miss Whipple strolled forward, moving our group in the opposite direction Snowe had gone. "And the sails at the very bow are called . . . ?"

"The flying jib, the jib, the fore topmast staysail, and the fore staysail. That one there . . ."

I only half listened thereafter, for even if I were put off ship at Cape Town, I would no doubt have a long time to learn the intricacies of the *Dignity*. And perhaps other information, as well. I did not know if I could maintain my forbearance.

Though Captain Malfort had to leave us soon, Miss Whipple and I strolled the deck for several more hours. We tried to stay out of the sailors' way but also to observe their business from a distance. Even when Miss Whipple declared that her head ached and retired to her cabin, I lingered on deck. I found everything fascinating, from standing at the battered rail to scan the horizon to watching sailors tying knots. The last observation occurred courtesy of Mr. Calow, the young midshipman who had directed me to Phineas at Gravesend. The lad seemed surprised to see me, though I was certain my presence aboard ship had become common knowledge once my place with the cattle was discovered.

He and the other five midshipmen had just concluded a lesson with Captain Malfort, who apparently quizzed them on finding latitude and longitude. Mr. Calow seemed to fare the poorest of the young class and was near thorough humiliation during a knot-tying competition. Captain Malfort seemed particularly harsh on the young lad, but I understood the need for the midshipmen to learn their lessons and learn them well. These were not mere studies on Greek and Latin; the lives of all aboard might hang on whether a sailor had properly tied a line.

Left to practice on his own, the dejected Mr. Calow worked doggedly with a bit of rope, tying and retying several mysterious knots. I dared a chance to sit beside him on the bench. He sprang to his feet, hastily swiping his eyes. "Miss Goodrich!"

"May I join you, Mr. Calow, to observe your work, or would that disturb you? I know nothing of knots myself, so I shall be in no position to comment."

"I don't mind if you sit here."

We sat, and he worked with the rope. I could see the

frustration on his face, and I knew above all else that he would not allow himself to cry. He could scarce have been above twelve years of age, probably not long from home, but he was obviously making a Herculean effort to appear the young man he was expected to be. Two senior officers stood at a distance, watching us, and their presence seemed to have a detrimental effect on Mr. Calow's confidence. His breath came in quick gasps, and his eyes appeared moist.

I could bear to see his suffering no more. "Do you have some extra rope for me?" I asked. "Perhaps I could learn."

He retrieved an abandoned line and handed it to me. "What knot is the easiest?" I asked. "I should probably start there."

With a minimum of words, he showed me how to tie a figure-eight, a square, then a clove hitch. He seemed to gain confidence as he explained them to me, and when I was capable of executing them with no help, I calmly asked, "What knot were you working on when I interrupted you?"

"The bowline." His shoulders slumped, and he jerked the knot free in his line.

"How does it begin?"

He held out his line to demonstrate. "There is an old story to remember how to tie this knot. Imagine that the free end is a rabbit, and the other end is a tree with a rabbit hole at its base." He twisted the rope, and I did my best to follow. "The rabbit comes out of the hole, goes around the tree, and back down into its hole again."

I laughed, letting my tangled line fall into my lap. "My rabbit apparently ventured to the backside of the tree, where he was promptly eaten."

Mr. Calow stared at the rope in his hands. "I did it," he whispered. He raised the rope higher for my scrutiny. "I did it!"

One of the officers moved beside us. "So you did, Mr. Calow. Job well done. But I'll not warn you again about speaking of those furry things on board ship."

Joy diminished from the lad's face. "Aye, sir. I'm sorry, sir. It won't happen again."

"Carry on, then." The officer tipped his hat and moved on.

When he was out of hearing distance, I turned to Mr. Calow. "What did he mean by 'furry things'? And why are you not permitted to speak of them?"

Mr. Calow leaned closer. "He means those animals in burrows," he whispered, then made a hopping motion with two fingers. "You know"—his voice dropped lower still—"*bunnies*." He clapped a hand over his mouth and looked around to make sure no one had heard. When he was not reprimanded, he relaxed.

I laughed. "Do you mean rabbits? Why ever are you not to mention them?"

Mr. Calow flushed. "Sailors believe they bring bad luck. None are allowed on board, even for food. We're not to mention their names, either, which is also bad luck."

"But Mr. Calow, surely you were raised in a Christian home. You do not believe in superstition, do you?" I was appalled that grown men should pass on such myths to a mere child. What foolishness was this?

"There are those who believe Christianity itself to be superstition, Miss Goodrich. The lad is merely following orders."

I looked up. Phineas Snowe stood beside me. Again I felt the intensity of his gaze, and I longed for him to retrieve those spectacles—no matter how horrid—and put them to good use on the bridge of his nose.

Though he said nothing further, he seemed to desire a private conversation. "Mr. Calow, I have intruded upon your time long enough," I said. "Thank you for sharing your knot-tying skills. I should like to discuss latitude and longitude with you some time. At your convenience, of course."

His mouth gaped. "You know about those things? Why, you're only a woman."

I raised my chin a trifle and rose.

"I beg your pardon," he said, rising alongside me. He touched his cap. "Good day, miss."

Mr. Snowe walked to the ship's rail, out of the way and out of earshot, for the moment, from anyone aboard ship. "I confess that I thought to reprimand you for bothering the crew, but I was present long enough to find that you accomplished quite the opposite."

I suppose that was his way of paying me a compliment. "Mr. Calow only shared his knowledge, and by so doing, he increased his own. As for bothering the crew, I am pleased that you find yourself in the wrong. I am determined to be of no consequence to anyone aboard ship."

I lowered my gaze. Oh, how Phineas Snowe could irk me, but he *was* a man of the cloth. "Unfortunately, I realize that I have now forced you to bear the burden of my decision to become a stowaway."

He leaned both elbows against the ship's rail, studying me like a lazy cat to a trapped mouse. "Indeed?"

Oh, I was a miserable wretch! Must I say it so plainly? "Yes." I nodded. "I am in debt to you not only for my fare, but for your efforts to protect me. I find them gallant, and I thank you for your efforts at offering me your protection as my, er, brother."

"I am not without chivalry."

"Yes." I cleared my throat. "However, you should know that I am prepared to defend myself physically, should the need arise."

"From me?" He quirked an eyebrow. "Miss Goodrich, I have already informed you that I have no intention of—"

"I was thinking more of an untoward advance from any stranger aboard ship," I said, flushing. "You are a missionary, Mr. Snowe, a man dedicated to holy work. It is true that you and I do not always see eye to eye, but your character must be impeccable for the London Missionary Society to accept you."

He waved a hand. "We were speaking not of my character but of your—what did you say?—your preparedness to defend yourself?"

I nodded. "Until recently it was a well-kept secret that I trained in martial arts."

"Indeed? Pray continue."

I could not tell if he mocked me or expressed genuine curiosity. "I have studied with a fencing master for nearly twenty years now, Signor Eco Antonio. He himself studied under the great master Domenico Angelo . . . but you probably have not heard of him."

"Actually, I have. Most impressive, Miss Goodrich . . . if it is true."

"Believe me, Mr. Snowe, I mention it not to impress but to alert you that I have little fear of caring for myself on this voyage and in China, as well."

"And yet you brought no sword for the journey."

So he did mock me! "I thought it best to leave it behind. A missionary should have no need of such training, is that not true? Particularly when it involves violence."

"Yet even Jesus remarked to the disciples that a man should sell his garment and buy a sword." He straightened. "Miss Goodrich, you are an enigma to me, yet one thing is clear. You have a heart for helping others, and for some reason, an earnest desire to serve in China. But I must insist that it is no place for the fairer sex."

"I was led to believe otherwise when I thought Julia Whipple part of your group. Nevertheless, I am determined to convince you that I am quite capable. Surely there are ladies and children in the Orient whom I could reach."

"You cannot speak their language."

"But you could teach me! I still possess the Gospel According to St. Luke that you gave me at the Ransoms' party, do you remember?"

He nodded.

121

"It is a long voyage," I pressed. "Could you not teach me even the basics? As my uncle informed you, I am learned in several languages already . . . French, Italian, German, Greek, Latin—"

He held up his hand. "That is enough, Miss Goodrich. I am familiar with your studies."

"Then you will teach me?"

He paused for a great while. Why must he deliberate? Was his time so valuable aboard ship that he could not spend it with me? If I failed to learn any Chinese (and of course that was unthinkable!) would it have inconvenienced him so greatly?

"Phineas Snowe, I have been looking for you." Julia Whipple stood beside him. "And you, Miss Goodrich."

"Are you feeling better, Miss Whipple?" I said.

She frowned. "Better?"

I tapped my temple. "Your headache? You left earlier to retire to your cabin."

"Oh yes. That. I am much better, thank you for asking." She glanced at Snowe, then at me. "I hope I am not disturbing you."

"Not at all," Snowe said, smiling. "We were merely having a brother and sister chat."

I sighed. "Miss Whipple is aware that we are not related. Must we continue the pretense?"

"But I think of you as a sister, Miss Goodrich," Snowe said. "Are we not related in our desire to do the Lord's work?"

Miss Whipple coughed delicately into her hand. "Excuse me. Phineas is correct, Miss Goodrich. It is better to keep up the pretense even with me. Dining with the captain tonight will be a good test . . . won't it, Phineas?" She brushed his shoulder. "I am rather looking forward to the meal. I am certain the conversation will be interesting. The captain is much concerned with truth and is knowledgeable about many things, is he not?" She gave him a decidedly pointed look.

"As is Miss Goodrich," Snowe said smoothly. "She has informed me that she is schooled in many languages."

"She and Captain Malfort will have much to talk about then, I imagine." Miss Whipple smiled at Snowe, then turned to me. "Miss Goodrich, if Phineas can spare your presence, I thought it might be interesting to show you my cabin. I brought quite a collection of embroidery with me, as I find it helps to pass the time. I would be delighted to share my cloth and thread if you enjoy such arts."

"I do, Miss Whipple. Thank you. It would be nice to stitch something that might be of use in the Orient, as well. Perhaps a cuff or a handkerchief?"

Miss Whipple smiled at Phineas. "Please excuse us."

Snowe bowed. "Miss Goodrich, we will speak again."

"I daresay we will, as we share a cabin," I said dryly. "Perhaps in the meantime you will consider my request?"

"What is that?" Miss Whipple said.

"I would like Mr. Snowe to teach me the Chinese language during our journey. I want to prepare to help in some manner once we reach Canton."

She cast a sidelong glance in his direction. "And he has refused?"

"Indeed, he has not answered. But I am sure it is not for lack of opinion."

Snowe said nothing, his face expressionless. Miss Whipple smiled at him then turned me away. "Come, Miss Goodrich. We will leave him to think, then, for though we have a long journey yet, every second brings us that much closer to our destination."

6

Miss Whipple and I admired her embroidery until it was time for dinner with the captain. Informed that this was normally at two o'clock, I proceeded shortly beforehand to my cabin to check my appearance. Dinner was as formal aboard ship as it was on shore, I had been told.

Though I possessed no mirror, I could tell that my hair was not at all to my liking. I supposed I must become accustomed to such since Flora would no longer be available to help me pin it up. Julia Whipple offered to help me, even loaning me several hairpins, but I vowed that I would learn to do it myself. A missionary should not be given to much vanity and should learn to care for herself.

However noble my efforts, I could not work the pins to my satisfaction. The lack of a mirror was one impediment, but the clumsiness of my hands was even more so. I would no more secure one strand of hair, and then another would come loose. Secure another, and the entire pile of hair tumbled loose into my hands. The pins clattered to the floor.

I sat down on the wooden crate, for I needed a moment to think. Flora. Where was she now? Had she made her way back to Oxford to report to Uncle Toby that I was gone? Surely he would not be cross with her for my decision.

The door opened, and Phineas Snowe entered. I rose quickly, startled. "I am sorry," he said with a bow. "I did not mean to disturb you."

"I think perhaps you have saved me," I said, trying to smile as I gestured at the misbegotten pins scattered about the floor.

He gathered them in the palm of his hand. "Sit," he said, gesturing at the crate.

"But I—"

One look from him, and I realized he would brook no argument. I sat.

"I do not fancy myself a hair styler, but I know that it can be difficult for a woman to accomplish this task with her own hands." He paused. "I have a younger sister."

"Indeed? Then you must realize my quandary. I want to appear presentable, since it is my first dinner with the captain, but I should learn to do it myself." I chattered because he stood a bit too close for my comfort. When his hands touched my hair, I felt my heart beat faster. "I . . . I do not imagine that there will be many formal occasions in China."

Snowe said nothing. He smoothed my hair then looped a section, deftly securing a tendril here, affixing another one there. Flora was the only person who had ever touched my hair before; certainly no man had ever done so. His hands, warm and smooth, brushed against my neck. I was aware that he stood just behind me. It was most unnerving . . .

He stepped back. "There. You may stand."

I did so, touching my hair lightly, breathing a sigh of relief but feeling curiously bereft of his nearness. "It feels quite secure. Thank you."

He stared at me—all of me—so critically that I paused. "Is something wrong?" I studied my dress, twisting about to see if I had acquired a spot or a tear.

"Your appearance is pleasing," he said. "That brown dress . . ."

"It is certainly a suitable color for being a missionary but not, I confess, a color to which I am much accustomed." I do not know why I sought Snowe's approval, but in truth, I did. "Is my appearance suitable . . . for dinner with the captain, I mean."

"Your appearance is pleasing," he repeated, this time with a bit more gruffness. "Miss Goodrich, there is something I—"

"Yes?"

Somewhere a drumroll sounded. "That would be the announcement for dinner," he said, sounding relieved. "If you are ready . . . sister, we should proceed. We would not want to keep Captain Malfort waiting."

He took my arm and led me from the cabin. It was only then that I wondered how a missionary such as himself had acquired the experience of arranging ladies' hair.

The cuddy seemed a different place from earlier, when Julia Whipple and I had strolled through. The table was laden with a fine linen cloth, silver candelabra, and the most attractive blue-and-white patterned place settings that must surely be Wedgwood. I remembered to keep my mouth closed and a pleasant smile on my face, though in truth my jaw longed to go slack and my eyes widen. I had never imagined such beauty and sumptuousness on a seagoing vessel.

An older officer—not one of the young midshipmen—seated Julia Whipple. She had changed into a lovely blue muslin with a floral print. As much as I tried to think Christian thoughts, I coveted that dress. Couldn't a woman be a missionary *and* dress stylishly? Surely it would bring comfort to the poor and downtrodden to have an angel of mercy clothed in fine raiment! I tried not to picture how like a mouse I must appear in my brown frock.

"Mr. Snowe, Miss Goodrich." Captain Malfort beckoned us to the table, bestowing us with seats of honor next to him. Snowe sat at his left hand, and I at the captain's right. The officer who had seated Miss Whipple sat to my immediate right, and she sat across the table. The midshipmen sat at the end of the table, removed, ostensibly, from the main conversation. I surmised from their schoolboy awkwardness and efforts to avoid fidgeting that they did not normally dine at the captain's table.

The captain made the proper introductions, and I learned that my companion was the chief mate, Thomas Gilpin. He seemed serious and proper and several years older than I. The same could be said of the second mate, whom Captain

Malfort introduced as Joseph Baggott. Perhaps one or both of these gentlemen were already married, but I wondered fleetingly whether an introduction to naval personnel years ago might have secured me a husband. It was most peculiar that Flora had not thought of this and dragged me to a port city long ago to introduce me into their society . . .

No matter. I was duty bound and determined in my current course. It was, after all, ordained by God. The Chinese translation, the slippers, and the tea had proven that to be true.

"Are you feeling better, Miss Goodrich?" Mr. Gilpin said.

"Yes, thank you. I believe that I am." I hoped that the evening's conversation would not center around my antics. I had already caused enough embarrassment. No need to rewarm it like second-day gruel.

Fortunately, the servants set the courses before us. What a feast! The sumptuousness of the table setting was far outweighed by the food on which we dined. I had suspected our fare for the entire voyage would be some sort of salted meat (and I worried that that was, indeed, the average sailors' meal), but we were served pea soup, mutton, chicken, ham, duck, and cabbages and potatoes. I was certain to be the most rotund missionary in China ere we arrived.

I tried not to smack my lips, but I still had hunger pangs from the time spent in the cattle stall. While Snowe conversed with Captain Malfort, and Miss Whipple apparently charmed Mr. Baggott, I tried to engage Mr. Gilpin in conversation between mouthfuls of meat and vegetables. This,

I hoped, would force me to eat more slowly. "Have you made more than one voyage with this ship, Mr. Gilpin?"

"This is my fourth," he said. "The *Dignity* is the most solid East Indiaman I have had the pleasure to serve on."

"Really?" Oh, fiddle, the peas! I wanted to shovel them into my mouth but was forced to pick them out carefully, as a lady should.

Mr. Gilpin sliced his ham with grave precision. I could not help admiring his attention to detail. It was plain to see why he had been considered officer material! "It may interest you to know that the *Dignity* was built in Bombay nearly seven years ago," he said.

At that moment, I am ashamed to say I was more interested in filling my stomach. "I should think all the East India Company's ships would be British built." I forked some of the stewed cabbage. Oh, heavenly leaf!

"Ships built with British oak are often eaten through by sea worms. The teak found in India is a better hardwood not only for construction but durability."

I was certainly in favor of a ship's durability. Particularly the *Dignity*. "Then she is not only beautiful but solid," I said.

It suddenly occurred to me why sailors spoke lovingly of ships in female terms. Men desired to have both ships and wives with the admirable traits of beauty and solidness. And an absence of worms, of course.

Mr. Gilpin laid down his fork and smiled. "She is a fine ship, Miss Goodrich. Steady and dependable."

There. I was right. "Miss Whipple and I strolled aboard

deck this morning. I have never been away from land before."

"How did you find the *Dignity*?"

"I am certain she is as fine as the *Victory*," I said.

"Oh, have you seen Nelson's ship?"

I shook my head, chewing thoughtfully (and somewhat greedily, I am afraid) on a portion of duck.

"It is moored at Portsmouth," Mr. Gilpin said, his voice lowering to a sad pitch. "My father was killed during the Battle of Trafalgar aboard ship. I visit the *Victory* whenever I am home in England."

I ceased chewing and sipped my wine. My appetite fled as I thought of poor Mr. Gilpin's loss. "How dreadful."

He smiled. "I am at peace with his sacrifice. After all, it is what prompted me to seek a naval career myself. I considered joining the Royal Navy but could not bear the thought of my mother losing another family member to battle."

"Yet merchant ships are not without danger too," I said, then winced. When would I learn to put thought before speech?

Mr. Gilpin's smile broadened. "Your honesty is refreshing, Miss Goodrich. Yes, that is true. There is always the danger of privateers, particularly in Eastern waters, but nothing for you to worry about. Come, let us speak of happier matters."

If it was nothing for me to worry about, why did he make mention? Must men always feel compelled to protect the fairer sex? I daresay we ladies would be better off by half if they would but tell us of worldly dangers and allow us to have a voice or hand in our own defense.

Captain Malfort turned to me. "Forgive me, Miss Goodrich. I have spent far too much time talking to Mr. Snowe and not you."

"Mr. Gilpin has been kind enough to discuss ships with me," I said. "I find them fascinating and would like to learn more."

"Then you are more interested in vessels than the cargo they carry?" He took a large sip of wine.

In an awkward moment, all conversation at the table ceased, and I found myself the center of attention. I smiled. "In truth, I had not given much regard to what would return with the *Dignity*, for I shall disembark at Canton."

"Ah, yes. Your missionary duties. So you have no desire to follow your brother and his work?"

The smile froze on my face. "Why, yes, of course. That is why I wish to serve in China. With, er, Phineas."

I could not see Snowe, blocked as he was by Captain Malfort's large frame, but I could sense his discomfort two chairs away. I could not understand the silence at the table. Bewildered, I glanced from one person to another. Their benign expressions betrayed nothing.

Except one. Julia Whipple looked at me with something akin to pity.

Captain Malfort smiled indulgently. "How do you expect to serve as a missionary alongside your brother when he will be about the business of the East India Company?"

My mouth went dry. "I beg your pardon?"

Phineas Snowe leaned forward just enough so that I could see his eyes, which warned me into further silence. "I have told you all along that your plan was foolhardy, dear Isabella. We should not discuss it again . . . particularly in the presence of others."

For a moment I considered pressing the matter then quickly discarded the notion. Estimation must be preserved at all cost, though I longed to know the entire truth of the situation. Without delay. Now.

What transpired the rest of the dinner is a blur in my memory. I am sure that I said the right things and responded with the correct remarks, particularly to Mr. Gilpin, who continued to be attentive throughout the meal. The plum pudding held no taste for me, however, and when Miss Whipple and I excused ourselves so that the gentlemen might indulge in glasses of port, I somehow made my way from the cuddy without, I hope, making a further fool of myself.

Once on deck, I turned to Miss Whipple. "You have known all along, haven't you?"

"Yes," she said, with no hint of pride in her voice. "I'm sorry."

I tried to gather my thoughts. What question did I want to ask first? Before I could speak, she leaned toward me. "I don't feel it's my place to say anything. You should speak to Phineas. He should be the one to explain himself."

"As well as your actions in Oxford? Both of you acting as missionaries for my benefit?"

She flinched then straightened. "Yes," she said firmly.

"He should answer for even that. I admit to being a participant, but the deception was his idea."

I wanted to be angry at her. Her pretense reminded me of Cathy Ransom and every woman like her who presented one face to her acquaintances in private and another to society at large. As I studied Miss Whipple, though, I could see that she begged no forgiveness, yet she also took no joy in her deception. I could never have applied the latter sentiment to Cathy. Miss Whipple also had apparently not had the benefit of upbringing or society to correct her. At least that is what I had been led to believe. Who knew what was truth?

"Is it true what Mr. Snowe says about your reason to travel to China?" I said.

"What does he say about me?"

Ah. Meeting directness with directness. None of the fawning or double-dealing to which I was accustomed from other women. "He says that you are a Cyprian and you seek new business in the Far East."

"That is true."

I had known it all along, of course, but I felt a sickness to my stomach. "Why?"

"London held no charms for me," she said. "It is a foul city. I thought perhaps that Canton might prove more advantageous for a woman in my position."

I wanted to know more, so much more, but delicacy prevented me from speaking further.

She studied my face. "You have no comment?"

"I hardly know what to say, Miss Whipple. I have much

to digest this evening." Certainly more than the meal I had gluttonously eaten in the cuddy.

"Miss Goodrich, I understand if you don't wish to speak to me further. We are of two different worlds, and—"

"And yet we are both bound for a new one," I said, noticing the surprise on her face at my words. "We each have much to think about on this ship for many months. I see no need to impose a restriction on our conversation. Within boundaries, of course."

"Of course," she said gravely. Was that a smile I detected her trying to suppress?

Snowe avoided me the rest of the day. I strolled on deck with Miss Whipple, neither of us speaking of anything of particular consequence save our current environment. At six o'clock we took tea, and at nine o'clock a supper of soup, cheese, and cold meat. By regulation, candles in the cabins had to be extinguished by ten o'clock, so I was well abed soon after supper.

I had anguished over dressing back into the nightgown that Miss Whipple had procured. It was certainly preferable to sleeping in the cotton dress when I would only have to wear it again the next day. Modesty, however, prevented me from donning bedclothes. Though I knew Snowe would not be able to see me in the dark, I knew I would feel un-clothed all the same.

I had hoped to fall asleep before he entered the cabin, preferring to save all my questions for the morning than to launch them in the privacy of our cabin. Yet curiosity prevented my falling into a deep sleep, and I lay awake swaying in my hammock, my heart beating a quickened rhythm.

The door to the cabin opened. Snowe entered, candle in hand. Before I had the presence of mind to feign sleep, I said, "It must be near ten o'clock. You should douse the flame."

Snowe stood still. "I did not think I would find you awake. Can you not sleep? Is the hammock uncomfortable?"

I raised up on my elbows as best I could. "The hammock is a tolerable bed and not at fault for my restlessness."

He shut the door behind him and set the candle on the trunk by his own hammock. "I suppose you want an accounting for the conversation at dinner."

"Yes. Please explain why Captain Malfort and everyone else believes that you are working for the East India Company."

He took a step closer to my hammock, and the candle cast his shadow against the far wall. "Because I do. I buy tea to import to England."

I closed my eyes, almost losing my desire to learn anything further. What a fool I had been, starting with the Ransoms' party and ending with dinner tonight. I had squandered my life on a dream that was not just smoke, but soot.

"You no doubt want to know why I misled you," he prompted.

"Would you even tell me at this juncture? Could I believe you?"

The ship's bells announced ten o'clock. Snowe sighed. "Miss Goodrich, allow me to provide a bit of modesty for our living arrangements. I have taken the liberty of rigging a torn sail between our beds, which we can raise and lower at our convenience." He pulled a rope and, indeed, a sturdy length of canvas raised between our hammocks. In keeping with the lateness of the hour, he blew out his candle, and our room was plunged into darkness save for the sparse moonlight through the porthole.

I heard him undress, whether fully or partially I had no notion. I trembled with anxiety, however, remembering that I now no longer shared a cabin with a man of the cloth but a man of the purse. He was a merchant and therefore under no obligation to observe societal norms beyond that of his own class.

The rings securing his hammock clinked as he lay down. "The *Dignity*, like other East Indiamen, shortens its sails at night," he said. "We should have calm waters and a good night's sleep."

"At least one of us will have such," I said into the darkness. "You, no doubt, sleep with a clear conscience."

"For the most part, yes," he said. "But if I do not, it is because you are on board this ship."

"Am I an impediment to your plans? The ones that included fleecing my uncle out of his money in the guise of bringing the gospel to the heathens?"

He said nothing for a moment. "I am more concerned with your welfare at this point. You will be put ashore at Cape Town and returned to your uncle on the next England-bound ship. If at all possible, I will even return your uncle's money with you."

"Aren't you afraid that I will sully your name when I relate around Oxford what you have done?" I paused, giving vent to the cry of my heart. "Why *did* you seek money from my uncle? Were you given funds by others as well?"

"No," he said quietly. "Only your uncle was charitable enough to contribute. Though I said as much, I truly did not seek funds, but he was so taken with my work that he insisted no matter how strong my protest. I had heard of his interest in missionary work, particularly among the Orient. I managed an invitation to Sir Ransom's party with the express purpose of meeting your uncle, to spread the truth about China . . . I did not plan on meeting you."

"Nor I, you," I said, refusing to squelch the bitterness in my voice. "I had been forewarned that there would be an eligible man in attendance, but I had no notion . . ."

I trailed off, thinking back. Flora had labored so diligently on my new dress. She had been so pleased to find the perfect pink slippers to match. Slippers with Chinese writing. I had been so certain . . .

"Why?" I said in a low voice.

"Why did I pose as a missionary?"

My eyes filled with tears. Uncle Toby and I had both been duped. Dear Uncle Toby . . .

Snowe let out a long sigh. "Do you remember that I was to attend the party with a husband and wife who sought to become missionaries? The Tippetts?"

I nodded.

"In truth, they are interested in further tea exploration, as am I. I believed that posing as missionaries would ameliorate our acquaintanceship. Mr. Tippett does not work for the East India Company, and I did not want to appear to be in collusion with any competition."

"But you are! You work for Britain's finest trading company, Mr. Snowe!"

"I have not forgotten," he said in a low voice. "But I seek new tea to sell and new methods of its purchase. The East India Company needs silver for trade. The Chinese are not interested in anything else." He paused. "Not much, anyway."

"Tea! You would deceive a lovely old Oxford dean, me, and all the people at the Ransoms' party for *tea*?"

"It is the lifeblood of the English," he said quietly. "Can you deny it? Do you know how much tea is imported on a yearly basis? The latest figures I have seen are over two hundred million pounds."

I pictured Uncle Toby's dear face. Did he linger, heartbroken, in his study at night? It was one thing to know that I had left him for a great calling, quite another when I realized what a sham it had all been. "You said you were with the London Missionary Society. You asked me if I had heard of Robert Morrison, the famous missionary to China."

"And you said that you had. I did not say that I knew nor worked with him or the Society directly. You believed only what you wanted to hear, Isabella Goodrich. For that, do not fault me."

"I can fault you for deception. I can fault you for playing the part only too well," I said. "I have not noticed you wearing your spectacles since we have been aboard ship. I suppose they were part of your charade?"

"Yes, I borrowed them from a friend. They were devilishly difficult to see through."

I could not believe what I heard. Not only did he seem to have no remorse for his scheme, but he was letting me in on his secrets as though I should be sympathetic. Or worse yet, impressed!

"Miss Goodrich, I will do everything within my power to make your stay aboard ship as pleasant as possible until we reach the Cape. That is all I can offer at this point."

Why was he being so congenial? Oh foolish girl, he had selfish motive indeed. His smooth talk had slowed me from realization, but I could comprehend it now. "You are afraid I will tell Captain Malfort about your deception, aren't you?"

"The thought had occurred to me, yes."

I shifted in my hammock, feeling a strange sense of power. "He could have you dismissed from the Company, I suppose, or at least send word to the proper persons in authority."

Snowe hesitated. "Yes."

I crossed my arms over my stomach, pleased. I could not believe my good fortune. "What, exactly, do you think you can do for me?"

"I have promised to see to your safety and comfort. Is that not enough?"

"And I have already informed you that I can care for myself."

140

He laughed. "With a sword, I suppose."

"If need be. I should like to have one, since that is the one possession I had the most difficulty leaving in England."

"Where would you find one here at sea?"

"Oh, come, Mr. Snowe, you are a man of many designs and persuasions. Surely you could procure such an insignificant item."

"Insignificant?" I heard him raise up in his hammock. He sighed then lay back down. "Very well. It is certainly an odd request from a woman, but I will try. If I find you a sword, will it barter your silence?"

"That and your assistance in proceeding to China beyond the Cape." I smiled into the darkness.

"What? No! It is unconscionable. Why do you desire to travel that far when you know that I work with no mission?"

"I have every confidence that I can find one. Robert Morrison himself is there with the London Missionary Society. They must need assistance."

Snowe sputtered. "China is not the size of Oxfordshire nor even the whole of England, for that matter, Miss Goodrich. We could not find him."

"You are no doubt a man of influence and intelligence. I am certain that you can help me."

He groaned. "I should never have taken Tobias Fitzwater's money," he muttered.

"But you did, Mr. Snowe. That is my offer."

There was silence on the other side of the canvas. Surely he could not have fallen asleep!

"I will match your offer with one of my own," he said at last.

"Proceed. I am listening."

"I will find you a sword. I will protect you for this leg of the journey. When we reach the Cape, we will revisit our agreement. Frankly, I am of the opinion that a few months at sea may change your mind."

"I do not think so," I said cheerfully, "but I can as easily inform the captain of your treachery in Cape Town as I can in the middle of the Atlantic."

"Then we have a pact?"

I settled into my hammock, suddenly weary. I had no choice. He had no choice. We were bound to each other's word to fulfill our individual plans.

"We have a pact, Mr. Snowe," I said grimly, wondering if I had just bound myself to the devil himself.

7

Our canvas divider was still in place when I awoke in the morning. I thought perhaps Snowe might have already left the cabin, but I could hear a gentle snore from the other side. It occurred to me that my wedding night anticipation of sleeping in the same room as a man had now been dashed. The snores persuaded me that I had probably not missed anything.

I was grateful that I did not have to change clothes but supposed that I would be forced to spend every day and night in the same dress. No, that was unthinkable. It was not even a question of fashion but of nasal condition. A lady must consider such things.

I tiptoed from our room to the deck. The air was brisk, the sun not yet on the horizon, though traces of pink and orange lit the sky. I stood transfixed at the rail, out of the way, wrapping my arms around myself against the chill.

"Good morning, Miss Goodrich."

"Mr. Gilpin!" I turned, smiling at the first mate.

He touched his cap. "I trust you slept well?"

"Very much so," I said. "The sea has a peculiar lulling quality that I find most conducive to sleep."

He smiled. "You may not say such when you have experienced a storm. It will make your early voyage seasickness seem quite mild by comparison."

"I have no doubt. I felt certain I was near death's door. But I suppose you have no difficulties with illness at sea anymore?"

"None to speak of. It is my life now. I find myself more sick when I am on land."

"Heartsick for the sea, I suppose?"

He smiled. "You are perceptive, Miss Goodrich. But here, you are trembling. Let me find you a jacket."

He disappeared and returned with a short blue sailor's jacket. "I apologize for its unfashionable nature, but it serves our seamen well," he said, holding it out to help me put it on.

"Oh dear." I shrugged into the sleeves. "I hope I am not depriving someone else of their own warmth."

"Not at all. And please keep this . . . I know you do not have any other clothes."

The jacket now warm around me, I leaned against the rail and studied the horizon. Fingers of pink and orange reached into the sky and reflected over the blue of the ocean. Then a sliver of the sun itself appeared, like a shy actor showing only one foot, then a leg, then a torso on stage. At last he appeared, his presence filling the theater, and I wanted to applaud.

As I watched the display, I felt alone with nothing between me and the edge of the world. Indeed, all things seemed possible in the beauty of such light and plane. I did not intend it, but a sigh slipped past my lips.

"The sunrise *is* beautiful," Gilpin said. "That is why I am usually on deck before my watch begins. I never tire of seeing a new day dawn."

I inhaled the chill air, the smell of salt tickling my nose. "It is all very new to me," I confessed. "I am certain I appear like a child."

"Never," he said, smiling. "I think it admirable that you embrace a new life. Most of our passengers complain the entire trip until we are once again on land. Speaking of passengers, I believe I heard the captain say that some of them are stirring today and feel up to partaking of meals in the cuddy."

"I look forward to meeting them. Everyone else seems so busy going about the business of managing the ship that I find myself with no one to talk to."

"There is always your brother, of course," he said.

"Yes, of course." No telling what I would learn from Snowe ere this voyage had concluded.

Gilpin put his hands behind his back and cleared his throat. "You and Miss Whipple have been congenial, I have noticed."

I felt myself on guard. "Yes, we have."

He rocked forward then stood motionless. "Miss Goodrich, I know you are a lady of character and breeding. It pains me to tell you this, but I would not want your own reputation sullied. Miss Whipple is not a fit companion for you."

"Indeed?" I did not know whether to be flattered or angered.

He nodded. "Her character is not on par with yours. Mr. Snowe's recommendation was enough to secure her passage, but all aboard know the limits of her character and have been warned against any association. Perhaps Mr. Snowe has already chastised you, but I can't help but think that my mother would want me to protect the reputation of any sister of mine . . . if I had a sister, that is."

"Thank you, Mr. Gilpin. I will take your words under advisement."

"Mama would want me to warn you."

The ship's bell rang. "Eight o'clock," he said, "and time for my watch. You will find breakfast in the cuddy. But if your teeth are of a delicate nature, beware the biscuits. They are usually extremely difficult to chew."

"Another warning from Mama?" I could not help asking saucily.

He did not take my humor. "No, from me." He touched his cap. "Good day, Miss Goodrich."

"Good day, Mr. Gilpin."

I made my way toward the cuddy, and whom should I find but Phineas Snowe. "Dear brother," I said, taking his arm, "I wondered if you would eat breakfast."

"I always try when I am aboard ship. And I, too, am delighted to escort you," he said.

I allowed him to lead the way, but it occurred to me that perhaps he was not so much trying to protect me aboard ship, as he had said last night, as making sure I had little

146

opportunity to divulge the truth about him. Nonetheless, we had a bargain, and he would have to learn to trust me. Though it pained me to think of Uncle Toby and his money, I would bide my time and abide by my agreement with Snowe.

Captain Malfort was already in the cuddy, speaking with two couples. One was close in age to Snowe and myself, deeply engrossed in a private conversation. The young lady's dress looked twice made over, but she had added a bit of ribbon here, there, and in her hair. The effect was complementary, though it did little to ameliorate the sharp angles of her face.

The other couple were quite elderly and dressed exceedingly fine. The woman appeared to be near dozing as she sat with her head propped in her hand at the table. Her husband spoke animatedly with the captain, gesturing wildly and evidently relating a great storm at sea. As Snowe and I approached, I could hear his heated words.

". . . rolling as though in a barrel, Captain. Really! Is there nothing that can be done?"

The captain was all patience. "I assure you, Mr. Harrison, that we had quite a calm night at sea. You have been with the East India Company for a number of years now. Have you not heard from other travelers that the seasickness will pass?"

"It is not I who was troubled so much as Martha," Harrison said, gesturing at his wife. Her head bobbed in her hand, and I thought I heard a tiny snore emanate. She did not appear to have any difficulty sleeping now!

"All will be well, I am certain," Captain Malfort said. "Ah, Mr. Snowe. Miss Goodrich. I trust *you* had a pleasant sleep?"

"Indeed we did," Snowe said.

"Remarkably well," I agreed cheerfully, the picture of innocence.

Captain Malfort introduced us to the Edward Harrisons, the elderly couple. I am sorry to say that poor Mrs. Harrison was rudely awakened by a curt jab in her shoulder from Mr. Harrison. "How d'ye do?" she said on cue, then promptly closed her eyes again. I could not tell if the burden of additional people in the room taxed her social graces or if she was merely trying to make up for the sleep she had apparently lost last night.

The other couple approached us, their shoulders barely touching, as decorum permitted. They tried not to stare at each other, but the furtive glances they shot in each other's direction told me all I needed to know. They were newly wed.

"This will be a long voyage indeed," I muttered.

"What's that?" Snowe said, leaning closer.

I smiled. "Nothing of consequence, brother."

The captain introduced the couple as Charles and Anne Akers, indeed newly married. "Brother and sister?" Mrs. Akers said, once Snowe and I had been introduced as well. "How very odd. I fail to see much of a family resemblance. It is always telling in the eyes, I say, but there is a distinct lack of similarity in yours."

"We both have brown eyes," Snowe pointed out, which

surprised me. I could not have sworn that he noticed the color of mine, for I had made no particular notice of his.

Mrs. Akers continued to study us. "Yes, but the shape. Something is different."

"We are only half related, after all," Snowe said.

"Really?" Mrs. Akers seemed delighted by the new tack of the conversation. I could tell she preferred a good gossip —under the guise of conversation, of course. "Exactly how are you related?"

I decided to let Snowe answer, but the captain—bless his briny soul—called us to be seated. "Breakfast is ready to be served."

We took our seats, Mrs. Harrison being prevailed upon to wake up enough to move to a different chair. We were a small group this morning, Mr. Gilpin being on watch, of course, and the midshipmen not present. I wondered why Julia Whipple was not among our group but thought it best not to ask. We were joined for this meal, however, by the ship's surgeon, Jonathan Mortimer. Mr. Mortimer had little regard for his general appearance, with unkempt clothes and stringy gray hair, and he spoke little. Yet somehow he carried himself with dignity and had the demeanor of a man well acquainted with his business. I did not remember his attending me while I recovered, and I hoped not to need his skills again during this voyage.

Misfortune prevailed, as I found myself seated next to Mrs. Akers. She immediately dominated the conversation, but thankfully her subject matter did not involve Snowe or me. I tried to feign attentiveness, but she spoke of such

149

trivial matters that I instead contemplated the meal—which I must add was shockingly not up to the standards of yesterday's dinner. We were served corned beef and tongue, questionable butter, curry (which Captain Malfort claimed was popular with those who had spent time in India), and the biscuits about which Mr. Gilpin had warned me. I regret to report that I took childish delight in the hardness of a biscuit forcing Mrs. Akers to cease all conversation for a moment.

"Why, these are as hard as a sea chest," she said after extricating the biscuit from between her teeth. She all but spit out the offending morsel. "Captain Malfort, are there none other available?"

"I am afraid this is all we have to offer," he said, and I could have sworn I saw a twinkle in his eyes. "You are not obliged to partake of breakfast, of course. Many passengers prefer to dip into their own provisions during this time."

"Nonsense!" Mr. Akers said, quelling his wife with a loving expression. "We are Englishmen, and we will eat what the company has seen fit to provide us." He gnawed on the biscuit with long, yellow teeth, which put me in mind of a rat. "Quite tasty, my dear. It gives the ol' incisors quite a go."

Mrs. Akers smiled lovingly, but while Mr. Akers was occupied, she set her biscuit to the side.

I tried not to smile behind a cup of tea. Mrs. Akers caught my gaze and frowned. I cast about for a topic of conversation to avert further questions about eyes. "Do you look forward to living in China, Mrs. Akers?"

"Goodness, no," she exclaimed, loudly enough for all to hear. "I understand it to be a dreadful place, full of yellow people who chatter in a strange language. In truth, when Mr. Akers informed me that the company was sending him on this voyage, I contented myself with the notion that at least I would see monkeys for the first time."

A polite pall settled over the table. "Surely you do not mean the Chinese themselves, do you?" I said quietly.

"But of course!" She laughed, glancing around the table for approval. "I have heard that they do not care for we Englishmen in their country, and I am happy to oblige. I look forward to living in Macao—a Portuguese colony, after all—during the trading season in Canton. Once Mr. Akers's business is tended to, we shall be on the first boat back to Britain. Were we not newly wed, I would be content to stay home. However, I consider myself a woman of the world and one entirely devoted to her husband and my new situation as his wife. I am sure I shall be as fine a traveler as any Englishwoman who has gone before me and a credit not only to my gender but to my country as well."

Such a speech might have been met with applause in her imaginary version of Parliament, but our little group sat quite shocked. Snowe, I noticed, sitting beside me, seemed almost livid. He showed no outward displeasure while he calmly buttered a biscuit with some of the dubious butter, but I could tell by the tightness in his jaw that he seethed inwardly.

What bothered me more—that Mrs. Akers believed as

she did or that I was learning to read Snowe's expressions and moods so easily?

"I am certain that the fairer sex will indeed be well represented in the Orient by all ladies present," Captain Malfort said, smoothing over the silence.

"Hear hear," Harrison said, holding up his teacup. Mrs. Harrison leaned against his shoulder.

"Miss Goodrich, I have not heard your impression about the Far East." Mrs. Akers buttered her biscuit and attempted another bite.

"I would prefer to save my opinion until I have actually seen it," I said, demurring.

"Isabella will disembark in Cape Town," Snowe said. "Perhaps, Mrs. Akers, you could do likewise."

She set down her biscuit. "What? I? Did you not hear me, Mr. Snowe? I have a duty in Macao, no matter how odious it may be. How could you disregard me in such a manner?"

"I beg your pardon, Mrs. Akers, but I *was* thinking of you. Perhaps you and my sister could be companions and travel back to England together."

Dear friend, I could not help myself. I am not given to violence unless it is of a fencing nature, but I planted my heel smartly but quietly against Snowe's instep. To his credit, he did not even flinch. I knew, however, that my message had been received from his manner of blinking.

Mrs. Akers waved her hands in protest. "Out of the question, Mr. Snowe. I am certain that Mr. Akers will hear none of it, as well."

"On the contrary," Snowe said. "Though he may agree

with you now, I suspect that by the time we reach the Cape, he will see the wisdom of my suggestion."

"You are kindness itself to be concerned with a newly married couple," Mrs. Akers said. "But I am afraid that we cannot be parted. Why ever are you on this voyage, Miss Goodrich, if you are only to disembark at Cape Town?"

Without so much as a sidelong glance at me, Snowe launched into an explanation of how I was determined to become a missionary, but he, as a loving brother, would not countenance it. Out of deference to me, I suppose, neither the captain nor Snowe mentioned that I had stowed aboard ship. Fortunately, Mrs. Akers was not quick-minded enough to ask why Snowe allowed me aboard in the first place.

When he finished, I marveled at Snowe's ease in concealing the truth, all around. I did not care for liars, but he seemed to have a certain skill.

"A missionary? Mr. Akers, did you hear that?" Mrs. Akers nudged her husband's arm, jostling the corned beef from his fork.

"Quite admirable, I must say." He calmly reclaimed the meat.

"Admirable? Why, I am all astonishment at your lack of propriety," she said. "For whoever heard of an unmarried *lady* missionary? In the Far East, no less!"

"Whoever indeed?" Snowe muttered, casting me an exceedingly penetrating sidelong glance.

Later Snowe, Harrison, and Akers met together to discuss East India Company business. It occurred to me that I did not even know what Snowe did for the company, other than to procure tea. How, exactly, did he do this? Did he send men out to pick the leaves? Did he lead an expedition himself? I resolved to ask him later.

I saw Mr. Gilpin on deck and mentioned that I already regretted the lack of books to read. I could not imagine the entire voyage without reading material.

"But I have the very thing," he said, smiling. "Mama sends me off on each voyage with a fresh armload of books. I have not the heart to inform her that my interest lies in navigation not in novels. I would be delighted to share from my personal library."

"Thank you, Mr. Gilpin, that would be wonderful. I am interested in any books you have available and certainly novels. I enjoy a good story as well as textbooks."

"Perhaps a book on navigation then?" he said, his lips curling in a smile.

"Why, yes. Mr. Calow and I discussed latitude and longitude recently, and I'd like to learn more. I confess to only understanding the rudimentaries."

"Don't tell me that you are thinking about applying to be a midshipman!"

I smiled at his earnest expression. "Nothing as serious as that. In truth, I would like to learn not only for my own knowledge but for Mr. Calow's as well. Everyone is so busy that I thought I might be able to tutor him if I had a chance to learn and understand the material."

For a moment his face looked inexplicably crestfallen. "You are well educated then?"

"I grew up at Oxford. My uncle is a dean, and I was tutored by others at the university."

"Oh." He cleared his throat. "I will have those books brought to your cabin as soon as possible." He cleared his throat again. "The pea jacket ensures your warmth?"

"Yes. Thank you again for procuring it for me."

"It will only be needed for the beginning of our journey. As we travel farther south, you'll notice that everyone sheds their outer clothing."

"I look forward to the warmth, as I look forward to many new adventures," I said.

He smiled, touched his cap, and left. I did not quite know what to make of Mr. Gilpin.

Miss Whipple appeared on deck later, vowing cheerfully that she only wanted to breathe some fresh air. I considered inviting her to my cabin, which at least had a porthole for fresh air, but then remembered Mr. Gilpin's warning. Snowe worked with Mr. Harrison and Mr. Akers, after all, and I did not want to bring criticism to him by my presence with Miss Whipple. I did not know if her reputation was known among the other passengers, but no doubt it soon would be. Being seen with Miss Whipple on deck could be accounted to coincidence, but a game of whist in the cabin clearly involved an invitation and willingness toward friendship.

Miss Whipple took one look at my navy blue sailor's jacket and wrapped her own stylish black pelisse closer. "I cannot believe you selected that out of choice," she teased.

"It may not be all the crack, but it is quite warm," I said. "Mr. Gilpin gave it to me only this morning."

"Ah, Gilpin," she said, smiling. "Now there is a naval man for you."

"I do not take your meaning."

She leaned against the rail, her eyes fixed on the ocean's gentle waves. "He is all that is right and good about the sailing profession. Duty, honor, charity. I suppose he has even mentioned his mother?"

"Why, yes, he has."

She smiled. "I would lay you odds that he cannot break free of her grasp," she said. "Why, he is probably interested in *you*, Miss Goodrich, but has no doubt already found something about your nature—or will find something—that would be troubling to dear Mama. And so he shall never approach you in anything more than a brotherly fashion." She paused. "Like Phineas Snowe."

I was not certain I cared for the turn of the conversation. "I am not after any man, Miss Whipple," I said. "Nor do I want them to approach me in anything other than friend-ship." *And that, with Snowe, is dubious indeed!* "I want only to complete my task, which is to get to China."

"And what does Phineas say about that?"

How much should I divulge about our agreement? How much did she know, anyway? "He does not want me to go," I said, choosing my words carefully. "He does not think it advisable, nor do the other passengers, apparently. Have you met them?"

She shook her head. "I have seen them from a distance. I

156

avoided breakfast for that express purpose, though we are bound to meet at some point during this voyage."

"What do you think they will say about you?" I said without thinking and, naturally, instantly regretted it.

She smiled. "I would hope they would comment on my fashionable dress or curly hair," she said. "What would you have them say about me?"

"I only wondered if they knew about your rep—that is, your life, your, er . . ." I trailed off, certain my face was three shades of red.

"I do not think it is stamped across my forehead," she said mildly. "If you choose to tell them, then of course I cannot stop you."

"I have no intention of such!"

"Then . . . why must we speak of it?" She smiled as if to say that I was forgiven.

Snowe joined us later, and Miss Whipple made some excuse to depart. I had the distinct impression that neither of them cared to be present together in my company, and I wondered if they were at odds. "Is your company business settled?" I said as Snowe and I strolled about the deck.

"For now." He said no more.

"Mr. Snowe, have you found—"

He stopped short. "Can you not refer to me as Phineas? It *is* my Christian name."

I glanced down. "That would be unseemly."

"We share a cabin. We pretend to be brother and sister. Would it not be better for our ruse to stay in character at all times? Suppose someone should overhear you call me Mr. Snowe?"

"I had not thought of that." It did make a certain amount of sense. "I suppose you will want to call me Isabella?"

"If I may," he said. His polite tone did not fool me; he would call me what he willed.

I pretended to agree. "Very well, then. As I was saying . . . *Phineas*. Have you found a sword for me?"

He sighed. "These things take time. I cannot simply conjure one out of the air."

"Of course not. I would not want you to."

We strolled side by side along the deck. The ship rolled gently along the water, and the sun warmed my unprotected head. Yet the touch of Phineas's fingers on the arm of my new jacket gave me a chill. *Who is this man?*

I cleared my throat. "Mr. Snowe—"

"Phineas."

"It occurs to me that I know little of either your background or your current affairs with the East India Company. You have the obvious advantage in that you know a great deal more about me—where I was raised, my family, for example."

"Very well, what would you like to know?"

"Tell me about your family. Are they alive?"

"I grew up in the north country, near York. My father was an East India naval man and is no longer living." He paused. "My mother, however, is still alive."

"You mentioned before that you have a sister. Is that right?"

"Yes. My mother remarried, and I have one sister, as I mentioned earlier."

"And your involvement with the East India Company? How did that come about?"

He shrugged. "I have long been interested in tea." He stopped again and turned to face me. "Tell me, Isabella. Over the no doubt many cups of tea you have drunk in your lifetime, did you ever chance to think about where the precious leaves came from? Or did you, like so many, never think of them as traveling any farther than from your servants' hands?"

Had I said or done anything to deserve such a rude tone? And did he think me so dull and uninquisitive as to never imagine life beyond Oxford? "Indeed, I often have thought on such. I have wondered about the hands that grew the leaves, nurtured them to fruition, picked them, carried them to who knows where to be purchased or traded then shipped to England."

"I—"

I had read about tea and was just warming to the subject. "You are right when you say it is our lifeblood. I know the history of tea in our country is varied. For example, did you know that green tea was the popular type imported at first, then gradually black tea became more popular?"

"Yes, of course," he said. "Have you ever had green tea?"

I shook my head. "I do not believe so, but I am interested in trying some."

"Tea has been popular much longer in China than in England."

159

"Indeed," I said. "How many voyages have you made to the Orient?"

He shrugged. "I cannot recall."

"But you speak the language well?"

"Fluently."

He proceeded to walk aft, and I was forced to rush to keep up with him. I could hear the chickens squawking up on the poop deck, and I wondered if Mr. Swinney, the poulterer, were tending them. I also wondered how Bossy and the other milk cow were faring and resolved to check on them later. "Mr. Snowe?"

"Phineas," he corrected.

"Phineas, then." I sighed. "I know this will be a voyage of great length. Mr. Gilpin has graciously offered to loan me some of his books so that I may read to pass the time. As well as to improve my knowledge."

"Really? I should think that you were quite near the end of your learning experiences."

"One can never learn all there is in the world. I am always anxious to improve myself. Which reminds me that I have another request for our agreement." I held my breath. "I would like for you to teach me to speak and read Chinese."

"We have already set our bargain and the terms upon which it is based."

"Nevertheless, I would like to learn Chinese."

He burst into laughter. "You are jesting, of course. Chinese is a particularly difficult language to acquire. I told you and your uncle that back in Oxford."

I did not so much as smile. "But I am in earnest. It is

a long voyage, and I have a skill for languages. I would particularly like to know Chinese so that I can better communicate with the people I hope to serve once we reach our destination."

"Your destination is Cape Town!" His eyes snapped fire.

Two seamen stopped their work in coiling a rope and turned to stare. I sighed. I might have known that Snowe would fight me. I lowered my voice. "Then think of it as a way for me to pass the time. And perhaps you as well. You must find these voyages tedious. I am sure that you would find me an eager, as well as capable, student."

He said nothing.

"Can you fault one Englishwoman for attempting to learn about another culture?" I paused. "We could even begin with the Gospel According to St. Luke that you gave me."

He looked at me with surprise. "Do you still have it?"

"Unless someone has moved it, it is probably still in the straw with the cattle."

He thought for a moment. "In truth, Isabella, I do find these voyages somewhat tedious. One can only discuss company business for so long."

"Then . . . shall we retrieve the Gospel from the cattle area?"

He sighed with resignation, evidently realizing that I was dead set on achieving my purpose. "Very well. Let us fetch the tract."

We made our way below deck. No man was present,

only beast. I preferred to believe that the cattle recognized me, but that would be mere fancy, of course. I recognized my favorite cow right away. "Bossy," I said sweetly and patted her gently on the broad, smooth skin between her eyes. Snowe waited while I entered the stall and retrieved the book, which was lying just where I had left it, hidden in the straw. Thankfully, it was tucked away near the railing and out of range of the cattle.

"Shall we read it right here or take it above deck?"

"As kindly as the cattle treated me when I was their unwelcome guest, I do not fancy staying here any longer," I said blandly. Bossy looked at me with her enormous bovine eyes and—I tell no falsehoods here—licked me as a lady's lap dog would show affection.

"It would seem the cattle, however, would have you visit," Snowe said, his voice tinged with amusement. He wrinkled his nose. "I admire the sight of pastoral scenes, but I am afraid the stench is somewhat overwhelming. Perhaps we could find a quiet place on deck or, barring that, our cabin."

Our cabin. I could not become accustomed to that phrase. Somehow it was easier under cover of bedtime darkness to acknowledge that we shared a room. I shivered a little at what would happen to my reputation were the truth known. "Perhaps we could use the cuddy," I suggested. "We would be out of the way of the crew."

"Very well." Phineas helped me back through the gate then latched it securely. He wrinkled his nose once more. "You stayed in here with these beasts for as long as you did?"

I nodded, raising my chin. I did not want him to think me some missish society woman. "I am not someone to trifle with, Phineas Snowe. I can live with one beast or another if it is required."

He smiled at me and stepped back to allow me first access to the steps leading above deck.

Snowe appropriated a shallow pan from Mr. Gilpin. At his further request, Mr. Gilpin also ordered a midshipman to relieve a sandbag from enough of its contents to cover the bottom of the pan. "Thank you," Snowe said, leading the way to the cuddy.

Hurrying to keep up with him, I was mystified. "I thought we were to study Chinese," I said.

"We are," he said over his shoulder. "Have I disappointed you in any way yet?"

Yet! Yet? Did he mean to make a future with me?

Snowe set the pan on the table and smoothed the sand flat with his hand. From his coat pocket, he withdrew a smooth black stick. I laughed. "Do you always carry that with you?" I looked closer. It was not only smooth but painted with tiny flowers and birds and was more pointed at one end and rounder at the other. Intrigued, I pressed closer. "What is that?"

"It is a chopstick," he said, holding it up for my inspection. "It is an eating utensil in China."

I laughed. "How does one use it to eat? It would seem difficult indeed to spear a pea."

He ignored my mirth and withdrew another stick. "You

163

eat with two of these, held between the fingers like this." He held them in his right hand so that they looked like natural extensions of his fingers, clacking them together to show me how they could grab and pinch. I was not certain how one could cut roasted beef, but perhaps he had something similar to a knife in his jacket as well.

He put away one of the chopsticks. "For purposes of our lessons, we will only require one."

"But I thought we would practice speaking first. Why do we need this sand in a box?"

"Paper is scarce aboard ship, and we must make do. As for writing instead of speaking, there are a multitude of dialects in China but the same written language. It has been the only way that people from different areas could communicate. I thought it would be the easiest for you to learn first."

With the thick end of the chopstick, he drew a character with three smooth strokes. "Chinese does not have an alphabet like English or other languages," he said. "It is based on pictures to represent ideas."

"And what is that?" I gestured at the symbol he had drawn in the box.

"Do you not recognize it? It was the symbol that was on your slippers the night we met."

I leaned closer. "I see it now." I glanced up at him, cocking my head. "You told me that night that the symbol meant love."

He stared at me for a moment, his dark eyes studying my own. I felt a peculiar pull between us, something foreign to my nature, something warm and enticing.

Abruptly, he turned and wiped the character away with his hand until the sand was smooth again. "I did not speak the truth that night, Isabella."

"Then what does it—" No! I would not ask. He heard me voice the beginning of the question, yet he ignored me while he drew figures in the sand. Which Phineas Snowe was I to believe? Had he lied the night of the Ransoms' party or was he lying now?

Snowe drew a short line, apparently prepared to attend to the business at hand with no other false starts. Well and good. At some point I would learn the meaning of the mysterious symbol.

He cleared his throat. "Isabella, are you paying attention? As I was saying, there are eight basic strokes. You must be careful to make them in the proper order for each character to appear correct . . ."

8

We never did open the Gospel that day. I wanted to learn words and characters right away, confident that I could memorize them as fast as he could create them in the sand. Snowe must have sensed my impatience, for at one point he admonished that I must learn the basics first before the bigger lessons would follow.

Though he would not speak it, he did seem pleased by my progress. By the time the crew politely shooed us from the dining room table to prepare the two o'clock dinner, I had learned the eight strokes and the proper order for making them. At first when I watched Snowe create the mysterious lines, I had thought it easy. Then I realized how carefully one must make the hooks and wings that completed some of the strokes. It was difficult enough using a chopstick in the sand. I could only imagine how difficult it would be to create on paper in ink!

Snowe said nothing of our lessons to me or anyone else at dinner; in fact, he seemed to go to great lengths to remove the sand from the cuddy before everyone arrived. He also tucked the chopstick back into his jacket without a word. I met his secrecy with approval for I had no desire to explain myself to Mrs. Akers or any of the others.

Miss Whipple joined our group that day, but to my estimation, none of the other passengers were aware of her reputation. Captain Malfort treated her with all courtesy as well, but I noticed that she did not have a seat of honor, only one below the salt. Unfortunately, so did Mr. Gilpin. I might have imagined it, but I believe that he glared at her the entire meal. Could he not be courteous, at least, in the presence of others?

After dinner, Snowe and I had every intention of returning to our lessons. I was eager to continue, and he, for once, did not seem reluctant. The crew was cleaning the cuddy, so we headed out to the deck. The midshipmen struggled at their lessons, and I noticed that Gilpin drilled Mr. Calow most religiously in knot making. Judging from the cheerful expression on Calow's face, I had to say that he must have been practicing. Unfortunately, it was far too windy for Snowe and me to contemplate any lessons using the box of sand, so we strolled the deck, staying clear of the midshipmen so that we would not disturb them.

A gust of wind blew at my hair. "Oh!" I clutched the pins so that they would not be swept overboard. I was certain that my hair was most displeasing to look at and said as much.

Phineas's expression softened. "I assure you that is not so," he said in a low voice, tucking a strand of hair behind my ear then handing me a bit of leather. "You can use this to tie back your hair. Would you like me to keep the pins in my pocket?"

"No, thank you, the leather should suffice." I secured my hair, frowning. "My, but I have never seen such an ill wind."

Phineas did not respond but stared at the horizon. I followed his gaze and saw billowing dark clouds. The wind seemed to howl, the waves increasing in size as they lashed against the ship. At a superior officer's command, the midshipmen scattered from their lessons, each one charged with a duty to secure the ship's safety.

Mr. Gilpin caught sight of us and approached. The wind had intensified so quickly that he was forced to shout. "The captain has ordered everyone below deck. We've encountered a squall. Mr. Snowe . . . ?"

"Right," he yelled. "I will see my sister to our cabin."

Gilpin nodded then turned to bark an order to the crew about the sails. Snowe led the way, and I obediently followed. The wind had increased so violently, the waves turned so treacherous. We had had such smooth sailing till now that I had been lulled into thinking that our journey would be no more dangerous than a boat ride on the Thames. The *Dignity*, though large, suddenly seemed quite vulnerable as she listed first to port then starboard, buffeted among the waves. To my way of thinking, it would take but one swell to heave her on her side. I had read of shipwrecks, of course, even East India Company shipwrecks, which suddenly pushed me beyond my books and daydreams into ruthless reality.

The ship rocked to and fro most alarmingly. Rain pounded our heads and backs like myriad dull daggers. I cried out, surprised by the painful force. Snowe turned back and wrapped his arm around me, raising his coat to shield me as much as possible from the onslaught.

We staggered safely below deck, but to my shame, I whimpered. "We are almost there, Isabella," Phineas said soothingly. "We will be safe."

He led me into the cabin and closed the door behind us. Rain and wind blew through the porthole, and he struggled valiantly to shutter it. Yet I could still hear the raging noise beyond.

I stood in the middle of the room, dripping, wetter than I ever imagined possible, and all I could do was cry. I was not a female easily given to tears, and I was embarrassed by the emotion that washed over me. I tried to turn away from Snowe so that he would not see my weakness. To my surprise, however, he touched my face. "You should get undressed," he said softly.

I stepped back in horror, tears abated. "Wh-what? I most certainly will not!"

He moved to his side of the room and raised the canvas between our hammocks. "You need to get out of your wet clothes, Isabella," he said. "Otherwise, you might take ill."

I heard a flint strike, then saw a candle's glow. "I will light this long enough for us to see by, then I'll douse the flame. We do not want to risk a fire."

Even though he could not see me, I nodded, already

divesting myself of the sodden clothing. I let them fall to the floor, not caring that the ugliest dress in Christendom would have to dry before I could wear it again. My nightgown was dry, and I slipped into it eagerly, shivering from the chill.

"Isabella, I have an extra blanket that I would like to bring you," he said. "Will you be alarmed if I approach your side of the canvas?"

"N-no," I said, teeth chattering as I climbed into my hammock and pulled my only blanket up to my chin. "You may approach."

Tentatively he lifted the end of the canvas, his eyes downcast so as to avoid mine. I tried not to look at him either, but I could not help notice that his hair was unbound and he was wrapped in a blanket. Whatever else he wore, I could not tell. In truth, I did not want to know!

He handed me the blanket and hastened back to his side. I heard him blow out the candle, and what meager light we had was now gone. I settled into my hammock, trying to find some warmth. Even the extra blanket did not seem to help much. Snowe must have heard my shivering. "Are you very cold?"

"I'm afraid that I am," I confessed. "I cannot get warm."

Rain, or perhaps waves, lashed against the porthole most cruelly. A flash of lightning jagged across the pane, and my hammock tilted at an alarming angle. I cried without thinking. "Phineas!"

"It will be all right, Isabella," he said, his voice an anchor of calm. "It is but a small storm, I am certain. It will pass, the sun will shine, and you will wonder why you were so frightened."

Aggravating man! "I know why I am frightened," I said, amazed at the high pitch in my voice, a distinct opposite of his own. "I am afraid of being killed. I . . . I do not want to drown. If you have any sense, you would be afraid of the same thing!"

"I will not let you drown. I promised to keep you safe, and I will not go back on my word."

I laughed in spite of my fear. "Your word? When am I to trust your word?"

"Believe me on this if nothing else, Isabella Goodrich. I *will* keep you safe."

The ship lurched, my hammock swayed far to the right then back again violently. I feared that it would be loosed from its mooring and I would be flung across the room. Even the canvas shielding me from Snowe's view flapped about.

Everything righted for a moment, and in the interim, I mentally took myself—and Snowe—to task. How could he be so calm and undisturbed over there? It was I who wanted to be a missionary and help the poor and downtrodden, yet I squeaked like a mouse at the first sign of danger.

The ship rolled, and I clutched the sides of my hammock, praying fervently. If the apostle Paul experienced and survived half my fear when his ship wrecked, I could well understand why he earned the title of saint!

"Isabella, you are interested in swords and fencing, yes?"

Where did *that* question originate? "Yes, of course!" I answered, keeping one eye on the porthole. Lashed by the waves and wind, it appeared that any moment water would burst in and overtake us.

"If you would learn about the Chinese, you should learn some of the stories they tell, great myths about powerful men and women who battle for justice against villains."

His words had the obvious desired effect of piquing my curiosity. "You speak of heroes? Women?"

"Yes, not only men. Often they were wanderers who were skilled in combat but only fought when necessary," he said.

"To right wrongs?"

"Yes."

"They sound much like knights of British myth. Like King Arthur and his knights of the round table."

"It is not quite the same," he said. "These heroes, called *hup*, were not nobility. They could be, of course, but could also come from a humbler background. They did not have quests, either, but were often wanderers."

"So they roamed the countryside with no purpose?"

"Their goal was adventure, and they could be hired, but they did not seek to line their pockets so much as to uphold honor and justice. Their word could not be violated."

That prevents you from numbering yourself among them, Phineas Snowe! I do not know why he spoke of such warriors when he was so far from them himself. However, listening to his description took my mind off the storm outside, and indeed, I believed I felt myself warming. "Tell me more," I said. "Do you know any actual stories, or is your purpose merely to inform?"

"I have heard a *mo hup* tale or two. *Mo* means having to do with martial arts, the military, or war, and *hup* is the hero of the story. It also means chivalry."

"Like King Arthur and his knights."

Snowe sighed. "As I said, it is not quite the same, Isabella."

If there was anything I preferred to fencing, it was a well-told story. Storm and danger receded, and I settled into my hammock. "Then spin a tale and let me judge for myself."

Spin he did, his words holding me spellbound. He told the tale of Wo-Ping, a *hup* who appeared in a village called Hu-King one day with little more than his sword. In exchange for food and a place to sleep, he worked for a farmer near the village. The next day another *hup* arrived, a woman, Mei. The villagers suspected her motives, and though she was lovely, she had a heart as hard as the soil after a rain. Unfortunately for the villagers and Wo-Ping, they did not know about the sword she kept hidden in the haystack nor how wrong they would be about the condition of her heart.

I did not know if Phineas merely recounted a story he had heard before or if he wove the tale even as he spoke it, but something happened to me that night as he sought to calm my fears of the storm. I no longer heard the voice of Phineas Snowe, but the narrator of a great tale. He drew me into the land and the characters with their struggle for *yi*, or righteousness. I was transfixed by the notion of a woman who hungered and thirsted for such.

Just as he reached a crucial point in the story, he suddenly stopped speaking. I was all but poised at the edge of my hammock, waiting for him to continue.

"We are past the storm," he said.

"Storm? There is no storm in Hu-King. Go on."

"I spoke of the *Dignity*, Isabella."

I blinked. I no longer saw the village or the woman with the sword but the canvas hanging between my hammock and Snowe's. I rolled over to face the porthole and saw that the sun was shining once again. We had survived.

"Are you warmer now?" he said gently.

"Yes, thank you." I spied my discarded clothing on the floor. "But I am afraid I have nothing to wear. I cannot be seen in my nightgown, after all."

I heard him rise from his hammock, then the rustle of clothing. "Perhaps Julia Whipple has something else that you may borrow. In the meantime, perhaps you should rest. I do not want you to catch a chill. I will bring you some tea."

"I do not suppose you have green to share?" I said hopefully, like a child. Indeed, I felt quite under his spell at the moment.

"I have some leaves in my trunk," he said. "After I have seen Julia, I will bring you some."

The door closed after him. Surely when he returned I would see what else was in the mysterious trunk besides, apparently, tea. I huddled under my two blankets, not from

174

the cold now, but from the memory of the story. I felt an odd sort of kinship with the man who had calmed my fears and fired my intrigue. Had it truly been Phineas Snowe who thrilled my imagination by taking me to a foreign land? I could not wait for Mei to recover the sword from hiding and use it to show Wo-Ping that she was not the heartless woman he thought her. Phineas had not even described what type of swords Mei and Wo-Ping possessed, and I longed to hear their descriptions. And what of the two *hup*? Would Mei be forced to fight Wo-Ping? What would be her initial approach? Surely she would be calm and allow Wo-Ping to exhaust himself by attacking with his sword first so that she could study his weaknesses and take full advantage. Or would he do the same with her?

I did not realize that I spent hours picturing the sword-play in my mind. At last I realized from the angle of the sun through the porthole that it had been quite a long time since Snowe had left the room. I could not imagine what had detained him.

Then I remembered that he had gone to Miss Whipple. *Julia*, he had called her. What else—who else—could have kept him for such a great length of time? My spirits sank, my enthusiasm dampened as greatly as the dress lying on the cabin floor. How could he weave a magical tale, drawing me into a world of his making, then abandon me for Julia Whipple?

When I heard the door finally open, I pretended sleep, even when on my wooden crate he laid a fresh dress and a cup of tea. Let it grow cold!

I felt betrayed. Indeed, Miss Whipple and Snowe seemed to have their heads together the rest of the day. They strolled the deck, laughing and conversing while the crew made busy repairing the damage the storm had wrought and mopping the deck. The sun shone brightly now, but it might as well have been pitch black and the ship storm-tossed for my mood. I did not understand why Snowe would seemingly abandon me for Miss Whipple's company. It is true that I was not, in fact, his sister, but we had shared something during the storm through his story, something akin to closeness that we had never had. I was bewildered at his reactions, and my own, as well.

The dress Miss Whipple had loaned me was gray this time, a light cotton that made me think of a dove or a pigeon. Naturally I was grateful to have dry clothing, but I could not help but desire something a little more fashionable to wear. It was difficult to remind myself that missionaries should have an attitude like the lilies of the field, but I believe that even flowers dressed more fashionably than I.

I took several turns around the deck, keeping an eye on Miss Whipple and Phineas. Midshipman Calow was kind enough to inquire about my health after the storm, avowing that it was not nearly the worst he had seen in his young life at sea. Mr. Gilpin joined us and agreed. They were both gentlemanly enough to reserve criticism when they heard of my distress at the tossing nature of the ship during the worst of the storm.

"Mr. and Mrs. Akers were both violently ill," Mr. Calow

reported cheerfully. "They did not even manage to toss their dinners into a bucket. One of the seamen is cleaning up their cabin now."

Mr. Gilpin gave him a silencing glance. "That is no fit talk for a lady, Mr. Calow."

"Aye, sir. I'm sorry, sir. I beg your pardon, Miss Goodrich."

I had rather enjoyed the strong image his words evoked regarding the Akers, but I suppressed a smile. "All is forgiven."

"Mr. Calow, climb up and check the rigging, if you please," Mr. Gilpin said.

"Aye, sir." Mr. Calow saluted then scrambled up the ropes.

I smiled. "I admire his stamina. Is he doing well as a midshipman? He seems quite young."

"It is a good age to begin," Gilpin said. "I was about that old when I began my career."

He cleared his throat and clasped his hands behind his back in his earnest manner. "Miss Goodrich, I took the liberty of sending those books to your cabin."

Julia Whipple tilted her head back and laughed at something Snowe said. I gritted my teeth. "Thank you, Mr. Gilpin. I look forward to reading them."

Gilpin turned and spied Miss Whipple and Snowe. The first mate shook his head. "I am sorry about your brother," he said softly.

"Phineas? Whatever for?"

Gilpin clucked. "He is shaming you by spending time

with her. Their association might ruin your reputation. He should be thinking about that instead of himself."

His solicitousness was irritating and altogether misplaced. "I have no concept of what society will be like in China, Mr. Gilpin. Perhaps such associations will not matter. Particularly if I live among the non-Christians."

He raised his eyebrows. "You mean the Chinese? Why, you will never be able to do that, Miss Goodrich."

"Why?"

"Because . . . because it simply is not done!"

"And why not?"

"Because you are an Englishwoman. Even though we are no longer on English soil, we are bound by her societal norms. You must not associate with Miss Whipple, and you will not live among the Chinese. No foreign women are allowed in Canton. You will, at best, live in Macao."

"I cannot very well be a missionary to my own people," I said. "What purpose would that serve?"

"Why, even we English need spiritual guidance. I am certain there is some useful work you can perform with the clergy who are already there."

His bossiness grated. "But I could have stayed in Oxford were that all I hoped to accomplish."

Mr. Gilpin shook his head. "Forgive me, Miss Goodrich. I know that your heart desires to reach the Chinese, but it is quite impossible." He glanced over at Snowe and Miss Whipple again. "I blame your brother for not advising you on this before you went to so much trouble to follow him aboard this ship. If you will forgive me, it is clear he has little regard for anyone save himself. Rest assured that he has some ulterior motive."

Why I desired to defend Phineas was beyond my understanding, especially since I was somewhat angry at him. "He *did* begin to teach me Chinese," I said, then could not resist adding, "for my benefit. I do not appreciate your words about my brother, nor your inference regarding Miss Whipple. She has been naught but kind to me. I will not slight her."

Gilpin glanced at Snowe and Miss Whipple, then touched his knuckles to his forehead in salute. "Forgive me, Miss Goodrich. Good day."

"Good day," I said, relieved to be rid of his company.

At the moment, I felt that I had not a friend aboard ship. Everyone seemed bent on telling me what I could and could not do. I confess that Gilpin's words about Phineas took root, and I could not forget them. Captain Malfort approached me, a genuine smile on his face. After we exchanged pleasantries, I said, "Have you known my brother long?"

"Several years now," he said. "Why do you ask?"

"I have not seen him in a long while, and you know that we were not raised together. What sort of man would you say that he is?"

"He has always been a man of stellar reputation regarding the East India Company, Miss Goodrich. I am afraid that is all that I know. But to me it speaks well for a man's character."

If Mr. Gilpin knew something about Phineas Snowe, then

it was not common knowledge. "Thank you, Captain. That puts my mind at rest."

He scrutinized my expression. "You do not have cause for concern regarding your brother, do you?"

I shook my head, affecting a smile. "No, Captain. It was only idle curiosity, nothing more."

He tipped his cap and went on his way. Miss Whipple and Snowe had drifted out of sight somewhere, and with a sigh, I determined to look for Gilpin's books by returning to my cabin. Provided those two had not already taken up residence in there!

Once again that night I retired before Phineas. I managed to hang the canvas curtain by myself, but I heard him enter, undress for bed, and lie down in his hammock. After a while I expected to hear snoring but was surprised to hear his voice instead. "Are you still awake, Isabella?"

What could he want? "Yes."

"You seemed distant this afternoon and evening. Are you well?"

"Since you have asked, I am experiencing some pain."

"Truly?" I heard him sit up. "What can I do to help?"

"You can tell me why you ignored me in favor of Julia Whipple."

He lay back down, a long sigh emanating. "She is alone on this voyage and has no friends. I feel sorry for her plight and merely try to bolster her spirits with my company from time to time." He paused. "She thinks highly of you, Isabella, did you know?"

180

If he sought to flatter me . . . it worked. "Really? What did she—" I broke off. "You two discussed me," I said, annoyance creeping into my voice.

"We discussed a great many things. It is not so large a ship that the primary travelers escape notice," he said. "And now, would you like to hear more about Wo-Ping and Mei?"

I must confess that I did and was willing to, if not outright forgive, overlook the slights I had felt were dealt me. "I would indeed like to hear more," I said, hating myself for giving in so easily. "But when will you reach the part about the swords? I am anxious to hear about Mei and Wo-Ping fighting. Who is the better swordsman?"

"That is yet to be determined," he said. "Remember, too, that there are many weapons in China, not just swords. Different areas of the country have different weapons, as well as fighting skills."

"What are some of the weapons?" I asked, temporarily forgetting the town of Hu-King.

"There are swords, which have two blades and can be broadswords, more like sabers, or heavier like cutlasses. Those with single blades are called knives. There are shorter butterfly swords, which are used in pairs. There are also *emei*, which have arrowlike points at each end. Then there are staffs, whips, and spears, not to mention axes, hammers, and cudgels. There are also throwing weapons—darts, arrows, sharpened stars, and blades."

I could scarcely breathe for excitement. So many weapons, and I had spent a lifetime learning only one! "Perhaps

Wo-Ping or Mei have skills in some of these weapons as well," I said. The story would certainly be improved if this were true.

"Perhaps," Phineas said vaguely. "Are you ready for me to begin?"

I wrapped the blankets securely around my neck, resisting the urge to kick my feet together like a child. "Yes, please."

He cleared his throat. "Mei knew that Wo-Ping had the sympathy of the farmer as well as the villagers, but she also knew that he could not be trusted. She would bide her time, for she was not only a skilled warrior, but she was patient and clever . . ."

We fell into a sort of routine, one day much like another aboard the *Dignity*. Phineas seemed persuaded of my earnestness in learning Chinese, and we passed much of each day in study. He taught me much of the written language, which, though complicated, seemed to make a great deal of sense. Two or more pictures could create one new word. I learned over a thousand characters, which, he said, would probably make me a functional reader in China. Not, he said, that I was actually going there, of course!

At my request, Mr. Calow secured some precious paper for me, which I used to laboriously copy the Gospel According to St. Luke in Chinese. My characters did not look the same as Robert Morrison's original, but I worked diligently and made several copies of the second chapter, the story of Jesus' birth.

Snowe seemed surprised that I learned so well, but at last he agreed to teach me spoken words. I did not want to resort to writing or reading characters when we reached China (and I *was* going there!), no matter how easily it could be understood in many regions. He taught me that Chinese was a tonal language, unlike English. Each word had a particular pitch, and using the wrong one could change the meaning from one word to something completely different.

He taught me by day, and at night he continued the story of Mei and Wo-Ping. An evil landowner threatened much of the village, and the warriors put aside their differences in preparation to defend Hu-King. I sensed an undercurrent of distrust between the warriors and still believed that one day they would fight, but though I had initially sided with Mei in all things, I now harbored great sympathy for Wo-Ping as well. He had been the first to see the true goodness in her heart, but he waited patiently for her to reveal it.

The story so overwhelmed me that during the day I often remembered two things and at night forgot to ask: how much time had Phineas spent in China that he was able to spin folktales, and why had he not yet procured a sword for me?

I would like to say that I became better acquainted with my fellow travelers, but I did not have much use for their company beyond what was required at mealtimes. Mrs. Akers continued to dominate all conversation, though thankfully she had moved on to other subjects beyond the lack of physical similarities between Phineas and myself. Mr. Akers kept busy with company matters, as did Mr. Harrison, who apparently had taken the younger man under his wing. Personally, I believe Mr. Akers merely threw himself into work to avoid the bride that he by now may have regretted taking.

We saw little of Mrs. Harrison, who seemed to be either sleeping or in a constant stupor. I began to believe that she had a physical ailment of some sort that prevented her from staying awake long, until I noticed that Dr. Mortimer gave her a tiny bottle almost daily. When I asked Phineas about it, he sighed. "It is laudanum, Isabella."

"From what does she suffer?" I said, alarmed.

"Malaise of life, I believe. I have my suspicions that Harrison chose China as a means of either ending his wife's life or giving her reason to fully recover. She has used the drug for a long time now, I have heard it whispered."

I did not have to ask who had done the whispering. Though he was more careful to spend most of the day with me, he still passed time with Julia Whipple. I had it in mind to speak directly with her, for I still felt it my duty to encourage her to seek a better life for herself once in China. I had heard that many of our fairer sex had to resort to desperate measures to survive, but I knew that there must be another situation for her.

Then one day I received an answer that I could only attribute to the Divine. While I had enjoyed the books Mr. Gilpin shared, I had not thought to use them for any other purpose save my own education and entertainment. But it occurred to me that perhaps I could loan them to Miss Whipple. Education, Uncle Toby had always said, was the key to unlock the doors of ignorance and poverty. While I would not deem her ignorant, for I thought her quite intelligent, actually, Miss Whipple could perhaps find a new life for herself as a governess if she but had the learning.

I found her one afternoon after dinner, lingering in the cuddy. Oblivious to the crew removing the dinnerware and leftover food, she stared at the wall as though a window would present itself. "Miss Whipple," I said.

She turned, and for one moment I saw great sadness in her eyes. Then something shuttered her vulnerability, and she smiled at me. "Miss Goodrich. Are you looking for Phineas?"

"Not at all. It is your company I sought."

"Have you and Phineas abandoned your lessons?"

"Only for a while. I find the Chinese words all run together if we spend too much time on them. I thought perhaps that different lessons might be in order."

Her smile turned sardonic. "And what is it you would learn from me?"

"Quite the opposite. I thought perhaps you might be interested in learning with me."

She laughed. "I have no use for Chinese, Miss Goodrich. The king's English will do for my needs."

I took a chair beside her. "Miss Whipple, may I be blunt?"

"Please do."

She stared at me so coldly that I felt compelled to look away for a moment, then resolve steadied my nerves. "Have you had much education?"

"It depends on the sort of education you mean."

I felt a blush creep around my neck. "Academic, of course. The truth is, Miss Whipple, that I have had the benefit of a good education. Some would say too much so, but that is neither here nor there. At any rate, I have no idea what purpose I will find in China, but perhaps it will be as a teacher. I have no experience as such, and I thought it might help me to practice, so to speak, with someone."

"And you see me as that candidate?"

I nodded.

"Why?" She folded her arms.

I blew out a long breath. "You have admitted your purpose for moving to China. I propose to change that purpose. With a bit of learning . . ."

"Miss Goodrich." She started to rise, apparently thought better of it, and sat down. "I have more learning than you will ever know. I believe you're a kind soul, but either you're too naïve to see life as it is or you choose to ignore its harshness. Either way, I feel sorry for you."

I blinked. "You feel pity for me?"

"You think it's the other way around, don't you? You feel pity for me and think I have no voice in my future."

"I have often thought that one's past did determine the future, yes, but pity? I feel more . . . sadness. I want better for you."

Miss Whipple leaned forward. "You're a fool, Isabella Goodrich," she said in a low voice. "You are being played for one, and yet you worry about my life. I should be the one to worry about you."

"I . . . don't understand." Her words confused me.

"You know that Phineas spends time with me. What do you suppose we do?"

My mouth went dry. "I . . ."

"We talk," she said. "Yes, that's all we do. Talk. But I have heard quite an earful since I met Phineas Snowe."

Tears stung my eyes. Afraid to hear more, I rose. "I do not think—"

She touched my wrist. "Sit down, Miss Goodrich. I'm telling you this because I admire you. Truly I do. You should know the truth."

I sat, believing her words to be for my own good. "I am all attention. What should I know?"

"Phineas Snowe will never let you go to China. He will have you put off at Cape Town."

I breathed a sigh. "I know that is what he says, but I believe he will change his mind."

"Do you know why he cannot have you travel to Canton?"

I shook my head.

"He is not who he claims to be. He has worked for the East India Company for the last few years, it is true, but the purpose of his voyage is not to procure tea. Not for the company anyway."

"Then what is it for?"

"He wants to find a special tea in China. Something that he believes will put the East India Company out of business. That is his life's purpose. Everything he has done in the past few years has been to that end."

"But why?"

187

"I'll leave that much for you to ask him. Know only that he has deceived you from the moment he met you and has not ceased. He plans to leave you in Cape Town no matter how impressed he is with your learning his native language."

"Chinese? *That* is his native tongue?"

She smiled. "Have you not noticed the structure of his face? His eyes? He wore spectacles at the party where he met you, did he not?"

"But . . . I do not understand." My head swam with her words, which seemed to make no logical sense.

Miss Whipple rose. "Ask Phineas to explain himself. In the meantime, do not worry about my future, but take care for your own."

9

She left me in the cuddy. I sat for a long time, numb, my mind all sixes and sevens. I could not believe that Miss Whipple would lie to me. Though we were not confidantes, I could not see what she would gain by speaking of Snowe in such a manner. Yet, could he lie to me again?

The answer came swiftly: yes. Though it grieved my heart, I knew that the truth was to my ultimate advantage, for now he could never put me ashore in Cape Town. While he believed Miss Whipple unwilling to reveal his deception to someone with the power to stop him, he knew that I would be more than so inclined.

But would I? I was terrible at bluffing in whist, the contents of my cards easily readable on my face. Or so I had been told. Higher stakes were certainly in play now, more than just a few coins between Catherine Ransom and friends and certainly more than a friendly game with Flora and Uncle Toby.

My dear loved ones. What would they advise me to do? Would they want me to see to my own safety and allow

Snowe to go about his nefarious business—whatever it truly was—or expose him? Or perhaps I should endeavor to work the art of persuasion so that he might steer aside from his wicked course of action?

"There you are, Isabella. I thought you would be ready to return to our studies."

I startled at the sound of his voice. Snowe stood so close beside my chair that I could almost feel the touch of his fingers against my shoulder. He smiled down at me, apparently unaware that his future was about to change.

"Please sit down," I said.

"If you will wait a moment, I will retrieve the box of sand and—"

"Please sit down. This is not about our studies."

He pulled out the chair Miss Whipple had recently vacated. Ten minutes ago I would have taken joy in advising him that I knew his scheme, but now I did not. Indeed he had shown me various kindnesses throughout our journey.

Yet, I reminded myself, ultimately he would separate me from my divine purpose because of his own double-dealing.

"What is it, Isabella?" he said. "You look pale."

"I have received some news that concerns you. And me."

The smile slid from his face. "Go on."

"You will not leave me in Cape Town," I said.

He laughed, probably from relief. "Come, Isabella, we agreed to revisit our decision when we reach port. It is early yet."

"But we are close enough now to speak of it. Particularly since I have learned of your true purpose for going, or should I say returning, to China."

He leaned toward me, his expression now hardened. "Julia has spoken with you."

"Indeed she has." I folded my hands atop the table. "Now I should like for you to explain yourself. You are owed that courtesy."

Muttering, he glanced away, rubbing the back of his neck. At last he returned his gaze to me. "I am sorry that she has spoken with you, Isabella, for I did not want you to be burdened with my problems."

"*Your* problems? You seek to undo Britain's premiere trading company, an act that would be near treason to the estimation of some, and it is a *problem*?"

"Do you know what the company is doing to China? To the Chinese?" he said in a low voice. "Do you know at what expense Britain gains her precious tea?"

"We trade for it, of course," I said. "Or purchase it outright."

"What do you suppose we trade?"

"I haven't the vaguest notion."

He shook his head. "I had hoped that you, of all people, would know. Yet apparently you are as ignorant as the rest of that godforsaken island."

I resented such reference to England. "Then enlighten me."

"The Chinese are quite self-sufficient and need nothing that Britain normally offers in trade, such as heavy woolens. Britain cannot rely on cash alone, for she is draining herself of silver to purchase tea outright. There is one thing that the Chinese have come to love, however, much to their detriment. When the British realized they could acquire it in India and trade for tea in China, they began the ruination of a great nation."

"What is the item?"

"Opium."

I blinked. "That is like the laudanum of which Mrs. Harrison is so fond?"

"Laudanum is made with opium, yes. Imagine a nation with hundreds, thousands, millions like her . . . gentlemen and ladies alike unwilling to do anything except stagger through life in a haze, their only desire to purchase more opium." He laughed bitterly. "All so that the East India Company can turn a profit and Britain can have her tea."

"I had no idea," I whispered. "Oh, Phineas . . ."

"Is your opinion now changed regarding Britain's premiere trading company?"

"I . . . I cannot speak to that. I can only think of the poor Orientals who are wasting their lives. Perhaps you should focus on helping them, Phineas. Perhaps together, we can—"

He smacked his hand on the table. "I am trying to help them! You seek to save their souls, but first their bodies must be saved. I want to put the East India Company out of business so that they can no longer bring opium into the country."

"How do you propose to do that?" I said softly. "The company is large and powerful. You are alone."

"The Tippetts are helping to finance the venture by entering the tea trade. More importantly, I will beat the company at its own game by finding a tea that outsells what they bring back to England. Just as green tea gave way in popularity to black tea, I will sell a new kind of tea for which the British will clamor. But the Tippetts' company will be the only one to sell it."

"Do you know of such a tea?"

He nodded. "I know someone who found it only a few years ago. It is a golden leaf that grows only in a certain part of China. The East India Company is restricted to Canton, a port city, and is dependent upon what tea growers bring there to trade. I can travel to the interior where the tea grows and bring it back to the Tippett company."

I studied his eyes. Why had I not seen their almond shape? Mrs. Akers had been more astute than I could ever give her credit. "How is it that you can travel inland?" I said softly.

He caught me studying him and smiled. "Because I am Chinese. Does that surprise you, Isabella?"

"I . . . did not see it," I said, faltering.

"I counted on that very thing from the beginning."

"The spectacles . . . ?"

He nodded. "A precaution for the party."

My heart felt as though it would break, and I could not entirely say why. Was I angry because Uncle Toby had been thoroughly duped? Was it because Phineas harbored such bitterness that had worked its way into revenge? Or was it because I had, as Miss Whipple kindly pointed out, been made the worst sort of fool?

"What I told you of my parents was not a lie," he said, apparently unconcerned with the condition of my heart.

"Then you grew up in York?"

"I did not grow up there entirely," he said. "I was raised in China by my mother and her family. My father was a naval man, as I said, but when he learned of my existence, he took me back to Britain to be raised in Yorkshire. I was eight at that time and lived in his family home, but I was not acknowledged as his son."

"Oh, Phineas." I could not believe I felt sorry for him, but I did. "How did you manage? You must have missed your mother terribly."

"I had the best schooling possible, and when I was of age, I saw my opportunity to return to China by working with the East India Company." He paused. "I traveled back and forth for several years, but when I saw how pervasive opium addiction was, I decided to continue to work for the company so that I could destroy it from within."

"And now you have your opportunity."

He smiled. "Yes. But the question is, what am I to do with you now that you know the truth?"

For one moment, fancy filled my imagination, and I pictured him throwing me overboard. Then I remembered that he had ample chance to disavow me but had done nothing save protect me at every turn, including my reputation. He had also lied to me at every turn, however . . .

"Isabella?"

"You must take me with you," I said firmly. "That is the price of my silence."

"No! Do you not see that I have further reason to keep you from China? It is dangerous, Isabella. I will not have you there."

"But it is my decision. Just as you have decided to avenge your countrymen."

"No."

"I am not above telling Captain Malfort still," I said. "Perhaps it would be you who is left in Cape Town, not I."

He narrowed his eyes. "You would not do that."

"I would." I lifted my chin. "You have been kind to me, but you have also used me abominably. I cannot help but feel that my posing as your sister is somehow a ruse for your revenge. It gives you more respectability and brings less suspicion on yourself, am I correct?"

His expression told me that my guess was indeed accurate, and I glowed inwardly. I had won. "It is yet again blackmail," he said.

"Then so be it," I said. "Your words make me more determined than ever to share the gospel in China."

He sighed. "I admire your courage and your enthusiasm, not to mention your faith, but I do not think your time in China would be well served trying to be a missionary."

"I would not be aboard this ship if I were not convinced of my destiny. I find it odd that you accept Julia Whipple's self-proclaimed destiny in China and yet you repeatedly chastise me for my biblical mission."

"Ah, Miss Whipple," he said, smiling. "Though she is oddly fond of you, and even more oddly, you profess to be so of her, I wondered what your true feelings might be."

I felt a small wave of regret for my hasty words. "I did not mean to criticize her, only to point out the inconsistency of your words and actions toward her and me. I find her quite intelligent, and I wish a better life for her."

"You cannot change the world, my dear Isabella."

"Oh? Isn't that what *you* are trying to do? Have you ever thought about letting God have his way with China instead of settling upon your own revenge?" I studied him closely. "What *are* your beliefs toward God?"

"I was baptized in the church, much to my mother's disapproval. She believed me coerced, but it was my choice. For that, I shall always be grateful to my father and his family."

"Then you must understand how I feel. I want to share my gratefulness with others. Perhaps if they know that God so loved the world—"

"And gave his only begotten son . . . yes, I know, Isabella. But imagine that a Buddhist in China desires to travel to Britain and convert everyone to Buddhism. Would you call him wise?"

"Of course not," I said. "But this is different."

He folded his arms.

"But it is. It is truth!"

"I agree, Isabella, but you cannot march into a country and simply announce that you have the answers to all their problems."

"But I do," I said stubbornly.

"They will not listen. They will not believe you."

"St. Paul was a great evangelist," I said. "He went to different countries."

"Yes, and he said that he was made all things to all men that he might by all means save some."

"Then that is what I shall do. Have I not endeavored to learn the language? Do I not have the tracts in Chinese? Phineas, I want to serve."

He shook his head, sighing. "That may be difficult. China is very different from your way of life. I hope that you are not disappointed by what you find there."

"And I hope that you are, for though your intentions may be noble, I cannot believe that your method of revenge is pleasing to God."

"Well, then." He smiled. "It will be interesting to see whose expectations are met."

"'All things are possible to him that believeth.'" I smiled in return. Phineas Snowe was not the only one who could quote Scripture!

As though nothing had changed between us, that night Phineas picked up the story of Wo-Ping and Mei. The two had become romantically involved, but they still kept their weapons a secret from each other. When the villain convinced each of them that the other was plotting the village's destruction, Wo-Ping retrieved his sword and Mei hers.

At last I would see them fight! I could see the intricate scrollwork on Wo-Ping's sword and feel the delicate balance yet razor sharpness of Mei's. When sword met sword, I saw sparks fly.

I forgot all about the *Dignity* and my own plans for China. I had fully entered the believable world Snowe spun, and it was as though I were an eyewitness to the battle. So it was with no small amount of bewilderment on my part when Wo-Ping suddenly ran, weightless, up the wall, and Mei followed him.

"What?" I cried aloud. "How can that be?"

"It is the story, Isabella. Accept it as it is. May I continue?"

I gave my consent somewhat unhappily. I had thought the story real. Yet more magical feats occurred than running up walls. Wo-Ping and Mei could all but fly, Wo-Ping made himself invisible, and Mei hurled balls of fire from her palms. Sadly, I stopped Snowe in midsentence. "I do not wish to hear any more."

"For just tonight or any nights hence?" he said.

"I am not certain." I felt shaken.

He was silent on his side of the canvas curtain. "It is but a story, Isabella. Do you believe that King Arthur truly tossed Excalibur into water, only to have it caught by the lady of the lake? Is Britain allowed her myths, but not China?"

I had no response.

"We are but a few days from Cape Town, where we will pass several nights. Perhaps we can resume the tale once we are aboard ship again."

I rolled over, turning my back to the canvas. I could not explain my disappointment, but it was there nonetheless. "Perhaps," I mumbled.

Other than the sound of water bumping the ship and the perpetual creak of timbers, our cabin was silent. At length I said, "You have yet to procure my sword, Phineas Snowe."

He groaned. "Go to sleep, Isabella."

The next morning I saw Miss Whipple strolling alone about the deck. The weather had indeed grown warmer as we sailed farther south, and she had abandoned her shawl. I thought that she looked quite respectable in a lovely blue muslin dress with a deeper blue ribbon in her hair. Mr. Gilpin did not seem to share my sentiments, however, as he passed her, barely acknowledged her presence, and moved on.

Flora would have boxed my ears for such behavior, but I could not stand to see Miss Whipple slighted. I fell in step beside her.

She glanced at me with surprise. "I was not certain if you would speak to me today."

"Why ever not?" I said, smiling. "Perhaps it is Phineas who will not speak to you."

"It would be of no consequence." She shrugged. "I could not stand another moment whereby I knew he lied to you. You two have spoken?"

"Indeed we have."

"The expression on your face indicates that the conversation was to your advantage."

"I believe it was to both our advantages. Phineas knows that I will keep his secret, and now I do not have to worry about being left behind in Cape Town."

"You should be careful, Miss Goodrich. He might yet find a way to change your plans."

"Thank you for the counsel, but I believe not."

We walked together in silence. Men overhead climbed the rigging, tending to some matter of a sail. Mr. Gilpin frowned at us, and I took Miss Whipple's arm in my own and turned us aft. "Let us go astern."

"Have you a peculiar desire to see the chickens on the poop deck?" she said, smiling. "Or do you hope to avoid Mr. Gilpin?"

"Both, if you must know."

We climbed up to the poop deck. Mr. Swinney, the poulterer, was nowhere to be seen. The number of chickens and ducks had diminished since we set sail from England, and I thought somewhat guiltily of our past dinners.

Miss Whipple sat near an empty cage and studied the wake behind the ship. After a moment, she spoke. "I have thought about your offer to teach me, Miss Goodrich."

I tried to conceal the smile from my face. "Indeed?"

She nodded. "If it would help you, I am willing to learn what you have to teach."

"Is there anything in particular you wish to study?"

"I can read well enough, but I know little of history. I know little of Napoleon, for all the talk I hear of him."

I sat beside her. "Is it the French who interest you?"

"To begin with. I would learn the history of England, of course. And the . . . what do you call them . . . ancient civilizations?"

"Mr. Gilpin loaned me some books on that very subject. We could start with those."

Miss Whipple was silent for a moment. "I imagine you wonder how I came to be the type of person that I am."

"It is not for my speculation, Miss Whipple," I said, lowering my gaze.

"I did not choose my life. I made a foolish mistake in trusting a man to lead me from Portsmouth to London, but he abandoned me." She paused. "I could not go home after that for fear of completely ruining my family."

I touched her hand, moved by her plight. "I am sorry."

She smiled bitterly. "Perhaps my story will have spared you from following after a man foolishly, though I think not. I believe that Phineas is not quite the same as the man who misled you originally, but he has misled you all the same."

"Yes, he has. But I do not plan to stay with him once we reach China. I intend to find an established mission or someplace where I can serve, but I certainly will not travel with him." I brightened. "Will you not go with me, Miss Whipple? I am certain that two ladies can help as well as one."

"I am afraid that I am only suited for a life with men. That is why Phineas confided his plan to me, even though we never—" She looked away, coughing into her hand. "I would still like for you to teach me, if you are willing. But perhaps you do not want to be seen with me. Gilpin—"

"Mr. Gilpin is not master of my soul," I said. "I would be delighted to teach you, but please . . . you must call me Isabella."

She looked at me fully for the first time since we had sat down. She smiled. "Only if you will call me Julia."

Mr. Calow solemnly informed me one morning that ships approaching the Cape of Good Hope were often besieged by violent winds. I could not imagine going through another storm. Indeed, he must have thought my expression particularly alarmed, for he hastened to add that hardly ever were the ships wrecked, though he repeated "hardly ever" as though reassuring himself as well. Fortunately for us all, we encountered no problems and soon sailed into Cape Town, docking at Table Bay.

I knew a little of the town, of course, but nothing prepared me for the joy I would feel at the sight of land again after so many days at sea. Particularly land as beautiful as this historic town. Phineas and I stood together on deck to watch as we docked, and I could scarcely say a word.

"It is beautiful, isn't it?" I murmured, glancing at the crystalline beach and a large mountain in the distance towering overhead.

"That is Table Mountain," Phineas said. "It appears clear today, but at times the top is shrouded in mist and fog."

I fanned myself with my hand. "I cannot believe that we have traveled so far and to find the weather so changed. I have read that the climate is different below the equator but never dreamed I would experience it for myself." I turned my attention from the scene and smiled. "But you must find me silly, for you have traveled this course many times."

He smiled down at me. "I have not seen the journey through your eyes. I find the view most enjoyable."

I caught my breath in hesitation. His dark eyes seemed to shine, and I thought that I had never seen him look so attractive. The outdated queue he wore now seemed quite familiar and . . . handsome.

I turned away, forcing myself to watch the seamen perform the laborious tasks of docking the ship. I did not quite know what to expect when we were ashore, but Cape Town seemed modern. I had pictured grass huts, perhaps, and natives running about in who knew what manner of dress (or undress!), but many solid buildings, some appearing British and some Dutch, comprised the city. The British buildings were easily recognizable, reminding me of home with their brick, pitched roofs, and sash windows. The Dutch buildings, on the other hand, had thatched roofs and high gables and were whitewashed with lime. The combination of the two styles was not displeasing, however, and seemed a reflection of the various peoples we encountered.

Phineas acted as a guide as we strolled around town, taking in the sights while he supplemented my knowledge of the area. He purchased bananas for us to eat, a strange yellow fruit. Laughing as I attempted to bite into it, he took it from my hands and showed me how to peel back its skin. The true fruit within was delightfully firm but easily chewed, the taste warm and golden.

We saw many people of all skin colors because so many different people had inhabited the area. The Dutch influence was prevalent because the town had been established by the Dutch East India Company, whose sailors used it—as we were now—to acquire provisions and, if necessary, mend their ships. They traded with the local native villagers, then sent Dutch colonists of their own several centuries ago to establish a town. Soon afterward they were joined by Huguenots, Protestants who fled France during an unsuccessful Reformation. Sadly, too, the area had known its share of slaves, not only those who labored there but those who were but mere cargo bound for other destinations.

Over the centuries, the town had been in the hands of the Dutch, the French, the British . . . in various order. Fortunately it had been controlled by Britain for the past few years, and though the town and its people bore signs of many cultural influences, it felt somewhat like home.

It was also good to be on land again. It occurred to me that I might actually have a real bed to sleep in tonight, as opposed to a hammock. "Where will we pass the night?" I asked Phineas.

He looked down at me again with his unfathomable brown eyes. "I know a husband and wife who accept lodgers."

A peculiar thrill tingled my stomach. We had been cabinmates for so long that I scarcely thought about it anymore. Particularly when everyone on board ship thought us related. Being on land reminded me that we were back in civilization. "We will . . ." My mouth went dry. "We will no doubt need to keep up the ruse about brother and sister."

"It is preferable," he said. "Were we to run into anyone from the *Dignity*, it might not bode well otherwise."

We would be in Cape Town for several days, but the remainder of that first day was spoiled for me. I worried about Snowe's intentions. I worried about my own, as well, for I did not trust the curious attraction I felt toward him. I would never betray my place as a lady, of course . . .

My fears were put to rest when we arrived at the lodgings, a home that could have been plucked from one of the finer sections of London. A lovely elderly couple, Mr. and Mrs. Eaton, were our hosts. They were British and had evidently known Phineas for a long time. "But you never mentioned a sister," Mr. Eaton said, smiling at me.

"How lovely you are, my dear." Mrs. Eaton turned to Phineas. "She must have Mary's room, of course."

"I do not wish to put anyone out," I said.

The room went silent. "Mary was our daughter," Mrs. Eaton said. "It has been some three years now since typhoid took her."

"I am very sorry," I murmured, glancing at Phineas, who revealed nothing by his expression.

I could think of little else while I waited for sleep that night. It was by far the most comfortable bed I had lain upon, and even though I was accustomed to a hammock these past many weeks, I do not believe I overtell my delight. However, I could not cease thinking about the poor Eatons and their daughter, which led me to think of Uncle Toby and Flora. Did they count me as one dead?

I tossed and turned. Perhaps the comfort of the bed did not matter. Perhaps it was the lack of a ship's motion just before sleep that would not allow me rest that night. Something was indeed amiss . . .

In the morning, after Phineas and I had quitted the Eatons' to tour Cape Town, he was forthright. "You should write your uncle to let him know that you are well," he said.

I was all astonishment at the prospect. "I did not know there was postal service available."

He nodded. "I would very much like to relieve your uncle's mind about your welfare. If you want me to write to him as well, I will oblige." He paused. "I was awake most of the night, worrying for his sake. Perhaps being ashore has brought my guilt to bear, but I feel I must make amends to him somehow."

"Can you trust anyone to carry money back to him in Oxford?"

Phineas stopped. "It is not his money that concerns me, Isabella."

"Then what?" I cocked my head.

"Do you not know?" He took my hand, the first time that he had ever touched me in a personal manner. A tingle raced through my fingers, and I watched as though outside myself as he brought them to his lips. "I regret that you became a means to my ends, Isabella Goodrich," he said softly. "Though it pains me to say so, I would still have you safe on board the next ship to England."

My gaze met his. "I . . . I cannot," I said, wondering even as I spoke whether my answer depended upon my missionary plans or the thought of being parted from Phineas Snowe.

Slowly he released my hand, and I held it with the other as though I did not trust it to ever again be as it should. I did not think that I would ever be.

"I do not want you hurt," he said. "I lay awake last night . . ."

206

Oh, I was foolish! I had plans, as did Phineas, no matter how misbegotten. Such talk was heartbreak to us both.

I glanced downward. "We have said enough. Perhaps we should return to the Eatons'."

He drew a deep breath, then took my hand again, only this time tucking it into his arm in a brotherly, gentlemanly gesture.

Once again that night I appreciated the softness of the high four-poster bed, but sleep eluded me. I thought of Phineas just down the hall, and I wondered if he found a better rest than the previous night. We did not speak of it the next day, nor the next, and I must confess that I was more than eager to bid Mr. and Mrs. Eaton farewell. I had enjoyed their company and certainly their hospitality, but I did not feel comfortable away from the ship. I found myself wondering about our fellow shipmates—Mr. Calow, Mr. Gilpin, even Mr. and Mrs. Akers. I did not dare ask about Julia Whipple, but it seemed to me that when we were all aboard again, ready to set sail, that she looked, if possible, even sadder.

A niggle of doubt troubled me the day we embarked, for I recalled her words to be on my guard with Phineas. He could contrive some reason to keep me ashore and, ultimately, from my purpose. But any fear was laid to rest, for it was he himself who held my arm and escorted me back onto the ship and stood beside me at the rail as we watched Cape Town recede.

I looked at Phineas, who stared solemnly as land faded

into the horizon. "I have missed our Chinese lessons," I said, affecting lightness.

He turned, his expression solemn. "I have missed a great deal."

Captain Malfort approached, Mr. Gilpin and Mr. Calow in his wake. "Miss Goodrich," he said. "I am delighted to hear that you are continuing with us on to Macao."

Gilpin and Calow echoed his sentiments, the former solemn as a vicar and the latter beaming.

"However did she win you over, Snowe?" the captain said. "The fairer sex often uses the most peculiar methods to get their ways. Some use tears, some silence, and others talk a man to death."

Snowe smiled at me like a begrudging brother; his demeanor changed from his previous intimate words. "Her persuasion was of a gentler nature."

"I'm delighted to hear of it. Ladies who act aggressively are not ladies at all. And now if you will excuse me and my officers . . ."

After they left, I turned to Snowe, curious as to his words. He was already bowing, however, to take his leave.

"I will never understand you," I murmured, watching his retreating figure.

That night after we retired and the candle had been snuffed, I spoke into the darkness. "Did you procure me a sword in Cape Town?"

Silence.

"You have not forgotten, surely," I said, suppressing a groan. "Phineas?"

"Your flight of fancy has not diminished south of the equator," he said. "Fortunately, mine has not either. Are you prepared to return to Hu-King? I believe Wo-Ping and Mei were engaged in battle."

"With each other," I added.

"Yes."

"And racing up buildings and becoming invisible and hurling fire."

"Yes. Thank you for the reminder. Do you wish me to continue? As I recall, the mythical elements seemed to disturb you."

I settled into my hammock, which cradled me far better than the Eatons' comfortable bed after all. "I am anxious to hear more. Please continue."

I fell into a deep contented sleep that night, happy to be back aboard ship. It felt like home, and I realized that I would miss it—and my shipmates—when we reached our final destination. I dreamed of Cape Town and Oxford and China, even though with the latter I had little upon which to base my dream. However, the Orientals were pleased that I could speak their language, and they were eager to hear the gospel.

Someone shook my shoulder, and I awoke with a start. Moonlight illumined the room, and I could barely see. Phineas put a hand over my mouth. "You must get below. Quickly. Not a word." He helped me from my hammock and led me toward the door. "Privateers," he whispered in my ear. "They are boarding the ship."

"What?"

"It is the French. You must go to the pantry with the other ladies."

On deck I came awake with the realization that this was no joke, it was real. A ship fired on us, and the *Dignity* answered in kind. Smoke filled my nostrils. Overhead, a topsail took a hit, rigging splintering around us, and I screamed. Phineas made haste to get me to the ship's pantry, all but dragging me. Julia Whipple, Mrs. Akers, and Mrs. Harrison already cowered there, the latter lady looking more awake than I had ever seen her, though she wore her bedclothes.

"You will be safe," Phineas said to us. "Stay here, and stay away from the opening lest a stray ball find its way through."

I grabbed his sleeve. "Where are you going?"

"I am going on deck to fight," he said. He looked at me for a long moment, then was gone.

Mrs. Akers clung to me, sobbing hysterically. "What are we to do? I am certain we will be killed!"

"Or worse," Mrs. Harrison said. "I've heard what pirates do with the ladies aboard."

Mrs. Akers swooned.

Julia Whipple held her upright, her expression calm. "Now, now, Mrs. Akers, let us not panic. Our men are brave, are they not? I'm sure we'll be quite safe. We have only to wait here. Look, the seaman who brought me below gave me this sword for our protection."

"Oh my!" Mrs. Akers swooned again.

"We'll probably drown anyway, for we are below the water line," Mrs. Harrison said dolefully. "All they have to do is sink the ship."

"You are a cruel liar, Miss Whipple," Mrs. Akers cried. "That sailor gave you the sword so that we might kill ourselves, lest we be ravished!"

A sound like thunder cracked overhead. Mrs. Akers and Mrs. Harrison screamed. Julia and I reached for each other. My heart pounded, but I tried to keep a steady voice. "It is only cannon fire, ladies. I am certain that we will be well."

"*Allez! Allez!*"

A voice rang out from the top of the stairs, then I had a quick view of thick black boots and faded gray-striped pants. A swarthy Frenchman brandished a cutlass as he descended the steps. A privateer!

He stopped, apparently surprised to find us instead of the ship's treasure, then grinned. "*Bon soir, mesdames et mesdemoiselles.*" He bowed with a flourish, sweeping his red stocking cap from his head.

Mrs. Akers screamed. "Mercy!"

Seized with panic, my heart in my throat, I ripped the sword from Julia's hands and brandished it. "*Partez, vous chien français!*"

Straightening from his bow, he smiled at me. "So you speak French? I speak a little English myself." He stepped forward. "But my heart breaks that you think me a dog."

I held out the sword, its tip pointed directly at his heart. "I would stand back were I you," I said in a low voice.

Glancing at my sword, he grinned then turned and walked back to the stairs, calling up the hatch. *"Mes copains! Venez ici—c'est les dames!"*

"What did he say?" Julia whispered.

"He's telling his friends there are ladies down here."

She stepped to my side, smoothing her skirt. "Let me handle them. I'm well acquainted with desperate men."

"No!" I pushed her back, gripping the sword while I used my free arm to shield the other ladies. *Think, Isabella! What strategy should I employ?*

Julia's eyes shone with admiration, but she gripped my arm. "Would you defend us? You'll be killed!"

"You will get *us* killed!" Mrs. Akers cried.

Mrs. Harrison sank to a barrel and sipped from a small brown bottle.

Three other scraggly looking privateers clomped down the stairs and joined their cohort. Their eyes lit with pleasure when they saw we four ladies. Julia stepped forward again, smiling. "I won't fight you," she said, lifting her chin. "Leave the other ladies alone."

The three newcomers looked at Red Cap for translation. He rapidly repeated her words in French. One with dark curly hair and a full beard smiled and moved forward, but I held out the sword. *"Arretez!"*

The stocking-capped privateer laughed. "She's feisty. That one is mine."

The sword felt heavier in my hands than that to which I was accustomed, but I gripped it with all my strength. "I am not yours nor are any of these ladies. I order you to leave."

"*Allez!*" The bearded one scowled and jerked Julia by the wrist, brandishing his sword in my direction.

Despite her previous bravado, Julia screamed. The pirate pulled her to his side and planted noisy kisses on her face. The other men laughed.

"*Show your opponent no mercy,*" Signor Antonio had drilled into me, and I heeded his words without hesitation. Into the gap between the pirate's sword arm and his hold on Julia, I thrust my sword in his midsection. He released her, stared at me in amazement, then fell to the deck, writhing.

10

"Robert!" One of the privateers rushed to aid the wounded man, but the other two turned to me. Anger replaced their amused expressions, and they moved closer, cutlasses brandished. Julia instinctively scurried to my side, and behind the protection of my out-thrust sword we backed toward the other ladies.

"That was not wise, mademoiselle," Red Cap said. "I must cut your pretty face in repayment." Then he proceeded to tell me what else he would do.

I do not mind revealing that I was more frightened than I had ever been in my life. I had had the element of surprise with the distracted pirate, but I would now have to rely on skill and strategy. Could I fight two men at once? I had never done so.

More men raced down the stairs, and my heart pounded. *It is over. My foolishness will get us killed.*

To my surprise I saw Phineas fighting backward down the stairs. He carried no weapon, yet he used his hands and feet, punching and kicking, to first knock the sword from a pirate's hands then to knock him down the stairs to the deck. Another combatant took the first one's place, and Phineas prevailed over him, as well. The pirate landed in a heap beside the first.

The two privateers menacing us turned toward Phineas. He was prepared, however, kicking the swords from their hands then punching them before they could defend themselves. They lay on the ground, moaning.

He saw me, and I was about to raise the sword in triumph when he barely had time to yell before another privateer was upon him. "Isabella! Take care behind you!"

I whirled around to face the pirate who had tended the wounded man. He held his cutlass at a deadly angle, slashing through the air as though to warn me. I suddenly realized that I had never actually fought Signor Antonio with the button removed from the tip of my sword.

I parried his thrust and could tell from his slashing that he fought with a great deal of drink inside him. He leered at me, his eyes rheumy with alcohol. I could not afford to let him tire himself out as would be my normal method. Though inebriated, he would fight too long and hard and would take risks that might work to his advantage. I hastily prayed for guidance and strength, then feinted, ducked, and after he followed through, drove my blade into his sword arm.

Cursing, he dropped the weapon and sank to his knees. Phineas rushed beside me, kicked him in the head, laying my opponent flat on the deck. We had barely a moment before we were beset by another miscreant, but between us, we sent him to join his companion.

We stared at one another, breathing heavily during the respite. I could not believe a man could fight the way Phineas had. Not a weapon did he have, save for his body, yet he had defended himself—and me—quite handily.

Mrs. Akers sobbed loudly, and even Julia had given herself to loud tears.

"Listen!" Still panting, Phineas held up his hand. "The cannons have stopped firing." He turned to the ladies. "Are you all to rights?"

Mrs. Akers could not stop bawling. Mrs. Harrison had nodded off with her head against a stack of barrels. The pirate I had dueled lay sprawled against a spilled sack of grain, completely still.

"I'll take care of Mrs. Akers and Mrs. Harrison," Julia said, wiping the tears from her face. "Go above and see what has happened."

I looked at the still pirate and felt my knees buckle. "I . . . I should stay to help."

"Go above with Phineas," Julia said softly. "We will be well."

Phineas took my hand and led me up the ladder. When we reached the deck, I smelled gunpowder. I tried not to focus on the prone and bloodied men on the deck, some of whom I felt certain were dead.

Smoke clung to the air around us. I could barely discern a much smaller French ship alongside the *Dignity*. The corsair sat so low in the water that its masts aligned with our deck. The pirate crew must have dropped onto our ship from their top masts, for one or two men still attempted to

216

board. One landed right in front of me, knocking Phineas and me to the deck. I held on to my sword and staggered to my feet, breathing hard. The villain grappled with me for a moment then drew back in shock. *"C'est une dame!"* The sight of the fairer sex wielding a sword must have frightened him, for he took another look at me and raced in the opposite direction, only to be caught by one of the *Dignity* seamen.

Indeed, the fighting had ceased. Our crew had rounded up the pirates and now encircled them, taunting with yells and displays of the captured swords and guns. Clutching his bloodied arm, Captain Malfort bellowed, "Throw them into the brig! And while you're down there, someone let the ladies know all is safe."

He caught sight of me wielding the sword, and his jaw dropped. "Good heavens! Miss Goodrich!"

Phineas glanced at me sharply. "You are bleeding," he said, touching my elbow.

I looked down and saw a bloody gash in the sleeve of the gray dress. "Thankfully, it is nothing serious. I should survive with a minimum of care."

"Which you shall have right now." He took me by my undamaged arm, the one still holding the sword, and moved me across the deck, bellowing for the ship's surgeon. "Mortimer!"

"I am all right," I murmured, unheard as he moved us toward the bow, where Mortimer knelt over a fallen man.

"She is wounded," Phineas said, thrusting me in front of the doctor.

Mortimer glanced up at Phineas, then me, taking in my wound with a surgeon's practiced eye before pronouncing, "It is nothing, man. Bind it up and leave me to tend to more serious matters." He gestured at his patient, who groaned then screamed as Mortimer adjusted the leg bent at a crooked angle.

"Mr. Gilpin!" I cried, clinging to Phineas for support.

"Take her away," Mortimer said with a sweeping gesture, "and leave me to my work."

Phineas steered me in the opposite direction, wrapping an arm around my shoulders. "Come away," he said gently now. "I have some fresh cloth to bind your wound, Isabella."

"But I must help!" I said, gesturing at the wounded men. "Mr. Gilpin . . . the others."

"You have done more than your part. Let us go back to the cabin where I can see to your arm."

I clung to the sword, in shock, I suppose, only releasing it when Phineas gently removed it from my hand once we were safe in our cabin. When he did, I could not help the rush of emotion that overtook me, and try as I might to prevent it, I wept fiercely. I had fought and won, but there seemed little glory. I had taken a life. A life!

Mindful of my wound, Phineas drew me into his arms. He said nothing, but pressed my face against his shoulder. When my tears dissolved into mere tremors then one undignified hiccup, he drew back, smiling. "Do you feel better?"

I did not, but I nodded, yet unable to speak.

"Sit," he said, gesturing at the wooden crate. I was happy

218

to leave someone in command, so I complied, numb, watching as he knelt to open the mysterious trunk. I could not see inside, for he shut it quickly, but he approached me with a white silk sash.

He knelt and bound the silk around my arm. "It *is* but a scratch," he said. "When I saw you wounded, I forgot myself and thought the worst."

He tied the cloth in place, then gently touched it. His eyes met mine, and my stomach trembled as it had in Cape Town. We looked at each other as though anew, and I felt a pull between us as thrilling but as dangerous as the currents of the ocean.

Phineas leaned forward then seemed to catch himself, rising and helping me to my feet. "Though it is past dawn, you should rest," he said. "May I bring you some wine?"

I shook my head, suddenly weary to the bone. I made my way to my hammock and crawled in. He drew the blanket around my shoulders then turned away. "Phineas?" I murmured.

He turned back. "Yes?"

"When I awake, will you brew me some green tea? I have yet to partake of any."

He smiled. "I shall brew you pot after pot."

"Phineas?"

"Yes?"

"Will you show me how to fight as you did?" I said sleepily.

"A lady with your sword skills wants to fight without one?"

219

"I will have to return the sword to its rightful owner, and then I shall be without a weapon again." With my eyes closed, I had no idea where he was, but I smiled anyway. "I am still waiting for my own."

I heard him raise the canvas, but he made no response.

I did not rise until nearly dinnertime, and I am not certain I would have awakened even then except for the memory of Mr. Gilpin. I wanted to ascertain that he was in good health. I donned the brown dress, since the gray would need to be mended in the sleeve, then I headed for the cuddy. The captain's cook was there, ordering others about to prepare for dinner. He stopped short when he saw me, clearly appalled for some reason.

"I did not mean to disturb you," I said. "Is there any news about Mr. Gilpin?"

"He's still breathing, if that's your meaning. Check with the doctor, if you like." He turned away as though he did not want to look at me.

Curious behavior! I headed for the stairs, to the surgeon's area below deck. I wondered how many other wounded men besides Mr. Gilpin I would find there.

Mr. Calow waited outside the cabin, and he bowed when he saw me, his young eyes twinkling. "Miss Goodrich!"

"Mr. Calow." I curtsied. "I am delighted to see that you are well."

He nodded. "Is your arm in need of attention?"

"It was a mere scratch. Phineas should not have troubled Dr. Mortimer."

Calow's smile fell. "The doctor is still with Mr. Gilpin."

"Then he lives?"

"Barely, Doctor says. His leg was broken. He was also wounded in the chest and bled quite a bit, but if he holds during the day, he may survive."

"Perhaps I can help." I reached for the doorknob.

Mr. Calow covered it first. "Miss Whipple has helped the doctor with Mr. Gilpin, as well as the other wounded men."

I turned. "Miss Whipple?"

He nodded. "She has helped Dr. Mortimer all this time."

"She must be exhausted," I said. "Perhaps I can relieve her so that she may rest."

"Did *you* rest well, Miss Goodrich? You must have been exhausted." Mr. Calow lowered his gaze. "I have never seen a lady fight before."

"I have not exactly fought before," I confessed. "Not with real blades, at any rate."

Smiling shyly at me, Mr. Calow opened the door and admitted me to the surgical area. Several men with various injuries—a bruised head, a sliced arm, a nicked shoulder— lay nursing their wounds. However, all appeared to be conscious and would no doubt be better in a few days, if not sooner.

Mr. Gilpin, lying in the corner bed, did not appear to have that luxury of time. His face was waxy, a contrast to the white bandages bound to the wound on the right side of his chest. He breathed, but scarcely.

Miss Whipple sat on the far side of his bed, applying a

wet cloth to his forehead. When she saw me, she looked startled. "Miss Goodrich!"

I took the chair opposite her. "How does he fare? Mr. Calow says that if he lives through the day, the doctor has hope."

"Yes. The bleeding has lessened, and we can only hope that he improves with rest. There is no longer anything to be done for him, other than prayer." She wiped his forehead again, and her shoulders drooped.

I felt great pity for her and admiration for her compassion. "You have been here all day?"

"How could I not? Dr. Mortimer admitted that he needed someone to help, and I was available."

"What of Mrs. Akers and Mrs. Harrison?"

Julia smiled bitterly. "I believe they took to their own beds, promising not to rise until they were fully recovered from being shoved into the ships's pantry in such an ungracious manner."

"You should have awakened me," I said. "I would have been glad to assist. Indeed, I would be glad to take your place now. You have been through a great deal."

"I have survived worse than being taken below deck for my own safety. Besides, it is you who have endured a great deal. It is all the crew can speak of, how Miss Goodrich and Mr. Snowe fought off many of the frogs and saved the *Dignity* from certain plunder and ruin. If not for you two, we would all be lost."

"The crew is too modest. They fought like tigers to save their ship. But what of the Frenchmen and their vessel?"

"Captain Malfort ordered one of the superior officers and some of the seamen to sail the vessel and prisoners back to Cape Town."

"It is a relief to know they are no longer aboard. Were there many wounded . . . and dead?" I suppressed a shudder, thinking of the men I had fought hand to hand.

Julia shrugged. "I did not hear. I only know that Captain Malfort said that the frogs were gone. Some of the crew are mopping the deck, as well as making necessary repairs."

"Would you like for me to watch Mr. Gilpin while you rest?" I offered again.

She shook her head, adjusting the bandage on his chest a trifle. "I find it good to be of use. Mr. Gilpin does not think highly of me, but he is a countryman. Captain Malfort said that he fought bravely." She raised her head. "As, I hear, did you."

"It was mere stupidity," I said. "I must have been beetle-headed to test my skills. Perhaps it was the element of surprise that gave me an advantage."

"You are too modest, I'm sure."

"Miss Whipple!" Captain Malfort's voice seemed to boom behind me, but when I turned, he was staring at Mr. Gilpin. "How is he?"

"There seems to be no change."

Captain sighed. "I do not like to lose anyone aboard my ship, particularly my highest officer. He is a man of integrity and courage. I believe he killed several frogs before one of them caught him by surprise. And speaking of surprise . . ." He turned to me. "It appears that you have caught us all off

223

our guard with your swordsmanship display, Miss Good-rich. May I ask where you learned to fight like that?"

"My uncle hired a fencing master for me."

"You and your brother both possess unusual, er, fighting skills. A most unusual family, I daresay. I do not approve of such activities for ladies, but in light of your help to all aboard the *Dignity*, I thank you." He bowed stiffly.

I nodded in return. Captain Malfort cleared his throat, clearly embarrassed. "Let me know if there is any change, Miss Whipple."

He left, and I rose. "If I cannot persuade you to accept my assistance . . ."

She glanced up. "I am happy to be of use," she said. I thought that she looked remarkably weary, but she seemed content. I left to find Phineas, for we had much to discuss.

I searched the ship high and low. Everywhere I went, sailors tipped their caps or otherwise acknowledged my presence. A few turned their backs as though expressing their disapproval of a lady wielding a sword. It made me realize how Julia Whipple must feel occasionally when she met with outright stares or received a cut direct. She and I had both stepped outside the lines drawn by society, and whether we could ever put both feet back inside remained to be seen.

I had nearly despaired of finding Phineas but found him in the last place I would expect. I had wondered if he had perhaps gone overboard when I retired to our cabin for a place of quiet to pray for Mr. Gilpin. When I opened the door, Phineas glanced up, startled, from where he knelt before his trunk. "Isabella!"

"I have been searching for you," I said. "I checked on Mr. Gilpin, and you and I must have somehow crossed paths."

He shut the trunk and rose. "Are you well? Are you recovered?"

"I am. The rest did me good."

"And your arm?"

"Your bandage still holds," I said, patting the slight bulk beneath my sleeve. "Thank you for tending to me."

His eyes searched mine as though for an answer. "Is something wrong?" I said.

"No." He stepped back, as though putting distance between us. "How is Mr. Gilpin?"

"He is alive, but he has lost a lot of blood, I am told. Julia is still tending him."

"She was much concerned with his health. The other wounded are not in danger, apparently. We are fortunate that only Mr. Gilpin was wounded badly."

"Still, it is a pity," I said.

"Yes."

We fell into silence, each of us scarcely able to look at the other. What was this awkwardness between us? Since the day we had met, we had always had conversation between us—spirited at best, antagonistic at worst—but always an exchange of words. We seemed as strangers at the moment.

"Isabella." He cleared his throat. "This seems the appropriate moment."

I frowned. "For what?"

He knelt before the trunk and lifted the lid, then drew out a long length of supple leather, wrapped tight. He laid it on the closed trunk lid and unwrapped it to reveal a sword. Double bladed and etched with delicate scrollwork, the steel gleamed in the sunlight beaming through the porthole. He placed it carefully in my hands. "It is yours."

I stared at it with awe. The tip was narrower and not as thick as the base of the blade. The hilt, which protected the hand, had short wings. The handle seemed just long enough for one hand plus a few fingers from the other, so it was primarily a one-handed sword. The grip was covered in some sort of skin, and the pommel—the end of the handle—seemed to hold all the pieces of the sword together. "It is beautiful, Phineas. The blade is quite unique."

"The tip is for stabbing or slashing. The middle section is for cuts and deflections. The closest section is for defensive action. It is made of several plates, with the middle hard and the outer, softer. "

I turned it over in my hands, then held it out to test its weight. It was heavier than what I was accustomed to, but it felt solid in my hands. "Where did you acquire it?"

"It has been in my mother's family for several generations."

I handed it back as though it burned. "I cannot accept this!"

"I have promised you a sword." He placed it solemnly back in my hands. "And it is yours."

"But Phineas—"

He touched my hands. "You have earned it."

My hands trembled. Suddenly the blade did not seem half as beautiful as it did cruel. "I . . . I killed a man, did I not?"

He nodded solemnly. "You also saved the lives of many aboard ship. To provoke a fight is unthinkable. To use your skill in self-defense, and especially in the defense of others, is noble. Remember that there is no greater love than to lay down one's life for a friend. Most of the ship is grateful." He covered his right fist with his left hand and bowed. "I am grateful."

My face warmed. I would have longed for this prideful moment many, many days ago. My entire perception of Phineas Snowe had changed so greatly during that time that now I only found myself embarrassed. "I do not think I should ever attempt such a feat again," I said. "I learned to fence only as mere folly. I was even foolish enough to dream of knowing a *botte secrète*—a perfect thrust. And now . . ." I thought about the dead pirate.

"When necessity demanded your skill, you accepted the challenge without forethought or hesitation. Some might call it destiny, Isabella."

"And what would you call it?"

His eyes met mine. "Do you remember the Chinese character on your slippers? The one that I said meant *love*?"

"Then you said it did not. Which time is the truth?"

"The second. I lied the first time because I believed you only interested in romantic notions, and I thought only to flatter you in jest."

227

"What did the character really mean, then?"

"Bravery. You have shown it every step of our journey." He bowed again. "The sword is yours, Isabella."

I laid it on its leather wrap and re-covered it. It was beautiful, but it was deadly. Yet it was a gift I could not refuse, for it had been given with the utmost sincerity and depth of heart. I turned back to Phineas. "I will accept it on one condition: that you teach me to fight as you did. Without any weapon at all."

He smiled. "We always seem to strike a bargain, do we not?"

"Will you teach me?"

"Yes." His gaze flickered over my form. "But you will need something more suitable to wear. You cannot kick wearing a dress."

"I am accustomed to wearing inexpressibles while I fence," I said.

He opened his trunk. "Then you will find these comfortable." He handed me a pair of light cotton inexpressibles and a loose-fitting cotton jacket that tied at the side. Their style was peculiar but comfortable looking indeed.

"What manner of fencing clothes are these?"

"They are not for fencing. They are what I often wear when I am in China."

"Where will we practice? Surely we should stay out of sight."

"Do you think the crew will be astonished at your learning martial arts after the way you handled a sword? Nevertheless, we do not want to be in anyone's way, so perhaps we could find more room in the cuddy than on deck."

So it was that I found myself in the middle of the Indian Ocean on an East Indiaman bound for China, learning Phineas's method of fighting. He called it *mo soot*. At first I found it difficult not to laugh at the stances he taught, which, he said, were based on various animal movements, such as the dragon, leopard, tiger, snake, and crane. It reminded me of being a child, when David Ransom and I had pretended to be animals roaming in their natural habitat.

What a lifetime ago it seemed, as though it had happened to another person . . .

As the days melded into weeks, Phineas and I began to speak Chinese more frequently, particularly during our training. I had learned to distinguish the various tones in the language, and with a little practice, I learned to repeat them well enough to be understood. I completed a few more copies of the second chapter of Luke in Chinese, and after the ink had dried, Phineas bound them with a ribbon Julia provided and stored them in his trunk. I was pleased, for I would pass out these tracts when we reached the interior of China.

Naturally, my reputation was quite ruined with our fellow passengers. Mr. Harrison appeared none too pleased with me, pursing his lips when in my presence. But as Mrs. Harrison was no paragon of a lady herself, he said nothing. Sadly, she appeared to be as addicted to the laudanum as ever, and I wondered at the wisdom of his taking her to a country where so many suffered from the same ailment. Phineas had described opium dens, and I shuddered to think of Mrs. Harrison's presence there.

Mr. and Mrs. Akers gave me the cut direct. Fortunately, neither they nor anyone else seemed wiser to the fact that Phineas and I were not truly brother and sister, but they would have nothing to do with me because of my behavior with the privateers. Mrs. Akers sniffed that it would have been far better for me to have been killed than to have participated in such wicked, unladylike behavior. "You want to be a missionary?" she said. "It is the Chinese who should seek to convert you. Perhaps it is well that you go there, though, for surely only heathens will have you. Britain certainly will not."

Her words stung that day and every day after when I passed her on deck or sat near her in the cuddy. She refused to speak with me, communicating only through someone else. "Mr. Snowe, would you please ask your sister to pass the salt?" Naturally, by this time someone had informed her of Julia Whipple's reputation, so she was never the recipient of Mrs. Akers's conversation, either. I cannot speak for Julia, but I learned to count it all joy.

Speaking of Julia, the oddest turn of events occurred while Phineas and I trained together. Alternately nursing the other wounded as needed, she spent the majority of her time at Mr. Gilpin's bedside. Perhaps because of much prayer, her steady compassion, and the medical skills of the doctor, Mr. Gilpin's health steadily improved. Soon he was able to tolerate broth, then to sit up and converse with visitors, and finally, to stand. One day Phineas and I were strolling the deck when we saw a shaky Gilpin on the arm of Julia Whipple, walking as far as the quarter deck before returning to the surgeon's area. Phineas and I both marveled at his improvement. We marveled even more when, as Gilpin was released from bed rest, he was seen in Julia's company more often than not.

"She has done much good for his recovery," Phineas said to me late one evening as we loitered about the deck. "A man will not fight to save himself half as much as when there is a lady involved."

"Perhaps the lady upon whom he thinks is his mother. He sets great store by her."

"Too much, perhaps. Though a man must, indeed, retain the highest regard for his mother, or he is no man at all."

"Indeed."

Though it was late and we should be headed for the cabin, we walked to the bow. I thrilled to watch the ship cutting through the water, pushing whitecaps to the side with such little effort. Ah, if only life could be so effortless. I turned to Phineas to express that very thought, but he was studying the horizon, not the water.

"A penny for your thoughts?" I said softly.

He turned, and I could see the moon reflected in his eyes. Solemnly, he took my hand. "Do you remember the night we met?"

"Of course."

"There was dancing that night."

I smiled. "As I recall, we were deep in conversation during all the dances, having one argument or another, I am certain."

"I wish . . ." He gently squeezed the fingers of my hand. "I wish that I had asked you to dance, for then I would now have the memory of holding you in my arms."

My mouth went dry. "Phineas . . ."

"Would you dance with me now?"

Oh, thank heavens, he was merely making a jest at my expense. I smiled again. "There are no musicians, indeed, no music."

"Then I will hum the tune. Have you ever waltzed, Miss Goodrich?"

The way he said my name formally, as he had once been accustomed, sent a shiver up my spine. "I . . . I do not know the steps, and indeed I hear it is a scandalous dance."

"It is easy enough to master if you can count one-two-three. Your hand goes lightly on my shoulder here, and my hand at your waist there."

"Phineas . . ."

He hummed softly, an unfamiliar tune to my ear. My feet—traitorous appendages!—willingly followed his steps. We were no longer aboard the *Dignity*, but at a ball. Instead of our dingy ship wear, Phineas and I wore the finest of garments and we waltzed across a parquet floor to the accompaniment of a four-piece orchestra. Candles flickered all around us, and the scent of flowers clung in the air. I sensed the strength of his body as he held me closely, yet his touch was so tender that I knew I need never fear.

"Isabella," he whispered, his breath stirring the fringes of hair covering my ear.

I opened my mouth to reply, but he held me even closer, and suddenly it seemed that we scarcely moved at all. Then I realized we did indeed stand still, and he was leaning even closer, if possible.

The ballroom faded away, the orchestra ceased its tune, and we were aboard the *Dignity* yet again. I had never felt such a stirring in my heart, and when his lips met mine, it seemed the most natural of events.

This—*this!*—was love. My heart beat with joy, and I allowed myself to be enfolded more closely in his arms as the kiss lingered on. Reason altogether fled but suddenly returned equally as swift. I released his hand and stepped back. "We cannot," I said softly, hating myself almost as much for releasing him as for regretting the words.

Shock then horror registered on his face. "Isabella . . . forgive me. I would never seek to compromise your character."

"I know," I whispered, and somehow, I knew that he would never trifle with me. I had been a willing, nay, eager accomplice. "It . . . it is late, Phineas."

"Yes, of course. Let me escort you to the cabin."

We hurried now, though I was certain we had ample time before the ten o'clock bells. The thought of putting the canvas sail between us promised security and perhaps, at least on my part, better reason. We passed several crew members, but no word or expression on their part indicated that we had been observed near the bow.

Phineas held the door open for me. "I will join you

shortly," he said, handing me the candle. "Extinguish the flame when you are ready for sleep. Do not leave it lit on my account."

I wondered at his words, but he was already shutting the door behind me. I readied myself for bed and did wait for a few moments, but when he did not appear, I snuffed out the candle. I tried to sleep, but my heart still pounded so that I was certain I would not be able to rest at all that night.

At last I heard him enter and saw him, briefly, before he ducked behind the canvas. I could not read the expression on his face, and he spoke not a word. When I heard the creak of his hammock and he blew out his candle, I thought then that he would say something. He did not.

Since the battle with the privateers, we had not returned to the story of Wo-Ping and Mei. It seemed an unspoken agreement that the reality of combat was too close to us still to return to the mythical land of Hu-King. Tonight, however, I needed myth not only as an escape but also as a reassurance for our own relationship. "Will you not tell the story tonight?" I said, hopeful and faltering.

"I do not have the heart," he said in a weary voice. "Though I regret that it is so. Tomorrow, perhaps?"

"Yes, perhaps," I echoed doubtfully. I could not believe that he was unwilling. "I hope so."

In the morning, I was not certain what to expect when we first saw each other, which was at breakfast. It was already a momentous day, for Mr. Gilpin joined us, looking somewhat pale but more fit than I had seem him in many days. We all welcomed him back with enthusiasm, but none more so than Captain Malfort.

"It is good to have you back, Mr. Gilpin," he boomed. "Cook will fatten up those bones in no time, as well."

"Thank you, sir," he said. He nodded at us all. "It is good to be in your company again. I look forward to resuming my duties."

"We are only a few weeks from Macao, then on to Canton and tea, then homeward sails the *Dignity*," Captain Malfort said.

"I do hope we'll encounter no further privateers," Mrs. Akers said. "A nasty lot, those Frenchmen . . . if men they can be spoken of at all!"

"I am pleased at your recovery, Mr. Gilpin," I said. "You gave us all a dreadful scare."

He glanced at Julia Whipple, who sat to my left, then back at me. "No matter how many times one faces privateers, it is always a test of fortitude. With God's blessing, we all not only survived but retained the *Dignity* under Britain's flag."

"Hear hear," Captain Malfort said. "And now, man, eat up, eat hearty!"

Phineas sat at the far end of the table, engaged in conversation with Mr. Akers, probably about East India Company business. Or what Mr. Akers thought was Phineas's interest in the company anyway. I wondered if Mrs. Akers or her husband would give Phineas the cut the way they did me if they knew his true intentions. Indeed, I had not thought

235

of his scheme in quite a while. Perhaps his silence indicated a willingness to abandon his thoughts of revenge. I could only pray.

After breakfast, our company dispersed. Mrs. Harrison was no doubt eager to retire to her bed (as usual), Mr. Harrison and Mr. Akers to make further business plans, and Mrs. Akers—I could not begin to say what she did with her idle time. I had never been invited to her cabin, but I understood that she had insisted upon bringing much of their furniture. Perhaps she spent her time rearranging it . . .

"Isabella."

I felt a hand at my elbow. "Yes?"

Phineas stood beside me. "May I have a word with you?"

He seemed so formal, so serious. Had I done something wrong? "Yes, of course."

Confused, I let him lead me to a corner of the cuddy where it was quiet. He had never asked to have "a word" before we began lessons. Oh my, in all the excitement over Mr. Gilpin's appearance at breakfast, I had forgotten about last night! Did Phineas seek an apology? Did he seek to berate me? I should never have agreed to the dance . . .

I studied him as he watched the last of our group heading out, Julia and Mr. Gilpin among them. The servants moved into the room to clear the tables, and Phineas spoke in a low voice. "I wish to speak to you about last night."

Oh dear. It *was* my fault. I knew little of men, but I knew enough to act as a lady should, and I had failed.

236

He cleared his throat. "I have done a great deal of thinking since our time together at the bow. I can scarcely believe a ship to be romantic with so many people occupied with their own business and lives."

I said nothing, still confused as to his intention. Why did he speak of romance? And why must he have such dark eyes? I could read nothing there whatsoever.

"The truth is," he said, then faltered. "The truth is that you must know I care greatly about your welfare. I hope I have exhibited that, if nothing else, during our acquaintanceship."

"I believe you have."

He looked relieved. "Then you will understand that I am in earnest by my declaration. I cannot bear the thought of either your unhappiness, your lack of security, or a bad reputation attached to your name." He drew a deep breath. "Isabella Goodrich, will you marry me?"

11

"I . . . You want to marry me?"

"Did I not say I was in earnest?"

"Water spaniels are earnest, Phineas. So are clergymen and Parliament. Well, perhaps we could argue about Parliament . . . But come, it is too early in the day to jest with me."

"I speak the truth, Isabella. I seek your hand in marriage. I have given it much thought, and I believe it is the only way."

"The only way for what?"

The servants clattered the dishes as they went about their work. Phineas drew two chairs into the corner and bade me sit. "I did not believe anyone saw us last night at the bow, but suppose they had? Brother and sister do not dance so closely. Nor kiss as we did."

I flushed. "That is true."

"And our entire charade about being related . . . suppose it were found to be false. What would happen?"

"We would not only be pegged as liars but as . . ." I

trailed off, my flush deepening. "Do you suspect that the truth has been discovered?"

"Julia Whipple informed me that one or two of the seamen suspect our relationship. She gave them a few coins, enough to buy their silence until we reach China, but even after that, gossip could prevail."

"So your solution is marriage?"

"Yes. The *Dignity* must leave Mrs. Akers, Mrs. Harrison, and Julia Whipple in Macao, as foreign ladies are not allowed in Canton. We, too, will disembark. There we will marry in secret and find another means of transportation to Canton."

"And from there?"

"You will find the missionary work you seek. It is the best plan to protect your reputation, Isabella. Even if someone should discover our ruse later, they will know we have done the honorable deed by marrying."

"If I find my missionary work, as you call it, where will you go?"

"With you, naturally. And you, with me. I know a Christian couple in Macao who are Chinese. They can help us."

I rose, trembling. "This is . . . this is too soon. It is too sudden. Sir, you take me quite unawares by your declaration."

Why oh why had I allowed him to dance with me? My foolishness had gotten me into trouble yet again. And what of him? Had he not enticed me into that most intimate of dances, one that I had heard was not even accepted without permission at balls at Almack's in London? For the first time in my life, I felt that I might swoon not only from the memory but from what he asked of me.

He must have noticed my faintness, for he helped me to sit again. I could not have been more embarrassed. To be caught in such a feminine act as swooning! Yet in truth I could not tell if it was fear or excitement that caused my head to swim so alarmingly.

"Isabella." He dropped to one knee before my chair, holding my hand. "You may think that China is a heathen nation where a lady's reputation does not matter, but I assure you that it is not so very different from England in certain regards. I seek to protect you from more than just idle gossip, however. You may speak the language tolerably well, and no one can doubt your ability to handle a sword in your own defense. But there are some instances in which the protection of my name, my position as your husband, would allow you more freedom to pursue your purpose."

I could scarcely hear what he was saying over the horror pounding in my heart. "Please do not kneel so," I whispered. "The servants are staring."

He sat in the chair, his eyes still beseeching. "As my wife, you can travel where no English lady can go. You can be the missionary that you have always desired—without being limited to Macao."

The thought did appeal to me. Though I spoke the language, Phineas's presence would allow me access to China. But something seemed amiss. Phineas never bargained without getting something in return. "What would be the advantage for you?"

He studied me for a moment. "I esteem my mother highly, of course, but she has long wanted me wed."

"To a Chinese maiden, I suppose?"

"Yes."

"That does not meet with your approval?"

He shifted uncomfortably. "I wish to travel between China and England at will. I cannot imagine a Chinese wife adapting to the change." He smiled. "However, I might have once said the same about you."

I folded my arms across my chest. "You would present me as your wife simply to satisfy your mother?"

He nodded. "We would both accomplish our purposes, and your reputation would be safe."

What he said made a certain amount of sense. What did it matter if I were married? Matches were arranged all the time at home. Hadn't David entered into one with Cathy for mutual advantage?

And hadn't I told Phineas when we first met that I never felt that young ladies were much concerned with love but with making a good match?

"This *would* be a good match for us both," I said.

"Match?" He looked at me quizzically.

I nodded. "You once said that a lady who settles for love generally settles beneath herself."

He raised an eyebrow. "Are you settling, Isabella?"

"I agree to your offer. I am entering into an agreement suitable for us both." I shifted uncomfortably.

He cupped my face with his hand. "Beautiful Isabella, on my part there is more to the offer than mere convenience. Do you settle for love as well as the arrangement?" He lowered his voice. "I would have it so."

His gaze and words transfixed me. I nodded, unable to speak.

He smiled then took my hand, and we rose. He did not look away from me, however, but continued to study my face. "Is something amiss?" I said.

He leaned closer, whispering. "I would seal our agreement with a binding kiss, but the servants may be watching. We must keep our engagement secret until we land at Macao and can wed quietly. Is that acceptable?"

"Of course." I could not believe that he would bypass what we had both desired last night. I laughed. "Are you certain you will wait for the kiss?"

"You may depend upon it, my future Mrs. Snowe."

Oh, how I longed for the arms of Flora in which to be hugged and advised. I was engaged to be wed, and yet I could tell no one, not even Julia Whipple. Uncle Toby . . . would he be happy by my news? Would he think a marriage of convenience to be better than none at all? But was it indeed only for convenience? Gentlemen desired wives, but not always for love. Companionship and intimacy, yet. But *love*?

As for myself, I was quite fond of Phineas Snowe, but did I love him? I had once imagined myself in love with David Ransom, but when he had married Catherine, I had not felt heartbreak so much as bewilderment that he had simply not spoken to me in advance about his plans.

No, Phineas sought only to protect me and to relieve his mother's worries. And I . . . I would finally be the missionary I knew I was called to be!

The days passed with extraordinary swiftness, a contrast to the weariness of all aboard ship. Mrs. Akers had been heard to snap at Mrs. Harrison, who, to the amazement of all within earshot, seemed to possess enough wakefulness to snap back. Mr. Harrison and Mr. Akers, in turn, pretended nothing was amiss, perhaps relishing the day they could bid *adieu* to their wives in Macao for six months while they lived in Canton during the trade season.

The sailors, of course, were ready for their own free time on shore. I wondered at the lives they led, those aboard ship and those on land. Their grumbling had increased the farther away from England we had sailed, yet apparently they returned to a life at sea again and again, so they must find some enjoyment.

Mr. Calow never flagged in his enthusiasm for seafaring, though I accounted it all to his youthful nature. Since the voyage began, he had not only become quite proficient in tying the required naval knots but had also, from all reports, excelled in navigation. I believe Mr. Gilpin had a distinct hand in the midshipman's tutoring, though the first mate himself seemed to have regained a sort of youthful enthusiasm of his own.

Julia may have had something, in turn, to do with his change of nature, for she remained his constant companion. No longer did I see her go below for hours at a time—for what purposes I had never asked, of course. She and I did not study together, either. Rather, she spent her time in her cabin reading one of Gilpin's books or listening as he read aloud to her while they strolled the deck. They seemed quite devoted to one another, but it was still with some surprise that I received her news one day when we chanced to meet alone on the poop deck.

"What do you think?" she said. "Mr. Gilpin has asked me to marry him!"

I could have fallen overboard and not been more surprised. "I knew that you had favored each other's company lately, but . . ."

"But he has made his opinion about me clear from the beginning of the voyage," she finished for me. "That *is* what you were going to say?"

"Well . . . yes."

"He said that no one could have given him better care while he was wounded, and he realized that it was not just physical care. He did not understand why I would want to change his bandage every day or help him with simple tasks like sitting or walking when he had never regarded me as a person of any character."

I sat silent, unable to speak. Had we crossed some sort of invisible line in the ocean whereby society's standards had been tossed overboard? "Please continue, Julia."

"I told him that though I was a fallen woman, I yet considered myself a Christian, and it was my duty to help those in need. Once we spoke plainly with each other, we found the freedom to discuss more, such as the books we read, where we had been raised, and so on. He was unaware that I came from Portsmouth and was so familiar with the sea. You can imagine that we had much to discuss on that account."

"Naturally," I said. "Mr. Gilpin seems particularly fond of the naval life."

"Yes, and I shouldn't wonder that he will be the captain of his own ship one day, for he works hard, as I am certain you have noticed."

I nodded. "What of his mother?" I said, disliking that my curiosity forced me to broach the subject, but it was a rather important one if they had discussed marriage.

Miss Whipple twisted her hands in her lap. "You know of her?"

"I have heard him speak of her, yes."

"We believe it best not to speak of my past in her presence, of course. He says that my personality is remarkably akin to her own. One of the purposes of a union between Mr. Gilpin and myself would be for me to live with his mother and care for her while he was at sea."

She did not have to mention the beneficial purpose to herself, which would involve the abandonment of her former way of life. It was peculiar that she had mentioned the word *purpose*, just as Phineas had done when discussing our own marriage. Thomas Gilpin would have a wife with a dubious past, but he would be at sea for a great part of each year, so he would not have to look upon her often enough to be reminded. She, in turn, would have a home, and the elder Mrs. Gilpin would have a compassionate companion in her declining years.

It seemed as calculated as the navigation Mr. Calow performed with his compass.

"Julia, you may think me forward," I said, "but has the

word *love* entered into your conversation with Mr. Gilpin at all?"

"Love?" She blinked. "That is a luxury for certain people, Isabella."

"Yes, of course," I murmured.

I wished that I could unburden my heart to her. There was no lady aboard ship my age, no one with whom to confer. I forced myself to smile, and in thinking on their future, I did find joy. "I wish you all happiness."

"We will marry in Macao, and I would consider it a great honor were you to attend . . . Phineas as well."

"I would not miss it," I said. "I cannot speak for Phineas, of course."

She peered at me thoughtfully. "I thought perhaps you two seemed closer these days. Is it so?"

I schooled my expression. Julia Whipple knew many of Phineas and my secrets, but this was one to which she could not be privy. Particularly if she was Thomas Gilpin's future wife. "Phineas and I are friends, naturally, but we have our own plans once we reach China."

"Then you will go your separate ways, I suppose?" She shook her head. "It is probably for the best, no matter how I had hoped . . . Never mind. It is of little consequence."

Our fellow passengers delighted themselves with the news. Unlike the proverbial leopard, the spots on Julia Whipple's character seemed to abruptly change. She was now hailed as the heroine of the *Dignity* for giving her time so unselfishly to the wounded—particularly Thomas

Gilpin. After the impending wedding was announced after dinner that day, Mrs. Akers took Julia under her wing without another mention of the past.

"I knew that those two were bound to wind up in matrimonial bliss," Mrs. Akers declared loudly to everyone at the table. "You can see that they are quite compatible and evenly paired in temperament. Mind, I do not consider myself a matchmaker, but I thought I detected a hint of marriage in the air among us. I must confess that at first I thought it might be Mr. Gilpin and Miss Goodrich, but after that unfortunate incident with those heinous Frenchmen, I knew I was wrong."

Captain Malfort cleared his throat, glancing at me briefly. "We are all pleased with the impending nuptials, which are to take place in Macao. The East India Company has a chaplain there."

"Indeed!" Mrs. Akers looked at Julia Whipple. "But you must have a true clergyman, my dear. Without, it is simply unthinkable!"

"Chaplains are authorized to perform marriage ceremonies," Miss Whipple said. "We thought it might be difficult to find a Church of England clergyman in Macao. After all, Catholicism is the dominant religious practice."

"Papists!" Mrs. Akers fanned herself. "Oh my, no! You are right, indeed. Besides, it is rather romantic to be wed aboard ship, for after all, it is where you met."

"Perhaps Miss Whipple and Mr. Gilpin did not intend to hold the ceremony on the *Dignity*," I ventured.

"Of course they will," Mrs. Akers said, staring at me

coldly as though I had suggested they grow gills and marry underwater.

"We have not decided on a location yet," Miss Whipple said, trying to smooth the conversation.

Captain Malfort raised his wine glass. "I would like to propose a toast, since this is our last dinner together before docking in Macao. To the new relationships that have been forged aboard the *Dignity*, in both hard times and good." He smiled at Mr. Gilpin and Miss Whipple. "May they be blessed by the Almighty."

"Hear, hear," we said in reply, raising our own glasses. I took a sip of wine, catching a glance from Phineas over the rim. While the others laughed, distracted, he held up his glass slightly in my direction.

After all the long days, weeks, and months at sea, we docked at Macao. Phineas had told me a little of what to expect of the port. It had been a quiet fishing village until the Portuguese colonized it hundreds of years ago. It was still under their control, though it was considered a peninsula, connected to China by a small strip of land. When we docked and all were properly ashore, I felt as though I were, indeed, in a new world.

The port bustled with activity—ships of various shapes, sizes, and nationalities lay at the docks. Sailors loaded and unloaded mysterious cargo, primarily chests and crates stamped with Chinese characters. I was disappointed that the buildings all appeared British or Portuguese in their structure. Dominating the scene, however, were the mingling sounds of different languages. English, of course, and what must be Portuguese and even Dutch. For the first time, I heard someone besides Phineas speak Chinese. I was accustomed to his patient tempo, for as my teacher, he had wanted me to understand every word. Yet the workers on the ships and dock spoke so quickly I could scarce understand a word. When I said as much to Phineas, he smiled. "You will pick it up in good time, I am certain. Do not try to translate to English in your mind. Allow yourself to absorb the Chinese language on its own."

We wandered the port together. I was no doubt as wide-eyed as a child, taking in all the sights. Birds squawked in cages, merchants hawked their wares to sailors in a peculiar language of animated Chinese and broken English. Phineas found a quiet, out-of-the-way place to eat, a tea house, where I sampled my first Chinese food—*dim sum*.

The building was crowded with other diners and noisy, like the vendors' birds. A man brought stacks of bamboo baskets, steam rising as he lifted the lids, for us to choose what we wanted to eat. Phineas chose for us, speaking so quickly in Chinese that I could not catch every word. Or perhaps I was merely enchanted by the sight and smell of the food. What a selection! Some of the foods were steamed—pork spareribs and *char siu bao*, which were roast pork packed into fluffy white steamed buns. Some were fried—spring rolls, which were thin flour skins filled with carrots, cabbages, and mushrooms, and *wu gok*, a light, crispy dough filled with something called taro. (I did not inquire about its nature.)

We also ate dumplings made of shrimp and wrapped with seaweed. Then dessert, my favorite, the custard tarts.

The food was sticky and sweet and fluffy and slipped from my chopsticks in my haste to eat and in my lack of skill with the foreign utensils. Phineas smiled and showed me again and again how to hold the two sticks between my fingers. Soon I was able to capture even a bit of rice.

All the while we dined on such scrumptious fare, we participated in the tradition of *yum cha*—drinking tea. Lots and lots of green tea, of which I could not seem to get enough. *Dim sum* means "to touch the heart," and by the time we had finished eating, my heart already felt touched in this new world.

I was accustomed to a society where people spoke in polite tones and acted civilly, at least on the surface. In between the smiles and polite words, however, one could say just about anything about another person. A quick observation of the Chinese men at the next table made me realize that there was nothing polite or subtle—by my British standards—about their speech. They yelled at, berated, and argued with one another to the point that I winced. I could only understand every other word, but perhaps that was to my advantage.

As if that were not enough, the men both spat small bones from their food—not to mention saliva—directly on the floor. I could not fathom such behavior!

Phineas smiled. "You are disturbed?"

I nodded. "They lack proper table manners."

"Those are proper table manners here. Just as you learned

a different language, so must you learn a different way of life."

A man at the table next to us rose, as did his voice. The pitch grew louder, but his words continued in the beautiful rise and fall of the Cantonese dialect. He gestured at his companion, then turned and stalked away, his long queue swinging. No longer appalled, I was now fascinated. I had sought adventure, and now I lived it.

Phineas took my hand. "We should speak of our wedding."

He received my undivided attention with those words, a reminder that adventure of another sort lay waiting. "Yes?"

"Julia and Mr. Gilpin will wed tomorrow, for he will be expected to go with the *Dignity* on to Canton as soon as possible. We should wed the following day."

"I leave the plans to you, of course, but a wedding only two days hence?"

"It is too soon?" he said, frowning.

"I thought only . . . oh, it is far too silly for a man to understand."

"If it concerns you, Isabella, then it concerns me too," he said. "What troubles you?"

In truth, I believed his concern. I smiled. "I was hoping to find a new dress for the wedding. I may have to clothe myself as a proper missionary for the rest of my life, but I want something special. I want to look truly beautiful for our marriage day."

He took my hand. "You always appear so to me. No

matter how fine the material or exquisite the design, the dress would only be secondary to your beautiful face."

Remember your mission, Isabella. This is a marriage of convenience for us both. Primarily . . . Probably . . . Possibly . . .

I cleared my throat. "Speaking of dresses, perhaps we had best return to the *Dignity*. I should help Julia arrange for her own wedding."

"I believe Mrs. Akers has taken it upon herself to help Julia. At least, I believe that is what I heard when we were disembarking."

His eyes seemed far too intent, signaling his desire to spend more time with me alone. Nevertheless, I had to discourage such emotions for they could only be detrimental to both our futures. "Perhaps that is so," I said, "but we should return at any rate."

"Very well." I could see the disappointment register on his face. I almost felt sorry for him, but then I recalled that one of us had to remember our ultimate purposes!

Back at the ship, we learned that Mrs. Akers had indeed arranged all things for Julia Whipple, from her dress to the location of the wedding. It was to be a civil ceremony performed aboard ship, with Mr. Gilpin asserting that his mama would probably prefer to see them wed in church back in England when they returned. Until then, a civil license would make things at least legal, if not elegant.

As for her dress, somehow a lovely white satin with tiny embroidered roses had been procured from a dressmaker in Macao, with the promise that it would be hemmed to fit by the ceremony. Julia described it to me in great detail, and it occurred to me that perhaps it was the most elegant dress she had ever owned. That was as it should be for any lady, of course, as it was her wedding day. Still, I wondered at Mrs. Akers's insistence on it being a fancy dress, as I doubted its serviceability for Julia after the ceremony. I could not imagine that she would have many occasions to wear such a lovely dress back home. Living with Mr. Gilpin's mother, she would have few occasions to dress formally since he would be at sea much of the year.

Julia looked as though she wished to speak to me, but every time she approached, Mrs. Akers seemed to recall yet another ceremony question. At last the younger woman gave herself completely to the older woman's care and let herself be led away. It was probably for the better, as I might be tempted to speak to her of my own impending marriage and thus reveal the secret.

I had no notion about what Phineas planned by way of a ceremony. I knew it would be Christian, for he was such, of course, but he consulted me on no matter whatsoever. Despite my expressed desire to find a dress, the issue seemed oddly unimportant now. My chief desire was to be wed and move into the interior of China where I could at last begin to be of some use. When I asked Phineas how we would slip away to be wed, he smiled.

"It is all arranged. As soon as Julia and Mr. Gilpin's wedding is over, we will slip away during the celebration afterward. I have already informed the captain and Mr. Harrison and Mr. Akers that I have business for the company to attend. They think that you will stay aboard ship, of course, as foreign women are not allowed outside Macao."

"But I will leave with you?" I said anxiously, envisioning his abandonment of me at the final minute.

"Yes, of course. But, Isabella, you must be certain this is what you want, for you cannot return to the *Dignity* without a full accounting for your whereabouts."

"It is what I want to do," I said, setting my lips firmly together. "This is what I have hoped for all along, and I will not turn back."

"Even if the accomplishment of that dream includes an unexpected husband in the bargain?"

"Even so."

He turned away but continued to speak, as if he did not want to look at me. "You cannot take anything with you, so if you have acquired anything during the journey that you wish to keep, give it to me for safekeeping in my trunk. They are expecting me to disembark, but not you."

I laughed. "The sword you have given me is still in your trunk, as are the gospel tracts. Otherwise, the only items I have acquired during this long journey are the very dress I wear and the horrid gray one besides."

He turned back to face me. "What sort of frock would you hope to wear for our wedding? You avowed that you wanted something special."

"Oh, Phineas. Truly, it hardly matters. I am resigned to wearing one or the other of my normal dresses. Mrs. Akers has carried on so over Julia Whipple that I have not the strength to seek a dress of my own. I am sure that they scoured the Macao shops that cater to European ladies."

"Will you trust me with the procurement? I think you will be pleased."

"Very well. You can hardly do worse than my cotton dresses."

He grinned. "I pray that I will not disappoint. Now would you care to hear how we will leave the ship?"

I nodded. When did this man ever lack for a plan?

I must confess that Julia Whipple's wedding dress was every inch as lovely as any I had ever seen, and I was near green with jealousy. Still, I reminded myself, clothes were nothing compared to the kingdom of God, and it was a passion I needed to forsake if I wanted to truly become one of his workers.

Naturally the ceremony was lovely as well, with the ship's deck decorated most festively with lengths of white tulle and as many flowers as possible. Julia Whipple flushed the most becoming pink, as did Thomas Gilpin. Perhaps their disparate natures would balance one another in one of those odd marriages of opposites that frequently seemed more companionable than those whose spouses had known each other for years.

Mrs. Akers managed to weep at all the appropriate moments, trumpeting loudly into her handkerchief so that I was certain it was past all future use, even with a thorough washing. She was also heard to announce rather loudly that the scene reminded her of her own dear wedding and that if the newly married enjoyed half the serenity and tranquility of her own marriage to Mr. Akers, they should consider themselves more than duly favored.

Mrs. Harrison leaned against her husband's shoulder the entire time, but I believe I saw her eyes flutter open briefly during the blessing of the ring.

The crew had been given shore leave, so only the captain and the most major officers were in attendance. Mr. Calow looked much older than his young years, dressed in his best uniform. I hated that I would not be granted a chance to say a proper farewell, and I hoped that he would remember me kindly.

After the ceremony, I kissed Julia Whipple—nay, Julia Gilpin!—on the cheek. I longed to bid her a proper farewell but settled for the deepest sentiment of my heart. "I am pleased for you both," I said. "May God grant you every happiness."

Love may not have been a companion to this marriage, but something certainly shone in her eyes as she glanced at her new husband. "I am certain that we will be most happy indeed."

For his part, Thomas Gilpin returned her gaze with a blush and accepted my best wishes as well. I caught no hint that he had perhaps wanted to place a ring on my finger, as Mrs. Akers had once asserted, for he seemed, if not overjoyed with his new bride, quite content. I prayed that his dear mama would accept her new daughter with graciousness and perhaps a bit of obliviousness as well.

Phineas, who had sat beside me throughout the ceremony

then drifted away afterward, beckoned me from across the deck. His trunk had already been removed from the ship, ostensibly for him to prepare for his journey inland. I had also laid a farewell note on my hammock, explaining that I had left with Phineas and not to worry for my safety.

Now it was time for us to disembark forever and perhaps, I felt in my heart, to leave England behind as well. Who knew if I would ever return to my homeland or to Uncle Toby and Flora?

I glanced at the shipmates with whom I had spent significant time for the past few months, and a lump settled in my throat. I could not bear the thought of never seeing or speaking with them again. Yet press on I must, for the higher prize.

And so Phineas and I slipped down the tulle-covered gangplank, unnoticed in the revelry, and embarked on yet another journey, one with no apparent return.

He took my hand and led me on foot along dusty roads to a waiting wagon and driver. Phineas helped me into the wagon then spoke a few words in Chinese to the driver in such a low tone that I could not comprehend his message. His trunk, I noticed, was stored in the back.

Clouds covered the night sky, and I could not see the stars. For some reason, this troubled me, and I shivered. Phineas put his arm around me, and I stiffened momentarily at the unexpected contact. "Are you warm enough?" he said, as if to soothe my fears.

His lips brushed my hair, and I shivered again. "Yes," I

said in a small voice, then cleared my throat. "Where are we going?"

He glanced at the driver, then put his fingers to his lips so that only I could see. I nodded my understanding.

Phineas and I rode into the night, forever it seemed. I grew weary and rested my head against his shoulder. Oddly, I felt safe and secure, as satisfied as a child who had just been allowed a cup of warm chocolate. However, I refused to allow myself to become accustomed to this sensation as we had no future together. None at all.

"Isabella," Phineas whispered in my ear.

I startled awake, bolting upright. "Yes?"

"We are here."

The driver had already descended from the wagon to haul Phineas's trunk outside what appeared to be a bamboo house. It certainly did not appear British or Portuguese in its architecture, as the buildings I had seen since we had landed in Macao.

"Where are we?"

"We are outside the walled city," he said. He dropped a few coins into the driver's hands, expressed his thanks, then rapped on the door. It swung open, and a Chinese man about the same age as Phineas bid us enter. He wore a long black queue and had his forehead shaved, a fashion I had seen many Chinese men sport in Macao.

Phineas led me inside. Once the door was closed, he gestured toward the man. "Isabella, this is Choi Sing-yiu, my good friend. Choi Sing-yiu, this is my bride, Isabella Goodrich."

Choi Sing-yiu means "To Gain Glory," but as he was a Christian, its implied meaning is "To Gain Glory for God." He bowed, then said in good English, "I am pleased to meet you."

A woman appeared from a back room, a baby on her hip. Glory ushered her forward, and she approached, smiling. Introductions were again made, and I learned that this was Glory's wife, Lui Chun-bo, which means "Precious Spring."

"Glory and Precious Spring are Christians," Phineas said. "Glory is, in fact, an ordained clergyman."

I blinked. Was this one of Phineas's deceptions?

Glory laughed. "I see by your expression that you do not believe him. But it is true. I studied in England. Phineas and I met in London."

"Like me, Glory has a British father," Phineas said. "He could have stayed in England, but he wanted to return here. He feels that his people need him. There are several Chinese Christians near this area."

"Phineas has promised to take you to them, yes?" Glory said.

"He has never said anything specific," I said, feeling confused. "I thought perhaps he was bringing me to you to help with missionary work."

Glory and Phineas exchanged a glance. Precious Spring appeared to try to follow the conversation, but it was apparent that she spoke little, if any, English. She did smile at me, however, which put me at ease. And her baby was adorable! Much better looking, I am ashamed to say, than my nephew

Lewis with his pinched, demanding face. This baby actually smiled at me, which was something that Lewis certainly never did in the entire year that I knew him.

"Is your child a boy or a girl?" I asked in Cantonese.

Precious Spring looked startled. "You speak our language?"

I nodded. "It was a five-month journey. Phineas was a thorough teacher."

Her smile broadened. "This is my son, Choi Ka-wai." A beautiful name that means "Honor of the Family."

Phineas took my hand. "Our time is short, Isabella. We have come here to be married, not to visit. We do not want to bring trouble to Glory and Precious Spring by your presence."

"Forgive me," Glory said, "but you are a foreign woman. Outside the city walls, you will be noticed. Our plan is to dress you in Chinese style so that you and Phineas can travel together to Canton. Your hair is dark enough so that with the proper attire and your ability to speak the language, you can pass farther inland."

"But I thought I was to help you."

"Precious Spring and I live here," Glory said gently. "Phineas himself can take you farther inland."

I glanced at him, and he nodded. "We can speak of this later, Isabella, but we must be wed and leave early tomorrow."

I looked at Glory. "So you will marry us? You are, indeed, a real clergyman?"

"I am." He smiled.

"Precious Spring has your wedding dress," Phineas said. "If you will make yourself ready, we can begin the ceremony."

Glory said something to Precious Spring, who took my hand. "Come with me," she said, smiling.

I glanced back at Phineas, who gestured me to go with her. No turning back, indeed!

12

"You are taller than me, but I believe this will fit."

I stared with awe at the beautiful skirt and tunic Precious Spring held up for my approval. The red silk could scarce be more opposite from Julia Whipple's modest white frock. The silk was interwoven with gold brocade designs of dragons and phoenixes, something a lady in Britain would never imagine herself wearing, of course! The high collar was unlike anything I had ever seen in fashion.

"This is a wedding dress," Precious Spring said. "Red is the color we wear for good luck."

"Why dragons and phoenixes?" I said, pointing to a wingless dragon and a flaming, crested phoenix.

"We believe they are also good luck and symbolize the emperor and empress, the balance of male and female power." She smiled shyly. "The Bible speaks of the submission of a wife to her husband, but Glory and I see the dragon and phoenix as symbolizing the balance of that submission to a husband's charge to care for and treasure his wife."

She looked at me anxiously. "Do you like it? Phineas asked me to find you a dress."

I could only imagine how Catherine Ransom would scoff at the color and style. Red, I understood without having to be told, was a symbol of joy, an emotion one should experience on her wedding day. I thought of Julia Whipple and her white dress, and I suddenly felt exceedingly sorry for her.

"It is beautiful, Precious Spring," I said. "Was this your dress?"

She nodded. "I hope you do not mind that I have offered you a borrowed dress, but there was no time to make one of your own."

"It is a great kindness, and I would be honored to wear it," I said. "Will you help me put it on?"

She smiled, and I knew then how much she had wanted to please Phineas. Precious Spring and Glory were obviously old and dear friends of his. That made me want to please him too, and I sensed that my wearing a traditional Chinese wedding dress would do so.

"No matter how fine the material or exquisite the design, the dress would only be secondary to your beautiful face."

His words returned to me as Precious Spring helped me dress. Was it possible Phineas not only thought me beautiful but more importantly loved me?

The silk brocade felt cool and soft against my skin, the heavier gold images chasing one another in a pleasing pattern. It had long, loose sleeves, and the tunic itself flowed past my hips, the skirt falling close at my ankles. I touched the cloth with wonder that I could wear something so fine. I confess that the color was foreign to me as I was accustomed to light shades, certainly nothing so bold and bright. Oddly, however, it made me feel daring and . . . dare I say happy?

Precious Spring stepped back to study me. Her frown alarmed me. "Is something wrong?" I said, anxious to look beautiful, indeed. Did I look ridiculous? Did the color not suit my complexion? Did I look too . . . British?

"I have forgotten the head covering. Will you allow me to style your hair? I cannot fix it properly as we should, but I'll try my best."

"Yes, of course." Vanity claimed me, and I added, "Do I do justice to your clothes?"

I had my answer in her smile.

Precious Spring fashioned my hair into a bun. "It is the style of married women," she said, standing back to admire her work. "Now we will add the head covering, and you will be ready."

A knock sounded at the door, then I heard Phineas speaking Chinese. "Is my bride not ready?"

Precious Spring's face beamed. "It is time for the door games, a wedding custom."

"What?"

"Ordinarily the groom would come to the bride's home, and her friends would play games to keep him from taking her. That means she is much loved and her family and friends do not want her to leave." She winked at me. "Watch. I must make him prove that he cares for you."

She opened the door, and Phineas stood there in full Chinese dress, an oddly shaped cap on his head. He blinked at my appearance, then smiled. He tried to enter, but Precious Spring blocked his way. "Who is your bride?" she said, her voice teasing.

"I am not certain now," he said. "Her name is Isabella Goodrich, but the woman in there looks more Chinese than her British name would allow."

"Why would you marry a British woman?"

"Because of who she is inside, not because she is British, of course."

"And who is she inside?"

Phineas dropped all teasing pretense in his voice. "She is a believer, foremost. She cares about others." His gaze found and held mine. "She is a strong woman."

I blushed and glanced away.

Precious Spring laughed, continuing the game. "Why would you want a strong woman? Do you want a boss?"

I waited for his answer. "I want an equal," he finally said, so quietly it was as though he were speaking only to me.

My heart soared. He smiled and handed a red envelope to Precious Spring. "If my answers will not convince you, I have money to buy my way in."

Precious Spring accepted it, pretending to consider for a moment. At last she stepped aside. She smiled at me. "Your groom seems to want you, Isabella." Phineas started to enter, but she shrieked and blocked his way again. "Wait! I forgot the head covering. Turn around, Isabella, quickly!"

She ran for a bureau and fished a red silk square from

the bottom drawer. She arranged it over my head, with the unfortunate result that it blocked my vision abominably. Phineas took my arm and led me through the door back to the main room. I squinted through the silk and saw that the wall now held a large red banner with the symbol for happiness—no, it was the single symbol, doubled. Extra happiness.

Precious Spring saw that I recognized its meaning. "May you both be happy," she said softly.

Phineas led me to a low table beneath the banner. Glory stood opposite us, and a teapot with cups sat between us and him. "You will kneel three times," Glory said. "In a traditional wedding, it is to the heaven and earth, your ancestors, and your parents. For you, let it be to God, your ancestors, and your living parents. Then you will kneel to each other."

We did so, solemnly. Glory poured tea in the cups. "Normally, the bride would offer the tea to parents and other relatives," he said. "In return, they would give you gifts like jewelry or money in a red envelope. Since you have no family present, drink to them, to God, and to each other."

I thought about Uncle Toby as I sipped the tea. Had he received the letter I had written in Cape Town? Did he know I was safe? He could not possibly dream that I was about to marry.

After we finished the tea, Glory stood. Phineas and I did as well. "Traditionally, you would now be considered married," Glory said. "But as we are believers, the rest of the ceremony will be from the *Book of Common Prayer*."

He cleared his throat. "Dearly beloved, we are gathered together here in the sight of God to join together this man and this woman in holy matrimony, which is an honorable estate, instituted of God . . ."

I had been in attendance at many weddings, all of which I had found to be quite lengthy. Glory read the entire ritual as written in the *Book of Common Prayer*, yet before I knew it, he said, "Phineas, wilt thou have this woman to thy wedded wife, to live together after God's ordinance in the holy estate of matrimony? Wilt thou love her, comfort her, honor, and keep her in sickness and in health; and, forsaking all other, keep thee only unto her, so long as ye both shall live?"

I thought Phineas smiled at me, but because of the head covering, I could not be certain. "I will," he answered solemnly.

Then Glory said to me, "Isabella, wilt thou have this man to thy wedded husband, to live together after God's ordinance in the holy estate of matrimony? Wilt thou obey him, and serve him, love, honor, and keep him in sickness and in health; and, forsaking all other, keep thee only unto him, so long as ye both shall live?"

"I will." *Oh yes. Yes. I am not certain when it happened, but I love this man.*

There was no one to give me away, so Glory himself clasped Phineas's right hand to my own. Then Phineas repeated after Glory. "I, Phineas, take thee, Isabella, to my wedded wife, to have and to hold from this day forward, for better for worse, for richer for poorer, in sickness and in health, to love and to cherish, till death us do part, according to God's holy ordinance; and thereto I plight thee my troth."

I was certain he could see right through my red head covering, for his gaze seemed focused completely on mine. Tears formed at the edge of my vision. I had dreamed of being loved and cherished by a man, but never one like Phineas.

Glory loosened our clasp, then bade me take Phineas's hand and repeat after him. I did not think I would be able to say the words, for a lump of joy lodged in my throat. "I, Isabella, take thee, Phineas, to my wedded husband, to have and to hold from this day forward, for better for worse, for richer for poorer, in sickness and in health, to love, cherish, and to obey, till death us do part, according to God's holy ordinance; and thereto I give thee my troth."

Glory asked for a ring. I turned to Phineas, certain he would be embarrassed at his lack. To my surprise, he laid a lovely green ring on the book Glory held, as I had seen countless grooms do. Glory took the ring and handed it back to Phineas, who placed it on the third finger of my left hand. "With this ring I thee wed," Phineas repeated after Glory, though the words sounded as though they were written just for us, "with my body I thee worship, and with all my worldly goods I thee endow: In the name of the Father, and of the Son, and of the Holy Ghost. Amen."

The rest of Glory's final words were a blur: ". . . God hath joined together let no man put asunder . . . consented together in holy wedlock, I pronounce that they be man and wife together, in the name of the Father, and of the Son, and of the Holy Ghost. Amen."

Though it was not in accordance with a Chinese wedding, after the Christian portion of the ceremony was concluded, Phineas lifted the red head covering to reveal my face. He looked at me as though it were the first time, then smiled. He kissed me sweetly, a soft touching of our lips, and when he straightened beside me—my husband now—I realized the enormity of what I had done.

Glory and Precious Spring laid out a great deal of food for us to eat: chicken, fish, a special soup that, naturally, was to bring us good luck. (I believe someone said it contained lotus seeds—whatever those were!) I ate it all in enjoyment, only afterward feeling much guilt. Glory and Precious Spring obviously did not have much money. I hoped we had not eaten a month's worth of their food. It certainly seemed as though we had.

While we were dining and laughing, I noticed that Precious Spring disappeared for a while. I assumed she was tending to Honor, who had slept peacefully through the entire ceremony. At last she returned and nudged Glory, who had just said something that made Phineas and me laugh.

"Glory, it is late." Her voice carried just a hint of scolding.

Glory rose. "Yes, of course." He motioned for Phineas and me to rise. Somehow he and Glory got behind us, maneuvering us toward the room where I had dressed. Smiling, Precious Spring opened the door. The bed had been changed to red linens, and a dragon and phoenix candle glowed on an adjacent table. Next to the candle sat two goblets filled with wine, attached to one another with a red string.

Still smiling, Glory and Precious Spring herded Phineas and me forward, forcing us to sit on the bed. Phineas may have understood this apparent tradition, but I did not. Surely my face reflected my mortification!

Glory and Precious Spring smiled fondly at us, as though we were two children. "You know that we would normally tease you both, but instead we will simply say good night," Glory said.

I rose. "But . . . but this is your room. We cannot take it."

"It is our only room for sleeping, so tonight it is yours," Precious Spring said, then winked. "Would you rather sleep on a mat?"

"Thank you," Phineas said, acknowledging the gift. "You have made this a wonderful day. A wonderful wedding."

Retreating, Glory and Precious Spring smiled, softly closing the door behind them.

I continued to stand, unnerved. "We have been alone together many nights," Phineas said softly, touching my hand, rising beside me.

"But not like this," I said. Tonight there would be no canvas sail between us. To change the subject, I gestured at the wine glasses. "What is the significance?"

He lifted one and handed it to me. "Can you not guess?"

He took the other, then crossed arms with me. He drank from his glass, and I drank from mine. Then we drank from each other's glass, smiling as we tried not to tangle the string between them.

We sat down again, side by side, and Phineas took my hand. "A Chinese legend says God ties a red string around the ankles of the man and woman who are destined to become husband and wife." He touched my cheek, his voice husky. "No matter how far apart they are, they will eventually get married."

I covered his hand with mine. "Phineas," I murmured.

"Do you not know that God has brought us together, Isabella?" He dipped his head and pressed a kiss to my lips. "We were born worlds apart, yet we are here together now. For many men, the first time they see their bride's face is when they remove the red veil at their marriage bed." His voice dropped even lower. "I am thankful to have known you much longer than that."

I nodded, unable to speak. My heart beat faster, then there was no need for words . . .

Later I lay in his arms, full of wonder and joy as bold as the red silk sheets. The dragon and phoenix candle burned lower, and I could barely see my husband's face. "You have not spoken of Wo-Ping and Mei in a long while," I said, teasing.

He laughed softly, kissing my temple as he twirled a strand of my hair between his fingers. "Didn't I tell you? They gave up fighting each other and joined forces to fight for righteousness. They had no need of secrets, and they kept nothing from each other."

My thoughts turned serious. "And you? Have you any need to keep secrets from me?"

He ceased playing with my hair. "What secrets do you wish to know?"

"Are you still harboring a desire for revenge on the East India Company?"

"That has not been a secret from you for a long time."

I raised up on an elbow. "Then that is still your plan? Despite that you know my feelings?"

"Isabella." He eased me back down. "Would I ask you to abandon your dream?"

"Mine is different," I said stubbornly. "Mine is God's work."

"Mine is too. You have seen the people addicted to opium since we have been here, have you not?"

I closed my eyes. Yes, I had seen them. They loitered near buildings with apparently no place to go, their eyes vacant, their feet only good for shuffling without purpose. I had not seen the opium dens where they smoked away their lives—and no doubt the futures of wives and children as well—but I knew they existed.

"You *have* seen them," he insisted. "Their numbers will only increase. Every year the British bring in more opium even though it has been illegal to import in China for nearly twenty years. The British will not suddenly acquire a conscience and stop the trade."

"I am British," I said, my eyes stinging with tears. "My

countrymen could not do such a thing. Do you think that Captain Malfort or Thomas Gilpin or Mr. Calow, for that matter, would harm a fellow human being?"

"They do not see this country as you do, Isabella," Phineas said. "They are not willing to share their true feelings with a lady, but their business—nay, their whole lives—are concerned with bringing Britain her tea. At any cost whatsoever."

"Then would you have Britain take over China and move here so that she might have the pleasure of *yum cha*?"

"I would not, but there are those in Britain who would gladly annex my country solely for her tea."

I could not help the tears that pricked my eyes. "Your country, Phineas? You told me you have spent over half your life in Britain. To which country do you belong—England or China?"

He lifted my hand and kissed my fingers. "I want only to belong to you."

"Then give up this foolish plan of revenge."

"If I do, it will mean that you give up your dream, for I am headed inland with my partners for the golden tea leaf. Was it not your plan to travel farther into China to spread the gospel?"

"Yes, but—"

"I am traveling to the Mo Tong mountains," he continued. "They are in the Hupei Province where there are many monasteries and temples."

"Monasteries and temples? No one there would listen to me."

"Perhaps you do not believe in your mission," he said.

I said nothing. How could I respond?

"The monks would not even see you—or me—for neither of us are fully Chinese," he said gently, covering my silence, "but the villagers in the province might. I do not believe any Christians have traveled to that area."

"What you offer, then, is a chance to fulfill my calling, yet at the cost of seeing you fulfill what you believe is yours. Even though I disagree with it strongly."

"That is the way of it."

All the joy of our wedding evaporated like cold water on hot stones. "Blackmail seems to have been the way of our relationship since the beginning." Moisture gathered in my eyes, despite my effort to stop it. "We have come so far, Phineas. I do not want to lose you."

"Isabella." Phineas wiped a tear from my cheek. "Isabella, please do not cry. I would see you happy, not sad. Our love will be well. But I have a duty—a calling—as you have yours. Can we not both be true to that?"

Perhaps we could, but I wept anyway because I did not believe that in the process we could be true to one another.

Morning brought a fair amount of awkwardness, for though we had spent countless nights in adjacent hammocks aboard ship, we had never been husband and wife. I found myself blushing when, in my early morning grogginess, I threw out my arm and hit Phineas across the chest. I am not certain who was more startled—he, because I woke him from sleep, or I, because he was so close beside me. He smiled at me and pulled me closer yet. It was still nearly beyond belief that I should find myself wed, but our first morning together made me more cheerfully accustomed to our situation.

My old gray dress lay neatly folded where I had laid it the previous day before donning the wedding dress, but Phineas retrieved new clothes for me from Precious Spring, a loose-fitting skirt and long blouse made of dark cotton. He handed them to me, and I ducked behind a screen to dress. He might have thought me overly modest, but he was kind enough to speak to me of practical matters while I donned the clothing. "You must look Chinese if we are to leave Macao," he said. "Remember that no foreign ladies are allowed to leave here. But with your dark hair styled properly and if you act like a proper wife, keeping her head down, no one should suspect you are not Chinese."

"How should I act?"

He grinned. "Though it will grieve you, you must obey me."

"That does not sound so very different from Britain," I said mildly. "Wives are expected to obey their husbands there as well."

"Are they expected to walk behind their husbands? For that is what you must do when we are in public, Isabella."

"Very well." It *would* no doubt grieve me, but I could act the role.

I emerged from behind the screen, and Phineas studied me as I adjusted the skirt and tunic. His frank gaze made me blush, but he smiled tenderly. "You should have a Chinese name. I cannot very well refer to you as Isabella when we are within the city walls of Canton."

"Is your family name not Wong? That should be mine too," I said.

"Names are not the same in China as in Britain. A woman does not take her husband's name but retains the name of her father's clan. It would be disrespectful to do otherwise. I only have my mother's family name because my father was British."

"But I have no Chinese clan at all," I said. "May I not take yours?"

He touched my shoulder, then smoothed the length of my arm. Again, I blushed. I was unaccustomed to such familiarity, though I confess I did not find it displeasing. "You may have my family name, for indeed we belong fully to each other now," he said softly. "I think Wong Si-yan would be a beautiful name for you."

"Wong Si-yan," I repeated, trying it out. "And it means . . ." I struggled to put the words together.

"Gracious Thoughts," he murmured, his fingers caressing the nape of my neck.

I closed my eyes despite myself. "I do not believe that your own thoughts are gracious at the moment," I murmured. "Perhaps they are of another nature?"

Phineas laughed softly then kissed me . . .

Precious Spring was feeding Honor when we entered the main room of the bamboo house. Her eyes lit like small firecrackers when she saw us, and she served us *congee*—rice porridge—for breakfast. I held Honor on my lap and played with him while Phineas, Glory, and Precious Spring discussed our impending journey. I picked up enough of their discussion to learn the details of our journey to Canton. They could not have been averse to my participation in the conversation, but in truth, I enjoyed Honor's company. He was a happy baby who gurgled and smiled most obligingly at the silly faces I presented him. I bounced him on my knee, and he squealed with pleasure. I confess that Lewis had never allowed himself to be amused in such a way, and Honor's reactions delighted me much more, I am certain, than I delighted him.

"He likes you," Precious Spring said, sitting beside me.

"I like him. He is a cheerful baby. You and Glory are indeed blessed." Phineas and Glory had finished their discussion and were watching us, so I reluctantly handed Honor back to his mother.

"May you have many sons," Precious Spring said softly.

"I would gladly have a dozen if they were each like Honor," I said.

Phineas approached, smiling, evidently having heard my words, though he did not speak of them. "We must leave, Isabella."

"So soon?" I did not want to impose on Glory and Precious Spring's hospitality, but I felt great contentment within their bamboo walls.

Phineas nodded. "We must be on our way to Canton."

"You are forgetting something." Precious Spring went back to the bedroom and retrieved a long switch of black hair. She motioned Phineas to sit, and she skillfully wove the hair into his much shorter queue. At first I thought the switch was from the tail of a horse, but when Precious Spring had finished her weaving, I realized it was Phineas's own hair.

"I had to cut the length when I left China, and I must wear it again when I return," he said.

"It is law that a man must wear a queue in China and is punishable by death if he does not," Glory said. "It is the same with a shaved head."

I glanced at Phineas, alarmed. "Will you have to do that as well?"

He smiled, obviously reading that I could not bear the thought of his losing any hair to a razor. "If I wear a cap, I think it will cover enough."

I sighed with relief.

We said good-bye, tearfully on my part, for I was not certain that I would ever see these wonderful people again. I wondered if their desire was to spread Christianity in Macao, for I sensed that the Chinese community in which they lived was much in need of the gospel message. Yet they had no tracts and politely refused the ones I offered them, declaring that they might be more needed farther inland.

For my part, I would never forget the kindness they showed Phineas and me, a stranger. It was with much reluctance that I left the red brocade dress, but it would remain a happy memory of my wedding to Phineas.

I also left behind the gray cotton dress, for I saw no need to keep any reminders of the life I had left behind.

Prearranged, a cart arrived for us, taking us back to the

harbor at Macao. The *Dignity* had left, I saw, and I asked Phineas if he thought we might see the ship in Canton.

"I doubt it. And even if we do, no one aboard will recognize us. We look Chinese to them and would easily pass under their eyes with no notice."

"How will we get to Canton? Is it a long journey?"

"Not particularly. We will travel up the Pearl estuary by way of sampan."

"What is that?"

Phineas pointed to a small flat-bottomed boat propelled by two short oars. I judged its size against the larger ships I saw in the docks. The East Indiamen and the equally large four-masted Chinese junks overwhelmed the little skiff. "Can we make it so far on that?" I said.

"Many people—entire families—live on sampans," Phineas said. "It will hold us."

The journey seemed to symbolize my current life, in which everything was new and exciting. I had foreign clothes and a new hairstyle, had been admonished to act Chinese, and found myself in possession of a husband. I was thrilled to be traveling where no British women were supposed to go. The future seemed endless!

"Where are we going first when we reach Canton?" I asked Phineas.

He glanced at me sideways. "To my mother's."

The future suddenly seemed rather unsteady.

The air was hot and sticky, and my cotton clothes clung to my skin. Phineas said that this month, August, was one of the warmest and that in Canton summers were long and the winters short. He warned me that sometimes monsoons occurred—devastating winds and rains.

The sampan belonged to a husband, wife, and two small children, and it reminded me of Phineas's words when we had visited the poor in Oxford: *"Yet even they would be richer than many in China."* I knew now what he meant. The family of four, with another child obviously on its way, lived on the tiny wooden boat with its partial cover, catching to eat and sell what fish they could on the Pearl. The husband's eyes widened when Phineas dropped extra coins in his hands. "You are going to much trouble to row us up river," Phineas said. I did not know how much the money was worth, but it must have been a goodly amount.

Besides other small sampans like ours, Chinese junks with sails that looked like folding fans sailed past. Dwarfing them were the foreign ships of commerce, much like the *Dignity*, belonging not only to England, but according to their flags, the Netherlands, Spain, and Sweden as well. We also saw stern-oared tanka boats. Both sides of the shores were hilly, and here and there I spotted small Chinese buildings. The river smelled of fish, water warmed by the sun, and the promise of commerce miles upriver in Canton.

When we were finally on shore, I was amazed again to hear so many languages. I was even more amazed that so much of it was English. Facing the harbor and the many ships crowding the water was a row of different buildings that various countries rented to conduct their trade. Each country flew its flag outside its building, all of which were enclosed by a wall. Phineas said that the European merchants were not allowed to leave this riverbank area, known as the Thirteen Factories.

"When the emperor allowed foreigner traders, he believed that if he could contain them to this area and within Canton, in the extreme south of China, that no harm would come. The Chinese merchants who deal with the Europeans must be licensed by the government in Peking and pay large fees. The government also profits from the European silver acquired in trade, the Europeans acquire their tea, silk, and porcelain, and all are happy."

His face darkened. "Until the Europeans started trading opium instead of silver."

"But the *Dignity* carried no opium," I said. "What will they trade?"

"No doubt they met with another East Indiaman in Macao, one that weighed anchor in India first for opium. Wong Si-yan!" he said to me sharply, under his breath. "Put your head down and walk behind me. Do not gawk at anything, for you must appear to be a submissive Chinese wife."

I raised my head even higher to argue, but his expression indicated that to brook an argument might be at my own peril. I lowered my head and dropped behind him a few paces. We were scarcely noticed in the crowd of people, who had important trade matters to tend to.

One man in British clothes bumped into me then tipped his cap. "So solly, missy," he said, grinning before he hustled away in the crowd.

Phineas smiled briefly, apparently pleased that our ruse

had worked, then continued pushing through the crowd. Outside the walled compound, he approached several men standing beside a sort of bamboo chair attached to two long poles. I could not hear his words, but I believe they haggled over a price. At last he gestured to me and, like a displeased husband, ordered me brusquely into the chair.

I had questions, naturally, but I wisely held my tongue, keeping my head down and my face away from the strange men. I did not want them to look too closely at me, lest they realize I was not Chinese. Fortunately, they seemed more intent on their business, one hoisting Phineas's trunk onto his shoulders with apparent ease, and the other two lifting the poles of my chair to their shoulders. My stomach lurched, and I found myself up in the air.

I glanced at Phineas, who grinned up at me. "Will you not ride?" I asked quietly, so that no one could hear.

"It would not be seemly," he said, equally as soft, then walked ahead as though happy to be shed of my company.

Once I accustomed myself to the jostling of the chair, I found it quite exciting and enjoyable. I was a good head taller than my chair bearers, so I could see over everyone we passed. The narrow streets were lined with many small shops, their steep roofs consisting of long tiles with the corners turned curiously up at their ends. Vertical banners hung near the street, proclaiming each shop's purpose. Vendors also sold wares and food—some with tantalizing smells and others a trifle peculiar to my senses. The streets teemed with people and the varying pitches of their voices as they proceeded with their commerce.

I would have continued to gaze in awe at everything the entire city had to reveal, but Phineas glanced back at me and frowned. I remembered to put my head down, focusing, sadly, on the dirt road instead.

We traveled a short distance, just long enough for me to wonder why I had not been allowed to walk. I was certainly capable! Perhaps it had something to do with class. I knew that there were different levels of society in China, just as in Britain, and I wondered about his mother. I had not thought to ask about her.

We stopped in a merchant area, and the chair bearers let me down rather roughly, to my estimation. I was unharmed, however, and certainly above giving them the satisfaction of knowing they had displeased me. I managed a quick glance at our surroundings before returning my gaze to the road. The buildings were set so close together that it was difficult to see where one shop ended and another began. Vendors and buyers haggled at makeshift tables set up to display wares such as squawking chickens, ducks, earthenware, and shoes.

To my disgust, it seemed that nearly every vendor and buyer managed to spit at least once. I can assure you that I kept a close eye on not only where I stepped but the lovely but serviceable black slippers Precious Spring had given me. The spitters took little notice of their saliva's destination, often to the peril of many shoes.

Phineas paid the sedan chair men and indicated that the man shouldering the trunk should follow. We headed off the main road, and I wanted to ask Phineas a multitude of questions, but with the stranger present, I could not. I remained the dutiful, unnoticed wife.

At last Phineas stopped outside a thick-walled compound. I could see several buildings past the iron gate, all with heavily tiled roofs and curling corners. Silently he paid the man, who hurried off—in search of another job, no doubt. Phineas glanced around to make sure we were alone. Assured that we were, he took my hand. "This is my mother's house."

I trembled. "What will she think of me?"

"She will be delighted that you have gone to such extremes to dress and speak as we do." He smiled and opened the gate.

"I was concerned more with her thoughts regarding our marriage. You said that she wanted you to marry a Chinese girl." My feet seemed resistant as we walked on thick stones past a tranquil garden and fountain.

Phineas squeezed my hand. "She will adore you, Isabella. Just as I do."

"What should I call her? I do not even know her name."

"Her name is Wong Siu-yin—Little Swallow—but you will call her Nai Nai. It is a term for a mother-in-law." With a final smile, he pushed through the door.

I believed I knew the answer to my question about her social standing right away. She was neither nobility nor peasant, but somewhere in between. A young girl approached us, and Phineas greeted her as a servant. "Please tell my mother that we are here," he concluded.

The girl cast a suspicious glance in my direction, then

headed into the interior of the home. I glanced around at the home with its gracious display of intricately carved chairs, tables, cabinets, and curiously colored vases. Two pots of peonies sat on three-legged stands. "Your mother does not want, does she?" I murmured.

Phineas seemed about to respond, but his gaze was drawn up the hall. A short lady with an elaborate hairstyle hobbled her way toward us, her green silk dress flowing. I could not divulge her age by her face, but her mouth set hard as though she had once been pretty and now resented advancing age. "Wong Yu-Chung," she said softly, smiling at Phineas.

I smiled as well, for I had not known his Chinese name. Its literal meaning was "To Take on the World Vigorously," and its implied meaning was "Success in Life."

"Leong Tsan." Phineas addressed his mother, placing his left hand over his right fist and bowed, as he had done when he presented the sword to me. His mother nodded in return.

No embrace? No welcoming kiss? Despite my curiosity at their peculiarly reserved exchange, I stood to the side grinning, I am certain, like an escaped inmate from Bedlam.

"I can't believe you have returned from that wicked, wicked country," she said. "I had nearly given up hope." Her gaze turned to me, and her expression altered like a storm cloud passing across the sun. "Who is this?"

Phineas drew me to his side. "This is my wife, Mother. Her name is Isabella. Her Chinese name, which I have given her, is Wong Si-yan."

I curtsied. "I am pleased to make your acquaintance, Nai Nai," I said. "I—"

She peered at me closely. "She is not Chinese! Why have you given her our family name, Ah Chung?" She referred to Phineas by the diminutive of his full name.

"She has chosen to identify with us. In England it is the custom for a husband's family name to pass to his bride."

Nai Nai sneered. "Your bride should have been picked by the matchmaker to make sure you would have luck together."

"Yes, Mother. She would have studied our birth years, days, and hours to see if we matched."

"You probably did not even consult the book that would decide whether it was a lucky day," she accused.

"We married only yesterday," I said, hoping to help. Surely the day before Phineas's return must be lucky indeed!

She narrowed her eyes, making no mention of the fact that I had spoken in Chinese. "Yesterday? It was particularly unlucky."

"Isabella and I do not believe in superstition," Phineas said. "You know that I am a Christian. Isabella is one too. In fact, she came all this way to—"

"That is your father's doing. And his family. They do not care that they have ruined my family."

"That was a long time ago," Phineas said softly. "Can you not be pleased that I am home again?"

She glanced at me then nodded at him, acknowledging that she would end the discussion. She led him into the house, and I followed in resignation, an obedient wife in borrowed Chinese clothing.

For the rest of the day, Phineas's mother spoke to me only when absolutely necessary. If I tried to insinuate myself physically closer to them or even into the conversation, she closed up tighter than an oyster. Phineas regaled her with stories of how diligently I had worked at learning Cantonese, how we had had—inasmuch as it was possible for our beliefs—a traditional Chinese wedding. Phineas introduced me to his younger sister, Wong Yu-fai, which means "Splendor of the World." I, however, would address her as Phineas did—Ku Tzi, which means "Little Sister." About the age of young Mr. Calow, she was all politeness itself, but underneath, I was certain, lurked a warmhearted girl. She nodded at me, dignified, but her eyes shone. Though she struggled as a young lady for proper behavior, the hint of a smile curved her lips.

Phineas's mother, on the other hand, sat as silent as a stone lion sculpture. Rather than displaying the power of mighty paws, however, she seemed to keep her claws carefully retracted for just the right moment until she could capture and shred her prey. The thought made me most uneasy . . .

Precious Spring had told me that marriages in China were not just the union of a man and woman, but the union of two families and fortunes. I could well understand that concept, for in truth many marriages in England were the same. A woman must marry a man who would improve her social standing and provide a good income, while a man must marry a woman with a generous dowry or, at the least, with a social standing that would not detract from his own.

The idea that Phineas's mother had envisioned an arranged marriage did not surprise me, but I had hoped that she would resign herself to the notion that her son had chosen otherwise. Apparently she would need some persuasion for this to occur, as her behavior the first day did not bode well for my future in Phineas's family. I consoled myself with the thought that we would no doubt soon leave her home and head inland. There were, after all, a multitude of souls to save, and I was anxious to be about my Father's business!

13

⁓⁓⁓⁓

"When can we leave?" I asked Phineas that night when we were finally alone in our room.

He laughed, stretching out on the four-poster wooden-canopy bed. "Is it that bad?"

"Worse." I sat beside him on the edge. "Your mother dislikes me immensely."

"She has not gotten to know you. Give her time."

"That is not the answer I had hoped to hear," I said petulantly. "I thought you were anxious to search for the tea."

He idly rubbed my arm with his fingers. "I must wait for the right moment in the season, when the leaves are golden and ready to pick."

"Will you meet your partner there?"

"Yes." His fingers traveled to my shoulder.

"Have you seen this tea for yourself?"

"Mmm."

"Will you—"

He dropped his hand in exasperation. "Is it your intention to talk all night, wife? Yes, I have seen the tea with my own eyes. Yes, we will leave as soon as possible. Yes, I know that my mother excludes you from my family, but you must avoid her barbs."

"Avoid them? Phineas, they already weigh heavily!" I said bitterly. "She will not give me a chance to speak. When you speak of me, she acts as though I were not even present." I crossed my arms. "I should like to take her to a party in Britain. She could teach the ladies of society a thing or two about delivering the cut direct."

Phineas sat up, laughing, embracing me with one arm. He kissed my cheek. "She will come around, Isabella. She worries about her only son."

I had not seen her husband nor been given any explanation for his absence, though I knew she had remarried after Phineas's father. "She is widowed?" I guessed.

He nodded. "Within the past five years. I was sorry to learn of it . . . for her sake."

· "What about your own father?" I turned closer to Phineas, intrigued. "How did she and your father meet?"

"She was the daughter of a merchant who dealt with the European traders—a member of the *kung-hang*, the officially authorized trading merchants. My father was the captain of an East Indiaman. My mother was allowed to visit the Thirteen Factories with her father, and she and my father met there. They fell in love—unheard of even between a Chinese man and woman. They were secretly married, and though she lived in her father's house, she and my father made plans to return to England."

He sighed. "Unfortunately, she learned she was carrying

a child. When her parents found out, they were furious. To keep their good name, not to mention her reputation, they arranged a quick marriage to another *kung-hang* member, an older man. I believe they told him about the child and paid him extra money to raise it . . . if it was a boy, of course."

"And if a girl?"

Phineas looked at me steadily. "They would no doubt have killed it."

I squeezed his hand. "You were that child."

He nodded. "Though forced into an arranged marriage, my mother was delighted to have me."

"And your true father?"

"He did not know what had happened to my mother, for she disappeared, and he sailed back to England. When he was able to return many years later, he used all his powers to find out if my mother still lived and discovered that not only did she, but so did I."

"He had not known you existed?"

"No. He was heartbroken at first, then angry at my mother for not telling him. He offered her and her husband a great deal of money for me, so that he might take me back to England to be raised. My stepfather had been kind to me, but I am certain that I was a daily reminder of what he felt was my mother's indiscretion with a dreaded foreigner. He eagerly agreed."

"And your mother?"

"She was heartbroken, of course, but she always clung to the hope that she would have other sons to raise. She wanted only to please her husband. After all, what could she do? She had no choice in the matter." He paused. "She gave me the sword as a sign that I would always, rightfully, be her firstborn son."

I leaned against Phineas for contemplation, but he did not give me any time for such. "We should enjoy our time here together," he murmured. "Soon we will be traveling again, and our accommodations will be spartan at best. This house is more than comfortable." He nuzzled my neck.

"This room is exquisite," I agreed, a catch in my breath, but I was not thinking of the furniture or the rugs. Phineas made me forget almost everything when he was so near. "Tell me . . . tell me about Hu-King."

He laughed softly. "Do you yet have need of a story to put you at ease when we are alone together?"

"Is that why you spun the tale?"

He pulled back so that I could see his smile. "It was also for my benefit. I could not sleep with you so near every night. I needed a distraction."

I kissed him, boldly. "Then let us save the story for the morrow," I whispered, just before he extinguished the candle beside our bed.

Phineas left in the morning to buy supplies for our pending journey. I wanted to hide in our room all day, but I awoke in such a pleasant, joyful mood that I disregarded my common sense. Phineas was right, after all; I should give his mother a chance to become acquainted with me.

"There you are," she said when I entered the eating area. "You are a lazy girl to sleep so late."

The sun had barely risen above the horizon, but I put on a smile anyway. She could not spoil my cheerful mood. "Good morning, Nai Nai."

She narrowed her eyes. "You don't have to pretend with me. Ah Chung is not here to be impressed with how you treat his mother."

Perhaps I was wrong about my cheerful mood.

"But I am not pretending," I insisted, eager to be understood. If she could only see my motive, she would no doubt like me! "I want to become acquainted with you, as I hope you do with me."

"I do not," she said. She poured tea from a ceramic pot into a matching cup but offered me none. "I only want you to leave my son so that he can marry a girl who is picked for him."

I sat down and calmly poured a cup of tea for myself. "Did you see a matchmaker? Was such a girl selected?"

Apparently she did not fluster easily. "No. I had waited for his return so that we could accomplish such a thing then hold the wedding. A real wedding."

"Our wedding was very real." I sipped my tea, smiling as I stared off, remembering.

"Stupid girl." Nai Nai slapped my face, and I dropped the cup in surprise. It fell to the floor, shattering, and I covered my cheek. I hated the tears that sprang to my eyes, but I could not hold them back. No one had ever struck me before, and I did not know if the humiliation or the physical sting hurt worse.

"Clean up that mess." She rose, towering over me.

I pushed back my chair and rose. Now it was I who had the advantage of height. "Not unless you apologize." God may have wanted me to show a meek and humble spirit to this woman, but this was not Catherine Ransom with her matchmaking tricks.

Nai Nai snorted. "Apologize for what? That you are a foolish girl who married my son? Bah! This is why we have matchmakers. They know better than the silly hearts of young people. I suppose you will tell me that my son loves you?"

Her words gave me pause. Phineas had never said that. Not in so many words, of course, but I had sensed it in his actions toward me. He had called me beautiful and married me, after all. Was there more to love? Were we lacking something?

"Ah," she said, nodding. "So he does not love you."

"It is only that he has never spoken the words," I said. And neither had I.

She folded her arms. "You should go back to England and leave my son in peace. Surely you aren't here just because of him, are you?"

"No, I'm here because I want to spread the good news of Christianity."

She put back her head and laughed. "How will you do this?"

"I have tracts," I said defensively. "Copies of the Gospel According to St. Luke that a British missionary translated from English into Chinese. People can read for themselves about—"

"Bring me such a paper," she said. Her expression had suddenly gone serious, like someone who only recently learned the world is about to end.

"Certainly." I curtsied without thinking, then hated myself for it while retreating from the room. I found the stack of hand-copied Gospels in Phineas's trunk, still wrapped in Julia's ribbon, and withdrew one. To my surprise, Nai Nai still stood at the table in the eating area. I had imagined that perhaps she had only meant to trick me.

I handed her the booklet, then watched as she studied it. "This was translated by Robert Morrison," I said, "and I—"

Nai Nai tore a strip from the first page and plugged it into the wall. To my horror, she tore another strip and shoved it after the first one. "Holes," she said simply, looking up at me. When she straightened, she called out, "Ting Fong!" The name means "Fragrance."

The young maid entered, and Nai Nai handed her the mutilated tract without so much as a glance in my direction. "Use this when you must start a fire."

Fragrance bowed at her mistress, but there was something defiant in her posture. As she turned away, she glanced at the broken cup on the floor then briefly at my face. She lowered her eyes again. "Would you like someone to clean this up, Madame Wong?" she said, her voice a trifle sharp.

Nai Nai apparently took no notice. "That won't be necessary." She nodded. "You may leave."

Fragrance bowed, a lazy gesture of submission, and complied. Nai Nai looked at me, a curious expression of triumph etching her features. I seethed inwardly, but I would not allow her the upper hand.

"Clean up the mess," she said in a low, dangerous tone.

I could be stubborn too. I turned my cheek, daring her to strike me again. "No." Without waiting for her reply, I turned and left, not looking back, leaving the cup and spilled tea still on the floor.

Any sympathy I had had for Phineas's mother withered and died. I did not want to hide in my room until Phineas returned, but neither did I want to risk running into her again. Fortunately, I found a garden with a wooden bench where I could sit. I studied the strange flowers and plants growing there. I had been told that Canton was called the City of Flowers, for they grew year round, but suddenly I missed the English gardens in Oxford. I had memories of playing among the hollyhocks and daisies and marigolds with Frederica when I was very young, then helping Flora plant flowers of our own when I was older.

I had worked hard to get to China, to learn the language and try to blend in with the culture, and one tiny woman with an enormous grudge was the near undoing of my plans! I could not believe that she would so heartlessly destroy not only the Scriptures I had so carefully copied, but the Word of God himself. Thankfully I was past tears, but I felt loneliness and heartbreak as heavily as ever I had experienced since leaving home. I began to wonder if I had been so very wrong about everything.

"Isabella!"

I turned, and Phineas stood at the opposite side of the garden. He smiled when he saw me, then hastened forward. I could not help smiling back. Would I do everything over again? Ah yes, here was my answer!

He cupped my elbows with his hands. "How pale you look," he said, then turned my face to one side. "But you are red here. What happened?"

I considered then discarded the notion of telling him the truth. It was not my nature to prevaricate, but no good could come from lowering his mother in his eyes. "It is nothing, Phineas. I was not paying attention and walked into a doorway. It will be fine . . . Did you procure the supplies?"

"Yes. As soon as the season is right, we can leave for Hupei." He kissed my forehead. "I know you are anxious to leave, yet your willingness to visit my mother completes my joy."

I was glad that he could not see my face, for he would surely find guilt written there. Guilt and an important question that his mother had raised. "I . . . I care about you, Phineas. You do know that . . . don't you?"

"Of course I do." He smiled. "Just as I care for you."

There! That was as good as saying the three magic words, was it not?

"Did you spend time with my mother this morning?" he said.

So much for magic. "We had tea together," I said, relating the only honest thing that I could.

"Good." He kissed the tip of my nose, then my cheeks, then my lips. "She is a lonely old lady."

She is a bitter *old lady. Violent too!* "Phineas," I said, before we were both lost in the moment.

"Shhh." He put his arms around me more securely, and giving in, I embraced him as well.

Someone cleared her throat, and Nai Nai stood at the opposite side of the garden. Phineas and I separated guiltily. Nai Nai's mouth worked open and closed like the orange and white carp swimming in the pond. "Yes, Mother?" Phineas finally said pleasantly.

Nai Nai glanced at me, then at Phineas, as though trying to ascertain how much I had told. I lifted my chin to let her know that I would never stoop to have my husband fight my battles for me.

"Is everything all right?" Phineas said, frowning.

She cleared her throat again. "Yes. I only wanted to see that you were home safely. You have not told me where you are going so soon when you have only just arrived yesterday."

So he had not told his mother about his plan! That was certainly curious. I glanced at Phineas to check his expression, but he revealed nothing. "We can discuss it tonight at dinner if you like," he said amiably.

"That would be suitable. Please forgive me for the intrusion."

"You have not told her?" I said when we were alone.

Phineas sighed and sat on the bench. "There is no need, Isabella. She and I seldom speak of my father, and she has no notion of the East India Company's commerce. Her husband never spoke of business matters with her, and she only knew that he dealt with foreigners."

"Has she forgotten about your father completely?" I sat beside him. "Does she not remember their love?"

"I believe she has chosen not to," he said. "Just as she would not remember me if I had not returned to China."

How cruel. How very cold and cruel! She was a heartless woman, indeed. I took Phineas's hand and held it as if I could keep him close forever. "My mother probably has some medicine for that mark on your face," he said. "Would you like me to ask?"

"No. It will be fine. Phineas?"

"Yes?" He smiled.

"I do not ever want to lose you the way your mother lost your father," I whispered.

"And you will not," he said, kissing me for good measure. "Isabella, I want you beside me. We are warriors together, yes?"

I nodded, thinking of the family sword he had given me. His mother would most likely halve me herself if she knew it to be in my possession!

The welt on my cheek disappeared, as did the broken ceramic cup and spilled tea. I never knew if Nai Nai had Fragrance clean it up or if she herself did the deed. It did not matter to me. I would not tell him myself, but I would have been happy to have heard Phineas ask about the broken cup and for his mother to be forced to confess.

I still could not fathom that she had destroyed the Gospel I had so painstakingly copied by hand. No doubt the characters were shaky and perhaps even a trifle illegible, but like the monks of old who labored at the Book of Kells, I had endeavored to make the rendering as accurate as possible. I wondered if the tiny bit she had stuffed into the wall was still there . . .

As for walls, something strange occurred to me one afternoon. Phineas had left for an errand for his mother, as ladies did not venture from their homes. I, being weary, decided on a nap. I had just headed down the hallway toward my room when someone pushed me against the wall and felt under my skirt for my feet, one of which was lifted. I cried out, more in surprise than pain.

Nai Nai jerked off my slipper and stocking. "Just as I suspected," she said in an accusing tone. "You have large feet."

"I beg your pardon!"

"Good women—women with class—have their feet bound when they are girls. Your feet are natural. Large."

She reached for them again, and I hopped away. "My feet are not large. They are rather small in nature, actually."

She shook her head, scowling. "Very large."

"Yes, well, would you please leave me alone now?" I said, reminding myself to lock the bedroom door. No telling if she would try to follow me to criticize more of my body parts!

Because of that incident, however, I made a note to study the feet of Phineas's sister and mother. Only Nai Nai walked with a hobble, but their feet stayed hidden under their skirts. Perhaps it was no accident, if they could hold such power as to pull men under their spell. Apparently the mere sight of their supposedly tiny feet might send some men into a swoon.

I did not have to wonder long, for that afternoon I again retreated to the garden. This time Little Sister joined me. She often followed me around like a shadow when I first arrived, quiet, but once I had been there a few days, she apparently felt free to ask a multitude of questions. When she learned I spoke Chinese, no matter how halting, she peppered me with questions about England, about the *Dignity*, about fashion and books . . . She was hungry for knowledge and conversation. I often said a thankful prayer that she had somehow managed to survive. Many Chinese parents murdered newborn girls because they would only grow up and marry into another family.

Little Sister sat beside me on the bench, tucking her feet carefully under her skirt before I could see them. "Why are your feet so large?" she said without preamble. "Did your parents not want your feet to be small?"

"Foot binding is not something that is done where I come from," I said, then paused. "Are your feet bound?"

Little Sister shyly pushed her feet out from behind her skirt. To my relief, they seemed normal. "Mother would have bound my feet," she said, "but when I reached the proper age, Elder Brother would not allow it. It was right after Father died, so Elder Brother's wish was followed." She looked wistful. "Mother says my chances to marry have been reduced."

She was so young to be concerned about such matters!

301

"They are still very small next to mine, are they not?" I said, holding out my own feet.

"Yes, Tai Soi." Little Sister called me Eldest Sister-in-law, giggled, then immediately sobered. "I'm sorry. I shouldn't have laughed." She tucked her feet back under her skirt.

I did the same. "It's all right, Little Sister."

"Are you and Elder Brother going to stay here forever?"

I did not know what Nai Nai had told the girl, but I determined to tell her the truth. "We will be leaving soon."

"Will you return?"

"I do not think so, Little Sister." The truth was that I was not certain what would happen to Phineas and me once we arrived in Hupei. After all, his plan was to find the golden tea leaf then use its sales to put the East India Company out of business. Which would, of course, mean eventually returning to England.

That, however, was not in my plans. Neither was staying at his mother's house much longer!

"You will return with me, naturally," Phineas said when I asked him about it that night when we were alone at last, preparing for bed.

"I have not thought of returning to England." I fluffed my pillow and burrowed my head into it. I yawned, exhausted. "My calling, I believe, is to stay in China."

Phineas laid his head on his own pillow, beside mine. "Even missionaries sometimes return to their homeland," he said.

"But—"

He put his fingers over my lips. "I know what you are about to say, Isabella. You do not want me to attempt to find this golden leaf tea and bring it back to England."

"I still do not fathom how your plan will work. I cannot believe you can compete with the East India Company."

"Perhaps not, but I must at least attempt it." He paused. "Lives are being ruined in this country, Isabella. People are dying. Surely you must understand the urgency."

I raised up on one elbow. "I do, Phineas, but I am not certain this is the best way."

"My mother also does not wish me to go to Hupei."

"Of course not. You are her only son."

"There is more to that than the relationship between Mr. Gilpin and his mother. In China, a son, even once married, lives in his parents' house. He is expected to take over the household, with his wife caring for the home."

"Then I should think her pleased that we were leaving so that she need not fear my usurping her authority," I said. No wonder Nai Nai had resented my presence, even before we met.

"You have read her fears, which are not uncommon to Chinese mothers of sons. That she has all but begged me to stay is an indication that she is willing to accept that fear instead of the alternative."

"And what is that?"

Phineas touched my cheek. "Being alone for the rest of her life. One day Little Sister will marry and move into her husband's home. Then who will care for my mother?"

"Can she not remarry?"

303

"It is possible but not likely. Widows generally stay widows in China and are not encouraged to take another husband. Their chastity is highly prized. I think, too, that she is not willing to face heartbreak yet a third time."

He blew out the candle and took me in his arms. After only a few days, I had come to rely on his physical presence, particularly at the close of day. In such a short time, I had learned what it meant to share my life with another. I was certain it was not something one could easily abandon, even after death. Lately the thought of losing Phineas, after all we had endured to gain one another, had hovered like a specter during my every waking moment. I could not shake it no matter how I tried to remove it from my thoughts.

"I am looking forward to our journey," I whispered. "Tell me about the Mo Tong Mountains. When did you first go there?"

"The mountains are home to many monasteries, as you know. I learned martial arts there several years ago when I first returned from England—as a man. My mother and stepfather were dismayed that I had embraced Christianity, so they sent me there, hoping the Daoist monks would influence me."

"And did they?"

"I am not fully Chinese, so I was not allowed in the temples or monasteries. However, one man became my *sifu*, my martial arts master, and I met many other students. My time there did not sway my beliefs. If anything, it reinforced them. The Mo Tong—the mountains themselves—have breathtaking valleys and cliffs and much vegetation and rocks on tall, steep peaks. Sometimes the mist shrouds the ancient buildings and stairways that seem to reach to heaven." He kissed the top of my head. "I felt very close to God there. I hope you will too. It is a beautiful place."

I shivered. We could not leave this home soon enough. I had wanted adventure for so long, and Phineas and I were near to realizing our dreams. In the darkness I held him closer as though I could hold him to the earth, our relationship a sapling threatened by a coming wind.

To prepare for our journey, Phineas insisted that we practice martial arts together in the grassy area of the garden. I smiled every time I thought of the expression on Flora's face if she could see how I had learned to kick at an opponent's head or punch much like one of the prizefighters at a boxing salon in London. Somehow I imagined that Uncle Toby would be pleased, for he had always indulged my hoydenish nature. Anything that allowed me to protect myself could only be good, in his eyes.

I wore the inexpressibles and loose top that Phineas had given me aboard the *Dignity*, and it felt good to have such freedom of movement. Such freedom was not without cost, however. Phineas refused to spare me from a harsh accounting, challenging my kicks and blocks in rapid progression. He spoke not a word, but I knew from the expression on his face that he meant to push my abilities. When at last he must have realized I was winded and spent (which indeed I was), he knocked me to the soft grass by sweeping his feet behind my knees. I dropped like a winged bird—unhurt, save for my pride.

He helped me up. I, grim-faced, assumed a defensive position. "Be prepared to counter that move," he said. He did not allow me the quick, heated retaliation I desired but slowly, patiently demonstrated several kicks and distracting arm movements. I forgot that I wanted to bring him to the earth the same way he had me and practiced the moves until he nodded his satisfaction. Emotion had little place in martial arts, I was learning, but I did not always heed the lesson.

He bowed. "I think that is enough for today, Isabella. You look peaked."

"If I am, it is only because I am anxious to fight you again." I smiled, assuming an offensive stance.

"That is enough for now," he said firmly.

"Can we practice with the sword?" I was not ready to finish our lesson.

He shook his head. "Your possession of the sword should be our secret."

"You do not want your mother to know that I have it, do you?"

"No," he said flatly. "I do not."

I bowed, defeated before we had even begun again. "Very well. I will change my clothes."

He winked at me. "May I go with you?"

"I think not." I laughed in spite of myself. "I am peaked, after all." Before he could respond, I left the garden and headed toward our room.

I hummed a cheerful tune, for every day drew us one

closer to leaving. Passing Nai Nai's room, I could not help noticing her open door. She had said little to me of late, perhaps resigned that I was taking her son away from her.

I meant only to glance through the door, as one's gaze flits involuntarily. But I saw her seated on a willow chair, shoes and stockings off, and it was then that I saw her unbound feet.

I had never seen flesh so hideous. I had imagined binding meant only a restriction of the feet's growth so that they were somehow only smaller lengths. But the arch of Nai Nai's feet was high and pronounced, the toes curled sideways under and to the soles like the folds of an ugly fan. She rubbed them carefully, and it was obvious from her unguarded expression that she was in pain though her foot binding had ceased many, many years ago.

Catching my breath, I backed against the wall lest she think I spied on her. Against my will, tears sprang to my eyes as they had when she slapped me. In truth, I felt as though I had been slapped again, but it was surely pain much less severe than what she had endured for many years. I headed blindly for my room, grateful for the steadiness of my own feet.

Fragrance passed me in the hallway, bearing a bowl of steaming water. I stopped short. "Is that for Madame Wong?"

She yawned. "Yes. But first I have to chat with the other servant girl. We have been planning a long talk."

"The water will likely be cold when you get it to your mistress," I said, frowning at her lack of concern.

"No matter." She shrugged. "That old lady isn't going anywhere. Most likely she'll smoke some opium. She'll fall asleep and forget she asked me to bring the water for her feet anyway."

I felt much as I had when Phineas knocked me to the ground. "She partakes of the drug?"

Fragrance narrowed her eyes. "What do you care? I know you don't like her. If it keeps her from bothering you, it's to your advantage, isn't it?"

Without waiting for an answer, she bustled away with the pan, sloshing water as she went.

Shocked, I took refuge in the room, sitting on the edge of the bed to gather my thoughts. My head and heart could not reconcile all I had seen and heard with what I had hoped for the future. My picture of Nai Nai was rapidly changing, but surely it did not matter. Phineas and I would be leaving soon. Her life would return to the way it was before we arrived. She had survived without us; she would manage again. Little Sister would no doubt be all right, as well. Besides, it was not my concern.

14

I tried to speak to Phineas about his mother many times. She had apparently kept hidden her opium usage, but perhaps she was even addicted. As for the deformity of her feet—did he know the extent of the damage? He obviously knew the practice to be barbaric or he would not have ordered Little Sister's feet left unbound. Did he know how his mother still suffered?

He had a right to know about her opium usage, yet I saw the tender way he cared for her. He loved her, and it was obvious she truly loved him. What could he do for her if he did not go to the mountains for the tea? Just as he would resent me for preventing his travel, he would resent her too.

I found it difficult to believe, but my heart had softened toward Nai Nai. I wanted to help her or, barring that, at least understand her.

"Perhaps we should delay our journey," I said to Phineas one morning as we dressed for the day. I needed more time to think about his family. I needed more time to think about us.

Phineas looked at me curiously. "I thought you were anxious to leave."

"I am, but . . ." I could not bring myself to speak the trouble that was in my heart. I am not certain why. Had we not agreed to have no secrets between us?

He frowned. "The leaves are only golden for several weeks. We must gather as much as we can, press them into cakes, and get them aboard a ship to take back to England." He sat beside me and took my hand. "Why do you no longer wish to go?"

No secrets. We must have nothing between us, no matter what the cost. "Your mother slapped me," I said, thinking to begin with that.

"What?" He rose. "When? Why?"

"Remember the red mark on my cheek days ago? I did not walk into a doorway, as I said. She slapped me."

He headed for the door. "I will talk to her. She cannot do this."

"Wait." I put a hand on his wrist to stay his departure. I had been prepared to tell him about the opium, but I lost my composure. "Your mother is . . . she . . ." I could not help it; I began to cry. These were no false tears, either, designed to persuade a man to do a woman's bidding. I wept because I suddenly felt exceeding sorrow for that old woman and all she had been through, all she was going through.

Misunderstanding my motives, Phineas took me in his

arms. "I am so sorry, Isabella. We will leave here at once. I had no idea she had treated you this way."

"She does not want us married, but that is not why I weep. I feel sorry for her."

He pulled away. "Sorrow?"

"Y-yes. She is old and lonely, and you have said that she is not likely to remarry. Little Sister will grow up and move away. Who will care for her then, Phineas? You have plans to find your precious tea leaves and return to England."

He turned away, running his hands through his hair. "I cannot stay here, Isabella. I cannot be who my mother wants me to be or even who you want me to be."

"And what is that?" I heard the sharpness in my voice but did nothing to prevent it.

"You want me to abandon my plan to gather the tea and sell it."

"I find the notion foolish."

"So you have said." Did his voice sound as cold as I thought, or did I imagine it?

"Do you deny that once you find the leaves you will return to England?"

He turned toward me. "Not England. America."

"I do not understand."

"Isabella." He sighed and took my hand. "Remember the couple who were to be at the Ransoms' party where we met?"

"The Tippetts?"

He nodded. "William Tippett looks to start a tea trading company, much like the East India Company, only in

America. Tea is quite popular there as well as Britain, and he hopes eventually to put the East India Company out of business. I have convinced him that the golden tea leaves are the best means of doing so. I was originally in London to discuss our business. We came to Oxford to research information about tea, and of course, I wanted to meet your uncle. When we were invited to the party, Mr. Tippett and his wife invented an excuse to decline. They did not want to answer a lot of questions about the nature of two Americans in England."

"With good reason. We are at war with them, Phineas."

"Yes."

I folded my arms. "That does not trouble you?"

"Not particularly, no. My concern is not with whatever silly squabble Britain has with the lost colonies. I am only interested in stopping the opium trade here in China."

"The way to help those who abuse opium is to prevent them from using more of the drug."

"The only way to do that is to prevent it from coming into the country altogether! Can you not see that? I have to stop the men who profit from its sale." He shook his head. "You are naïve, Isabella. Do you think that I can stop everyone in China from partaking of the drug?"

"And do you think that you can stop all the tea in China from getting into British hands by way of illegal trade?" My eyes stung with tears. "You and your precious golden tea leaves . . . You are the one who is naïve."

He stared at me, hard, and I knew instinctively that I had wounded his pride. "You are not fit to be a missionary," he said in a low voice. "You cannot care for others when you have doubted, nay, insulted, the one person you should care for most."

"And you have never said that you loved me," I said, reacting impulsively to his own wounding blow.

He stared at me again, then he left the room, closing the door firmly behind him.

I sank to a teak chair, holding my head in my hands. I could not stay, I could not go. Most of all, I realized, Phineas was right. What had I been thinking? I was not fit to spread the gospel. I could not even please my own husband.

I am sorry to recount that we avoided each other for much of the day. Phineas spent time with his mother, and I entertained Little Sister. She and I sat on the bench in the garden, and I entertained her with tales of England and what my life had been like there. She especially enjoyed hearing about my clothing, and I smiled to remember the pink slippers with the Chinese symbol.

Since we were at odds, it pained me to recount the Ransoms' party where I had met Phineas, but I thought she might enjoy hearing about the dresses all the ladies wore. She seemed most interested in mine. "You wore white?" she said.

"Yes."

She shuddered. "What a strange country you come from, Eldest Sister-in-law. We don't wear white except at funerals."

Phineas stood at the entrance to the garden.

313

I smiled at the girl. "Little Sister, you must leave. We can talk more later."

She returned my smile and left. Phineas walked to the bench but did not take her place. "I have spoken to my mother, and she is sorry for slapping you."

"I did not mean for you to speak to her about it," I said.

"Nevertheless, it needed to be discussed. She assures me that it will not happen again."

Then he sat beside me, though stiffly. "Isabella . . ." He cleared his throat. "Isabella, I am leaving tomorrow. It is time to travel to Hupei."

My heart pounded.

"I would like for you to leave with me," he continued, though I could ascertain no enthusiasm in his voice. "I know we have spoken of this day for a very long time and that you have worked hard to prepare the tracts you wish to hand out."

I clenched my teeth to stall the tears.

He turned toward me. "Will you say nothing?"

"I cannot go," I said in a small voice.

His expression did not alter. "I have said that I want you with me."

I shook my head. "Though I have my doubts about that at the moment, I know that they will pass. I know little of marriage, but I know that any two people who have pledged to share their lives must encounter some argument along the way. That we should find ourselves at such a point after mere days of being wed is disheartening but not, I am certain, the end of our relationship."

He looked relieved. "Then you are not angry with me?"

"No. Nor you with me?"

He took my hands. "Of course not," he whispered. "So you will go with me?"

"You know that I cannot countenance this silly tea business, particularly now that I know you are working with Americans."

He dropped my hands, exasperated. "Isabella—"

I placed two fingers on his lips. "It is more than that, Phineas. No, I cannot countenance it, and so I do not wish to be a part of it, no matter how much I want to be with you and to travel to these mountains. Beyond that, there are higher considerations."

"Such as?"

"Your mother and your sister. Who will care for them?"

A shadow crossed his face. "Who will care for them when we leave China? Perhaps they should become accustomed to the idea now. They knew I—we—would not stay in Canton for long."

But Nai Nai cannot be relied upon to care for herself, let alone Little Sister! "Your mother has no one, Phineas. Even the servants show her little respect, have you noticed?"

"Yes, I have. I can speak to them." He sighed. "If this is about what I said earlier about you not being fit to be a missionary . . ."

I shook my head. "It is not. But it is about my caring for your sister—and mother—while you are gone. When you return . . ."

I stumbled on the words because I suddenly felt a wave

315

of apprehension—the old fears—that he would somehow never make his way back to Canton and that we would be parted forever.

"When I return . . ." he prompted.

I drew a deep breath. "When you return . . . we will leave together as you have planned. My place is with you, whether in China, Britain, or America. But for now perhaps, at least, I can help your mother to . . . to establish some sort of order in her home in the meantime."

He touched my cheek. "I was wrong. You are not naïve, only tenderhearted. How can I leave you here?"

"How can you have any other choice? You have seen that I can care for myself, so you need not worry about me."

"But I will," he said softly. "Every minute."

I smiled, trying to lighten the moment. "Then it will motivate you to gather the leaves and return to Canton as quickly as possible."

He moved closer, his face only inches from mine. "And will you worry about me?"

I trembled. "Yes, of course," I whispered. "Every minute."

He kissed me then, longing welling between us. Later that night we held each other close, whispering to each other in Chinese and English, sharing memories, foolishly planning for a future that we both unspokenly knew might not be. At dawn we awoke, and as I drowsily struggled to awaken, Phineas whispered in my ear. "Isabella, I love you."

I opened my eyes.

He smiled at me. "I have loved you for a very long time. Have you not known that?"

I should never have let his mother's words cause doubt to fester in my heart. "I have known it," I whispered back. "I love you too."

"Nothing can separate us," he said. "You know that I will return from the mountains, don't you?"

"Yes." I lied to hide my fear. "Though perhaps you will board another ship and try to evade me again?"

He laughed softly. "And you will follow," he said, joining in the tale. "But this time I will know exactly where to look. You have a fondness for cows, I believe."

I could not help the smile that curved my lips. My days with Bossy seemed so very far away and long ago.

His expression sobered. "If I had known you to be the kind of woman I know you are now, I would not have wanted to lie about the Chinese symbols of bravery embroidered on your slippers. Your character is evidence enough of that trait."

"I don't know if I can be brave," I said. "Even before you have gone, I find myself already afraid."

"But you *are* brave"—he kissed my temple—"and unselfish. You are like Ruth who followed Naomi to care for her."

"The Bible does not say whether Naomi was lovable or irritating," I said. "Perhaps she was a gentle companion for the younger Ruth and therefore no burden."

"My mother will be a burden for you. I am aware of her faults. I have an idea that Julia Whipple will have a much

317

easier time with Thomas Gilpin's mother than you will with mine. But I love her dearly." He kissed me again. "And I thank you for caring for her in my absence. Particularly as you are giving up the future you have worked so hard to obtain."

I wished he had not mentioned my plans. I had told myself that I was being noble for abandoning them, but in truth, all I could think of at that moment was that the only loss that mattered to me was him.

He touched my hair, smiling. "You are indeed a spontaneous creature, Isabella. Will you change your mind about me while I am gone?"

"Never," I whispered. "My spontaneity has brought sorrow to those I love. I see now that I was selfish in leaving Uncle Toby and Flora, that I thought only of myself. I pray that they forgive me."

"You are not selfish. Quite the opposite. You wanted only to help others."

I realized then the fear Uncle Toby must have felt when Flora returned without me. What if Phineas did not return? Who would give me even an inkling of his fate? It was a long journey . . . Mountains were steep . . . Bandits might lurk at any bend . . .

I held him close, fear overtaking me. "Please come back to me," I whispered.

"We will be together again," he insisted, kissing me. "You have my pledge."

His words meant no deception as they had when we had first met, but I did not know that I could trust them still. So much in life was beyond mortal control—destiny, some would call it, God's will, others. I suddenly realized that I had traveled this great distance not to find adventure, but love, and I wondered if Phineas and I would have been better served—safer—to have found that love back in England.

He left soon after the sun rose, and I could barely speak, so heartbroken was I. I doubted my motives for staying in Canton when his mother merely nodded at him as a farewell. Surely she did not need someone to look after her! Naturally, I felt instant shame at the notion, but I do confess that my heart longed to journey with him and leave her to fend for herself.

At last Phineas drew me aside, and after giving me a final kiss, whispered, "I cannot bear to be parted from you. I promise to return as soon as I possibly can. Do you believe me?"

I nodded mutely, accepting a final embrace, then watched as he left the safety of his mother's home. After he had disappeared from view, Nai Nai gave me an evil glare, then went inside the compound to the house. Little Sister lingered with me for a moment, slipping her hand into mine. She had come to adore Phineas in the short time they had become reacquainted with one another, and I sensed she would miss him greatly.

Still hand in hand, she and I walked back into the house, silent. How would we three pass the time until he returned . . . if he did at all?

I decided to secretly take stock of the house—was everything in order? Were the servants performing as they should? Was there a secret stash of opium somewhere?

Naturally, Nai Nai caught me scouring her room for evidence. To say that she was livid would be an understatement. "What are you looking for?" she demanded as I guiltily closed her dresser drawer.

"What might I be looking for?" I challenged her, hoping that she would confess right away.

"Money, probably. That must be the only reason you married my son. You bewitched him into marrying you so that you could steal my money."

In truth, this woman rivaled all the selfish thinking of Mrs. Akers! "Were you aware that Phineas did that very thing to me? He flirted with me to gain my uncle's money."

Her face reddened. "He would never do anything like that. He is a good son."

"He is sorry for what he did, yes."

"See?" She folded her arms. "I know that you didn't leave with him so that you could stay here to torment me. You want to take over my house."

"I only want to help," I said. "I did not want you and Little Sister to be alone."

"Bah! We have been alone for a long time now. We are fine."

I wondered if it was too late to try to join Phineas. Surely it would not be difficult to find the Hupei province! How large could China be, anyway?

I took a deep breath. "Nai Nai, I know that you are using opium. I would like to discuss it with you."

"If I would not talk about it to him, what makes you think I would talk about it with you? It is none of your concern, and if you try to interfere, I will throw you out of my home."

She flounced out of the room, or would have, if her tiny feet had permitted a faster gait. I was glad to see it, though, for it reminded me to be sympathetic and charitable. I was inclined that way as long as I could focus on her feet—so to speak.

The rest of the first day was, I believe, painful for all three of us. Nai Nai moved through the house in stony silence, snapping at the cook, Fragrance, and the gardener. Little Sister sat at a chessboard most of the day, staring at the pieces. I asked her if she knew how to play, and she shook her head. "My father was going to teach me, but he died."

"Would you like for me to teach you?"

"Another time." She shook her head again and went back to studying the pieces, picking up each one as though it were for the first time.

I could not sleep that night, so heartsick was I. I had shared a room with Phineas for so long that the loneliness overwhelmed me. I curled up in a ball and finally fell asleep near daybreak. Of course I slept much later than usual, prompting many critical words from Nai Nai. I gritted my teeth and ignored them.

For the next few days, she found fault in everything I

did, from how I arranged a vase of camellia blossoms, to my chess playing with Little Sister, to even how I looked.

"Why my son married you, with such hideous feet, is beyond my understanding," she said, eyeing my slippers as I tucked them under my skirt.

Yes, and I can at least walk at a normal, civilized gait! "Phineas married me for more than my feet," I said smugly.

She laughed. "Chinese men like women with small feet."

I prayed she would speak no further on the matter, and thankfully, she did not. She returned to her embroidery work, which I must confess I admired greatly. She stitched the tiniest of flowers and animals on red silk. I had seen her handiwork on decorative pillows, and I wondered how she would employ the silk of this project but did not dare ask. I had asked Fragrance for my own embroidery materials, but Nai Nai had criticized my efforts so much that I decided to work on them only when alone.

We coexisted thusly for several weeks. I found I spent more time with Little Sister than Nai Nai, who disappeared for hours on end. When she did, the servants became lazy and insolent, refusing to obey not only me but Little Sister. Our meals seemed less fresh and appetizing, as though thrown together with scraps. Sometimes Nai Nai did not eat with us, and I wondered if she was taking meals in her room. One day she did not appear at all, and when I inquired about her, Fragrance only smiled mockingly. I feared that much was amiss, and I awoke one morning determined.

What was needed was for me to take over the household. Phineas had said that daughters-in-law often did so, and while my courtesy was to allow Nai Nai the management of her own home, someone had to stop her opium use as well as the laziness of the servants.

The first thing I did was to question the servants to see if they had noticed anything amiss. I started with Cook. He was displeased at my presence, never mind my endless questioning: Did someone go to market every day for fresh food? Did Madame Wong leave much of her food untouched? (I had heard that opium addicts lost interest in food.) Was he preparing as much as he should for Little Sister and me? Yes, yes, yes, he said, finally brandishing a cleaver and admonishing me to allow him to return to his work.

Fragrance was of more help. She said that Nai Nai had only begun to smoke opium within the past few months, but obviously it had begun to affect her management of the house. Fragrance often had to remind her of many basic details, such as seeing that everyone (particularly the servants, she noted) was clothed and fed on a regular basis. I found it interesting that she made no mention of neither Nai Nai's nor Little Sister's welfare.

When I inquired where Nai Nai secured the opium, her gaze flickered downward for just a moment.

"Oh, Fragrance, how could you?" I said. "She is your mistress."

She raised her head defiantly. "She asked me to find it for her. I do as I am told."

When you feel like it, apparently. "And do you also pocket a small sum for its procurement?"

"I don't know what you mean."

"I think you do," I said, folding my arms.

She sighed. "Very well. My betrothed knows some of the foreign traders near the port, and Madame Wong buys it from him through me. Of course I get a small sum for my trouble."

"I want you to stop. Now," I said firmly. "You will be the death of Madame Wong, and then where would you go?" For some reason, I thought about Julia Whipple and breathed a prayer of thanks that she had found a happier life.

Fragrance laughed. "I will go with my betrothed."

And I am certain that he has a lovely home and a charming life for you. "Until such time as you are no longer in the employ of Madame Wong—and that time may come sooner than you think—you must buy no more opium. Is that understood?" I drew myself up to my full height. "I am in charge."

I must have employed the precise amount of command, for she bowed.

For a first day's work, I felt rather pleased with myself. Now to speak with Nai Nai.

I found her in her room, sitting on a chair and staring out the window, hands folded in her lap. Her eyes seemed dull and unfocused, the smell of a sweetish smoke clinging to her clothes. I knew that she was probably under the drug's influence.

I turned to leave. "You have assumed command of my house," she said.

I entered the room and stood beside her. "I thought it best."

She turned to me, unblinking. "Best for you, of course."

"You are . . . troubled lately," I said. I saw no reason to discuss her drug use when she was currently under its wicked spell.

"I am troubled for my son. You are not the proper wife for him."

Thank you for your thoughtful words! "He believes that I am," I said. "Marriage is the choice of a man and a woman where we live." I thought of David and Catherine Ransom and added silently, *Most of the time!*

"That is what his father told me too. He was wrong."

I knelt before her chair. "Nai Nai, I am sorry for what happened so many years ago. I am certain that you have endured much grief. A heart once broken is not easily mended."

"I will endure even more when my son returns. He tells me that you and he plan to return to your foreign land again."

I paused. "I do not wish it so."

"You would remain in China?"

"That is why I traveled here. To stay."

She closed her eyes, and I thought I saw a dreamy smile cross her face. Within a moment, her head nodded forward. I rose, alarmed, but then I heard a gentle snore and knew her merely to be asleep.

I called for Fragrance to help me, and we saw Nai Nai into her bed. Fragrance departed as quickly as possible, but I remained to see that Nai Nai was adequately covered. Her face had a waxy yellow cast, and she appeared older than I had ever seen her.

"Is Mother going to be all right?" Little Sister said from the doorway.

I turned, wondering how much of the truth Little Sister knew. I held my fingers to my lips even though I doubted we could disturb Nai Nai. I tiptoed to the door for effect, however, and beckoned Little Sister outside. "She is not feeling well," I said.

Little Sister made a face. "She has not been feeling well much at all lately. I wish Elder Brother were still here. She was happy then."

Little Sister shuffled down the hall, her head hanging low. Anger rose in my heart that Nai Nai could be so selfish as to ignore her daughter this way. It was time for something to be done, I determined, and I would tell Nai Nai—whenever I next saw her—that that smoke had been her last.

Fragrance grudgingly led me to Nai Nai's stash of opium, of which I personally oversaw the destruction. As much as I liked the opium-infused Nai Nai for her quiet and mild state more than the normal, bellicose Nai Nai, I was determined to confront her. She did not appear for breakfast, and I lingered over my *congee*, thinking of Phineas.

The fear that he might not return had not abated. Nor had my longing for him. Was he so focused on obtaining the tea leaves that he had forgotten me? Would his desire for me be overwhelmed with the sense of purpose he had had ever since we first met? Would bandits waylay him along the road?

Fragrance appeared at the table, startling me. "My betrothed, Chow Wah, is here to see you, Mistress." She beckoned him toward the table, and a scruffier fellow I do not believe I have ever seen. How could she bring him here? Surely she knew the proper etiquette would have been for me to have met him in a more formal setting. I was still at my breakfast, for goodness' sake!

She did not even bow, but stepped back, a little smile on her face. Chow Wah stared at me coldly, acknowledging me with no greeting. "Fragrance has told me that you have destroyed Madame Wong's opium."

"That is true."

His face brightened. "Then perhaps she will buy some today. My interest is not in a completed sale, but in future sales."

"There will be no future commerce between Madame Wong and yourself," I said firmly. "She does not need what you sell."

"That is for her to decide."

"It is for me, as her daughter-in-law and the only one who seems to care about her welfare." I frowned at him. "You are fortunate that my husband is not here, for he would give you an earful about trading with foreigners who do not care for your country or its citizens."

He laughed. "I don't care about what my customers do with the product. I am only interested in their money."

"Obviously. Now you must leave."

He folded his arms. "Not without speaking to Madame Wong."

"Very well." I turned to Fragrance. "If you do not show Chow Wah out, you may pack your bags and go with him."

Her jaw dropped. "But I—"

I raised a brow.

"Very well." She bowed at me, then gestured for Chow Wah to leave. He gave me one final glare but thankfully departed.

When Fragrance returned, I asked her to call all the servants. She kept her expression carefully hidden, so I could not gauge her attitude. They appeared in short order, however, and I stood before them like Captain Malfort in front of his crew aboard the *Dignity*. Indeed, this household was not much different than a ship, and if we were to stay afloat, we must all labor together toward the same purpose.

"A man was admitted to Madame Wong's household today, a man by the name of Chow Wah," I said. "I am certain that you know him, for Fragrance claims him as her betrothed."

Fragrance glanced downward, but the others stared at me, attentive.

"He is not to be admitted to this home again, and anyone who does so will find himself unemployed and on the street. Is that clear?"

They all nodded. From some of the expressions on their faces, I gathered that they were already familiar with Chow Wah's charming nature.

"Fragrance?" I prodded.

She looked me in the eye, and her gaze could have cowed a lesser lady. I, however, would have none of it. I met her expression measure for measure until she glanced away. She gave a quick nod.

I relaxed. "Madame Wong is not well," I said. "We must all take extra care in our duties, particularly keeping her and Miss Splendor in mind. This is their home. We must do what we can to make their lives comfortable. I will brook no laziness, neglect, or disrespect. Is that clear?"

Again they nodded, Fragrance with them this time. Some of them actually looked relieved. Uncle Toby had been an easygoing man, but once or twice over the years, I had seen him speak sternly with an indifferent servant, and both had always been the better for it.

"You may go about your work," I said, then before they dispersed, I called them to attention. "One more thing: on behalf of my husband and myself, thank you for your faithfulness to Madame Wong. Now you may go."

They bowed politely, and I saw not a trace of disrespect in their posture. They had all been with the Wong family for many years, and I was relieved to see that they did not appear on the verge of mutiny after all; they simply desired reassurance of a firm hand in control.

I would like to say that Nai Nai shared their desire, but unfortunately, her opinion took an opposite tack. Later that day the opium seemed to have worn off, and she actually sought me out in my room, Fragrance apparently having informed her that the drug had been destroyed.

329

Nai Nai threw open my door, her eyes hard as unburned coal. "Why have you usurped my authority?"

I rose from the chair, where I had been trying to embroider. "You are not yourself, Nai Nai. Someone needed to—"

A scream sounded throughout the house, followed by the sound of shouts and running feet. Fragrance, white as death, pushed an equally frightened-looking Little Sister into my room. "I am sorry," she said, bowing quickly at both Nai Nai and me. "My betrothed has sent evil men to this house. They are wrecking everything, and I fear they intend damage to us as well!"

Nai Nai shrieked, leveling accusing eyes at me. "You did this! Now we will all pay."

Little Sister cried. Fragrance wailed as well. I could scarcely think from all the noise and my pounding heart, but calmness took over. "Stay in here and block the door after I leave," I commanded.

"That is good. Let them have yourself," Nai Nai said, her voice bitter.

Ignoring her, I opened Phineas's trunk and withdrew the sword. I released it from the leather wrap and prepared to do battle, if necessary.

15

The sword was heavier than I remembered, and I had to carry it with both hands as I ran down the hall. Oh, how I longed for the inexpressibles Phineas had given me to practice in, for my flowing skirts did nothing to aid my progress toward the vandals. I could already hear them throwing ceramics and smashing wood.

Three men were in the main room, hard at work destroying the Wongs' home. They wore their hair long and loose instead of in neatly bound queues and wore peasant clothing. The chess set Little Sister and I enjoyed lay scattered against the far wall. Vases were smashed against walls, camellias and peonies crushed underfoot, water soaking the floor. These were pirates as surely as the French privateers we had encountered in the Indian Ocean, and my anger boiled.

"What do you think you are doing?"

They stopped as they were. One held a large ginger vase over his head, another held the remains of a smashed chair, and the third stood with a knife plunged into one of Nai

Nai's beautiful embroidered pillows. Taken by surprise, they watched me for a moment, obviously perplexed to see a British woman in Chinese clothing holding a very old sword.

The one with the knife smiled. He left the blade plunged into the cushion and straightened. "Go cower, little girl. Then maybe we won't hurt you."

"It is you who should leave, and maybe I won't hurt *you*," I said in a low voice.

The three bandits looked at one another then burst into laughter.

Narrowing my eyes, I sliced the air with the sword several times, then neatly cut a candle in two to emphasize my resolve. "Leave Madame Wong's house!"

Scowling, the man retrieved his knife from the cushion. "This is your last chance, foolish girl. I am not afraid to use this if I must."

I pointed the sword at him. "Neither am I."

He nodded to his two companions, who started toward me. I waited for them to come closer, for I had learned that the strength of martial arts was to use your opponent's own *hei*—energy—against himself. And after all, it was fools who rushed in, though I confess I prayed heartily for angels to do some mighty treading on my behalf.

These two had no weapons, so I would only use the sword if necessary for my defense. The first man, who was large and doughy, did not know martial arts at all, for he came at me slowly, hands out, as though he expected me to surrender the sword. I could easily have inflicted

332

much pain, but I settled for cuffing him on the side of the head with the flat edge of the sword's blade. While he was distracted, I feinted toward the second man as though to plunge the sword into his heart, then neatly employed the leg sweep Phineas had used on me just weeks ago. The man fell to the floor with a thud, and I stood over him with the point of my sword at his throat. "Get out."

"Drop your sword."

The point of the knife touched my own throat, and the bandit's left arm encircled me, pinning me fast. I could feel his hot breath on my neck, and I chided myself for not considering his presence. I hesitated, gathering my wits. Phineas was not here to save me this time, as aboard ship.

"Drop it now!" The knife tip pierced my skin, and I felt a trickle of blood.

Phineas's training returned to me instinctively. I jabbed my right elbow into the miscreant's ribs and stomped on his instep as hard as I could with my heel. For good measure, I punched him in the groin, and he screamed with pain. The knife clattered to the ground, and he released me, cursing. I whirled out of reach and swept the sword from side to side, covering the intruders. I kicked the knife across the room, where Nai Nai—to my shock—retrieved it. Little Sister and Fragrance cowered behind her, but I turned my attention to the bandits.

"You came here to harm us, but you have not succeeded," I said. "Go back to Chow Wah and tell him that Madame Wong no longer desires to purchase what he sells. I will be lenient toward you this time, but next time you will not be so fortunate."

I stepped backward and pointed the sword toward the door. "Now leave!"

The bandits scrambled to their feet and hurried toward the door. I followed to make sure they had truly left, laughing to myself as I saw them run through the gate and down the street without glancing back. I reentered the home and shut the door firmly. "Good riddance," I could not help muttering, feeling pleased.

When I surveyed the damage they had wrought, however, my heart no longer laughed. Nai Nai's beautiful home was in shambles. The servants had come out of hiding, and they stumbled through the mess, weeping and moaning.

"There, there, it is over," I said, comforting them one at a time. "Let us pick up this mess together and forget what happened. All of these things can be replaced, and we are safe."

Little Sister rushed to me, her face shining. "You were so brave, Eldest Sister-in-law. I cannot believe you fought those men . . . and won!"

Nai Nai still stood with the knife in her hand, apparently in shock. Blinking, she let it clatter to the floor, and she stared at my hands. "What is that you hold?"

I held out the sword, flat, and presented it to her with a bow. I had no right to keep it when she did not accept me into the family. I hoped that Phineas would not be angry. "I am certain you recognize this, Nai Nai, for it belongs to your family. Your son gave it to me, but perhaps it should return to you."

She stared at it a moment, and her gaze jumped to mine. Her eyes flickered with admiration then shuttered again. She turned away. "What would I want with such an old thing?"

Relieved, I gripped the hilt of the sword for a moment then set it aside. I wanted to hug Nai Nai—indeed, I moved forward on impulse to do so—but I stopped short at the last minute. "You understand why these men were here?"

She nodded, no trace of regret in her expression. It seemed likely she would never acknowledge the danger she had placed us all in.

"You must stop smoking opium," I said. "I understand it may be difficult, but Fragrance and I will help you." I lowered my voice, glancing at Little Sister, who was sobbing over the scattered chess set. "I pray that we may keep her from learning the truth just yet, for she is too young to be so burdened."

Nai Nai gave me a slight bow in agreement—surely, not deference!—and shuffled to comfort her daughter. I watched them together, gaining a tender glimpse of Nai Nai that I seldom saw. She usually looked to Phineas for support, but with Little Sister, she allowed herself to be the one to reassure. She had a gentle side yet!

I clapped my hands to gain everyone's attention. The servants stopped crying and looked to me for guidance. "We must all work together to clean this mess," I said, excusing the cook to prepare something special for dinner. It would help our moods if we had a festive meal to reward our efforts. Fragrance I took to one side. She admitted that the bandits had forced their way through the door and that she would never have allowed them admittance otherwise. If I wanted her to leave, she was prepared to pack her bags.

I put my hand on her shoulder. She was but a little older than I, and I wondered if she had the same pressure to marry as ladies our age in Britain. Perhaps the notion of being a servant to Nai Nai and her family for the rest of her life frightened her. Yet perhaps the alternative frightened her more. "I do not believe you meant any harm to come to anyone in this household," I said. "If you promise to have nothing to do with Chow Wah anymore, you may stay."

She nodded, her face tearful but joyful to learn that I did not plan to put her out on the street. "Madame Wong will need our help in the coming days if she is to rid herself of the poison in her body," I whispered. "Have you any experience with such?"

She nodded, whispering back, "Yes, Madame, and I will be there to help. I do not think that Madame Wong has taken so much opium that she will have physical problems, but she will crave it all the same." Without being told, she moved immediately to help the other servants dispose of the shattered ceramics and roll up the damaged rugs for cleaning.

I picked up the sword and carried it back to my room, rewrapping it in the leather. I thanked God for his protection and that I had not had to hurt anyone beyond what was necessary to protect the household. If there was one thing I had learned from Phineas's stories about Wo-Ping and Mei, it was that warriors stood firm.

I smiled. Wouldn't the three bandits have been surprised if I had run up the walls or floated to the ceiling as they did in Phineas's story—and in Chinese folklore? Perhaps the bandits would spread the word that Nai Nai's house was supernaturally guarded. Indeed, I had certainly felt it so.

With the sword tucked back in Phineas's trunk, I lingered in my room for a moment. I needed to rejoin the others to help, but I also needed time alone. I could do little but bow my head in thanks, which led to fervent prayers for Phineas's safety. No doubt the dangers that lurked between Canton and the mountains in Hupei were greater than the three bandits who had visited us today.

We had just enough time to put the house back to some sort of rights, but late that evening I was awakened by Fragrance. "The desire for the drug is upon Madame Wong," she said after apologizing for awakening me. "She will suffer now for a while until she is free from its hold. I thought you might want to be with her."

I certainly did not! Like most sheep, I yearned for peaceful green pastures and crystal blue waters, knowing that my loving Shepherd guarded me. But my Savior did not want me to live a fat and lazy life, and after all, he had called me specifically to this region, perhaps for this very purpose. "Thank you, Fragrance. Please make her comfortable, and I will be right there."

I opened Phineas's trunk yet again and retrieved the

337

original Chinese translation of the Gospel According to St. Luke that Phineas had given me so long ago. I did not know of what use it would be, as I would be more likely required to tend physical needs, but it felt good to hold.

Nai Nai paced the rug in her room, turning abruptly when I entered. "I do not want those horrid men back in my home, but I must have some opium. You must see that, even though you are a particularly stupid girl."

"I know what you want, but it is not what you need. I have been told that you will go through a time when you crave the drug, but if you will resist its pull, you will be free. I am certain you want that."

She laughed. "Why would I? I was happy under its spell. If you foreigners have done anything useful for China, it is bringing this wonderful drug."

She must not venture forth very often or far, or she would see the results it has wrought. "Nai Nai, your son has gone to the Hupei Province to find something that would stop those who bring this drug into China. It is for people like you that he is willing to risk his own life to travel so far." I paused, uncertain how much she would believe. "I want to help, as well."

"You? What can you do?"

I smiled. "Once when I was afraid, your son told me many stories about China. They prevented me from worry and helped me to sleep at night."

She sighed, clasping and unclasping her hands nervously, then lay down on her bed. "I know all the old stories. What new ones can you tell?"

I held out the Gospel According to St. Luke so that she could see Chinese characters. "I will read to you from this." I pulled a chair beside the bed and began. "'Forasmuch as many have taken in hand to set forth in order a declaration of those things which are most surely believed among us . . .'"

It took several days and nights for Nai Nai to feel settled again, by which I mean she stopped talking about opium. Fragrance whispered her thankfulness that her mistress had been spared the physical withdrawal symptoms of the drug—nausea, chills, fever, and sweating—but I knew Nai Nai would fight the mental desire much longer. I tried to encourage her to take an interest in Little Sister, but she seemed ashamed somehow, though we had all managed to keep the truth from the girl.

My thoughts turned to Phineas, as always, and I found myself frequently gazing at the jade wedding ring he had placed on my finger not so long ago. I remembered our conversation about Naomi and Ruth. What, particularly, had Ruth done for her mother-in-law, other than to travel to her homeland? Surely she had not stumbled over Scripture in her mother-in-law's native language, as I did with Nai Nai. How she laughed at my stumblings and fumblings as I tried to read my own poor copy of Robert Morrison's original. My ears burned at such times, but I continued to read until she asked me to cease. Other times, I was delighted with how long she suffered my reading, as though she were absorbed with the story.

I was not certain that she still listened when we reached the story of the Last Supper one night while she lay in bed, trying to find sleep. I found myself yawning with weariness and sought to stay awake. "In another story similar to this one, the author recounts that Jesus washed his disciples' feet," I said, scarcely without thinking.

Nai Nai frowned. "It is good that his disciples were not women, for such a thing should not be done."

"What do you mean?"

She seemed embarrassed, and indeed, I believe I saw her blush. "Men are much taken with ladies' feet. It is part of the intimacy process between a husband and wife." She paused. "Surely you must know that."

It was my turn to blush. Thank goodness I could truthfully deny it. How odd! "It is not part of our culture," I said diplomatically.

She looked puzzled. "In China, men don't care about a future bride's face, but they'll make sure her feet are small and delicate like golden lotuses."

Oh my! Is that why she examined my feet in the hall that day? She wanted to know if I was suitable for Phineas? I cleared my throat. "Then that is why girls have their feet bound?"

She nodded. "My feet were wasted on my son's father . . . What is wrong with men in your country that they do not care about such a thing? Golden lotuses bring pleasure to the husband."

Because his wife's toes have been broken? "I confess that feet are not thought of much in my culture. In the times of Luke, when our story takes place, feet were thought to

340

be dishonorable. People lived in a hot, dusty climate and wore sandals. Naturally, their feet became dirty and were thus considered dishonorable. For a teacher to wash his disciples' feet was a sign of submission." I paused, and the words spilled from my mouth. "Would you like me to wash yours?"

Nai Nai pushed back the covers and stuck out her feet. "Yes."

I blinked, suddenly wide awake. "What?" No polite refusal or even a gracious hesitation?

She gestured at her feet covered with tiny bed slippers. "Yes. Wash mine. You talk about submission all the time in this story. Show me."

I cleared my throat. "Very well." I called for Fragrance, who, though already dressed for bed, brought us a pan of warm water and a cake of soap. I had Nai Nai sit on a chair, and I knelt before her. I gently removed the red slippers she wore to bed. Startled, I recognized the embroidery she had been working on, the silk covered with dainty flowers and animals. One of the servants must have made the slippers for her. How many hours she must have spent on the handiwork, hours of loneliness and grief.

I began removing the cloth that bound her feet. I could not believe they were so necessary after all these years, but perhaps to leave one's feet unbound was even more painful. "I had the smallest feet in my family," she said proudly. "All of my sisters said so. They were very jealous."

I took a deep breath and removed the last of the bindings. Golden lotuses her feet might appear when she hobbled

341

about, but grotesqueries of flesh were all I saw. They were even more disgusting up close than they had been when I viewed them from her doorway. Her big toe made a point at the end of each foot, with the other four toes pulled down and to the side until they nearly met her heels, like a piece of paper turned down at the corner. How anyone could find desire in such mutilation was beyond my understanding, and bile rose in my throat.

St. Peter had been unwilling to have the Master wash his feet, but he probably would have had no problem with washing Nai Nai's. I, of course, was made of lesser stuff than the apostle, but I knew this moment was not only important for my future relationship with my mother-in-law but for my own future, as well. Had I not said, nay, boasted, for months that I had been called to be a missionary? What sort of Christian ambassador would I be if I could not perform this task for the mother of my own beloved?

Taking one foot in my palm, I dipped soft cloth into the soapy water and gently washed. Somehow I did it without dwelling upon its grotesqueness, but in thinking about how much I wanted to please Phineas and, more so, Jesus. I slowly realized that I wanted to please Nai Nai, as well. I could read her the Gospel According to St. Luke, even in Chinese, till I was blue in the face, but what would she understand more—words or a demonstration of how much our Lord loved us all?

When I finished, I patted her feet dry. I held the bindings in my hand, unwilling to re-cover her feet. I wanted them to be free, I wanted them to be whole again.

"Bah! Give those to me." Her words, though sharp, belied the fact that she took, rather than snatched, the bindings from my hands. "Let me do that. I have been doing it for longer than you have lived."

I smiled up at her, and she paused. Again, I saw something flicker in her eyes, and I sensed that she wanted to return my smile. She frowned at me, however, and bent her head to wrap her feet.

Taking up the used pan of water, I rose to return it to Fragrance. When I was at the door, Nai Nai said, "You and Ah Chung are suited for one another. You have the same beliefs, even if they are peculiar."

Flora would have called that a left-handed compliment, but I believed it to be a beginning of sorts for Nai Nai and me. "Thank you," I said, then hastened from the room before I could spoil the moment by saying anything more.

Days passed into weeks. I tried not to be concerned about Phineas, but the more I did that, the more concerned I became. Of course, Jesus did not say *"try* not to worry" but simply "do not worry." I confess to often missing that mark.

If he returned safe and sound, Phineas would want to return to England—or rather, America—as soon as possible. I could not believe I found myself thinking such, but I could not bear the notion of leaving Nai Nai and Little Sister. Though their lives were running smoothly again without the presence of opium and with the servants' full cooperation, who would help Little Sister prepare for becoming

343

some man's wife? More importantly, what would happen to Nai Nai once her last child had left the home?

One afternoon, Nai Nai and I sat in the parlor, working on embroidery. She had grudgingly showed me how to duplicate the tiny stitches on her shoes. I thought to make something for Precious Spring's baby, Honor, with such delicate patterns. Or perhaps, I smiled to myself, to set aside for my and Phineas's own child one day, should we be so blessed. I thought happily of such things when Fragrance burst into the room, forgetting all decorum. "See who has arrived!"

I rose, fearful that the bandits or some other miscreants had returned. "Who is it, Fragrance?"

My husband stepped into the room, and I dropped the silk. His clothes were ragged, he wore an unfamiliar leather pouch, and he looked weary, but he was still my husband. Alive and home at last. "Phineas!" Forgetting proper behavior myself, I fairly lunged across the room and into his arms. "Oh, Phineas!"

"Isabella," he murmured, embracing me closely, kissing my face and neck. "I made you a promise, did I not?"

I nodded, hugging him again. When we had our fill of rejoicing to be so close again—though I secretly thought I might never grow weary of his embraces and kisses—we reluctantly separated. It was then that I noticed Nai Nai standing quietly in the background. Her face registered shock at our behavior, but her eyes danced with barely suppressed joy at her son's return. She did not draw attention to herself, however. Phineas could not seem to remove his gaze from my face, so I gestured toward his mother with my eyes.

He released me and went to her. "Mother," he said, bowing.

She nodded. "Ah Chung," she said softly, as though he were a ghost who might disappear.

He kissed her on the cheek, earning her surprised look. "Thank you for taking care of my wife," he whispered, though it was loud enough for me to hear.

She glanced at me briefly then nodded. "You're welcome." She seemed to will a smile to his face. "You look weary. You would probably like to rest. I will have Cook make something special tonight to celebrate your return . . .?"

I do not believe that Phineas noticed the questioning tone at the end of her sentence, and I am certain that he did not see his mother glance at me when she asked it. I nodded slightly, and she beamed, rushing off to discuss the meal.

Little Sister greeted her brother as well, then headed toward the garden for some afternoon sun.

Alone at last, Phineas put his arm around my waist. Without speaking, only staring and smiling at one another, we headed back to our bedroom. Inside, he removed the leather pouch he had slung around his neck and dropped it into a chair. He took my face in his hands and kissed me long and deep. "I have missed you so much," he murmured.

I ran my fingers through his queue, loosening his hair. "And I, you. So much has happened. I have so much to tell you."

His put his fingers to my lips. "First, let me speak." He

reached into the leather pouch and removed what appeared to be a large golden cake. "Do you know what this is?"

I shook my head.

He smiled. "Do you not recognize tea leaves? These are the golden ones."

I touched it with awe. No wonder he had sought these leaves. They shimmered in the light of the room like beautiful treasure. I did not know if they were as delicious to drink as he had said, but they were wondrous to behold.

"This represents the labor of my time away from you," he said.

"This is all? One cake?" I smiled. "For this you hope to bring down the East India Company? It might fetch a nice sum at auction but hardly enough to put that venerable firm out of business, I believe."

"And your belief is accurate." He frowned, sinking wearily to a chair. "This is all I brought home."

I knelt beside him, my hand on his knee. *So it is over.* "The Americans have taken the rest? They will sell it and begin to work against the East India Company?"

He closed his eyes. "I no longer care."

"What?" I rose. "It is what you have worked for so long."

Phineas took my hands and rose to face me. "The Americans," he said bitterly, then tried again. "The American trading company will be no better than the British. They too are bringing opium to trade in China. Indeed, it is how they acquired the money to finance our expedition.

I told them I would have nothing further to do with their venture."

"I am sorry," I said and meant it, though once it would have been a lie. "You worked hard for what you believed was right. I am also sorry that the Americans have taken the tea leaves for their own."

"It does not matter, for I learned a secret from one of the monks in Hupei. Tea leaves undergo different processes to achieve different colors. Black is heated the most, green only lightly so, and white, even less."

"White? I have never heard of such."

"It is a tea primarily for royalty in China," he said. "It is made from tender new buds plucked from the top of the plant. Much like the golden leaves, which grow only in a certain part of the mountains."

"But that is no secret. You were aware of that already."

He smiled. "The leaves are golden but undergo no heating at all. Which means that they will never make the long voyage to America—or England—without withering and becoming useless. They must be used quickly and thus can only be drunk in China."

"Will you tell this to the Americans before they leave Canton with their supply?"

Phineas folded his arms and grinned.

I smiled in return. He took me in his arms and held me close. I felt his heart beating solidly. "I do not wish to be parted from you again," I said softly.

"Nor I from you. When I learned the truth, I thought about what you have said these many months regarding revenge. I saw how foolish I would have been, even had my plan succeeded. I do not want to tilt at windmills when it would be time and effort spent apart from you." He cupped my face. "You are the love of my life, Isabella. I want nothing more than to live with you, raise children"—he gestured at the cake of leaves, smiling—"and *yum cha*."

He kissed me before I could say anything in return; indeed, there was nothing I *could* say, for he had expressed my desires as well. His attentions made my head swim, and I knew that all my news would have to wait, for I was about to forget everything.

"We can return to England if you like," he murmured, scarcely ceasing with his kisses. Oh, he was a fiend with his kisses!—never allowing them to stay in one place for long, but placing one on my cheekbone, then one at the corner of my mouth, and another near my ear. "I am certain you are ready to leave this house," he whispered. "Macao, Cape Town . . . wherever you wish to live."

I shuddered, trembling. "I want to live here."

"Canton?" His lips moved to my temple.

I could scarcely speak now! "Your mother's house," I finally managed to whisper.

He laughed softly, whispering against my ear. "You will have to tell me about this madness later, Wife, for it appears you have cast a spell on more than just me. I, however, am completely bewitched at the moment."

With that, he lifted me into his arms. The tea cake dropped softly to the floor, where it remained until much, much later.

Every culture, nay, every generation, has a story to tell. Mine has been that of two cultures and hopefully many generations yet to come. Phineas and I still have the dog-eared original and copies of the Gospel According to St. Luke. Like St. Francis of Assisi, we believe in preaching the gospel at all times—and if necessary, to use words. St. Francis's statement is what I learned being a true missionary often means. We also still have the sword that has been in Nai Nai's family for many years. We pray that it will never be needed again, but we are prepared, like Wo-Ping and Mei, to battle for righteousness.

And now, dear friend, I close my tale with the happy report that tea is also still important in our lives. Every year, Phineas and I travel together to the Mo Tong mountains to gather golden leaves, which we brew and drink with everyone we love, from the oldest to the youngest.

Jane Orcutt is the author or coauthor of twelve books, including the bestselling *Porch Swings and Picket Fences*. She lives in the Fort Worth, Texas, area with her family.